ANGELS OF LIGHT

P. B. Lamb

authorHOUSE®

AuthorHouse™
1663 Liberty Drive
Bloomington, IN 47403
www.authorhouse.com
Phone: 833-262-8899

Published by AuthorHouse 11/02/2022

ISBN: 978-1-6655-7454-9 (sc)
ISBN: 978-1-6655-7455-6 (e)

Library of Congress Control Number: 2022919892

Print information available on the last page.

Any people depicted in stock imagery provided by Getty Images are models,
and such images are being used for illustrative purposes only.
Certain stock imagery © Getty Images.

This book is printed on acid-free paper.

Scripture taken from the Holy Bible, New International Version®. Copyright © 1973,
1978, 1984 Biblica. Used by permission of Zondervan. All rights reserved.

Dedication:

I dedicate this book to my entire family. Without the support system I have this would not be possible. To my children you are my entire existence, without you my life would be incomplete. To my husband, my love, thank you for supporting this endeavor.

Love, P.B.

PROLOGUE

"Wake up! Please GOD Wake Up!!!!" I was screaming at the top of my lungs holding the body of my lifeless mother in my arms on the floor of my bathroom. My mother was a beautiful woman, tall, blonde, always tan with baby blue eyes, every man's fantasy girl. I on the other hand was the attractively curvy, brunette with pale skin and dark green eyes. I wasn't fat by any means, but certainly not model skinny like my mother. She could light up a room anywhere she was so full of life, she was always the quintessential southern woman who lived to charm the pants off men. Literally.

Now she was laying limp on my bathroom floor, how long had she been here I did not know. I had known something was bad, unbelievably bad. Something did not feel right in the atmosphere. I know that people would think "oh great here we go another self-proclaimed psychic," if they knew about my visions and feelings. They would be wrong. I do not discuss what I see or feel with anyone, not even my best friend. I happen to see people after they are gone from this world. Other times it's just a feeling like I can sense the air in the room or a person's aura. In this case, while sitting at my desk in my office, I just knew something was definitely wrong in my own home. I knew it was dark and that it was going to change my life forever.

I sat in disbelief and shock as the police and EMS workers buzzed all around, eventually taking my mother away from me. How could this honestly be happening to me! Seriously! This is not how I wanted to end my year! I stared off, lost in my own thoughts as the police officer asked me questions. She was gone. My mother was gone.

CHAPTER 1

November in Southern Maryland is a tricky time of year, as you never know what to wear when you walk out the door. Some days it may be warm enough that you can get by with a long sleeve, light shirt, or a short sleeve shirt and a light jacket. Then on other days it may be close to freezing, and you need a parka just to walk to your car from your front door. Today was one of those parka days it was a beautiful, clear blue sky, yet bitter cold with a forecast of temperatures dropping below freezing at midnight. My mother was gone. I was supposed to entertain family in my living room waiting to go to the funeral home. Accidental overdose was the official ruling in her death caused by a lethal combination of pain pills and alcohol. No, my mother wasn't an alcoholic, nor was she a drug addict. Sure, there was speculation that she popped pills a little more often than she should have, but who were we to pass judgment?

Sitting on the edge of my bed, looking at myself in the mirror wearing black thigh-high stockings with a black garter belt, which I had recently bought at Victoria's Secret, along with a matching black bra and panty set. I could not decide what else to wear. Mother always did preach the importance of being perfectly put together, all the way down to our under garments. My issue was what to put over them. I was much more comfortable in jeans and a T-shirt or sweatshirt, but today I was going to be representing my family in her honor. I decided on a black pant suit with a dark-grey blouse, my simple, classy black heels, and a long silver necklace with a silver heart locket on it.

The locket had been my grandmother's and held a photo of my brother on one side and me on the other. Our younger sister was not included in the locket since my grandmother did not officially recognize her as her grandchild. She harbored ill will toward my mother for having a child out of wedlock. Needless to say, there was no love lost between my mother and my grandmother. Have you seen the movie *Divine Secrets of the YaYa Sisterhood*? That just about accurately describes the relationship between my mom and her mother. Two polar opposite women related by birth. Each attempting to live life all while irritating the heck out of one other. I pulled my hair up into a neat bun and dabbed on a little eyeliner and lip gloss. No sense in putting all my makeup on at this point. My mother would probably roll over in her grave over my decision to not put "my face" on. Oh well, she was certainly quiet right now.

I was not sure if she would be one of my visitors in the coming days, but I was hoping she would at least say goodbye. When my best friend died in a car accident several years before, she appeared within a few days of her death. That was my first experience with a "visitor" from beyond the grave. At first, it freaked me out. I thought I was hallucinating, and that I was going insane. I mean, I have always been a spiritual person raised in the church my entire life, but I had not honestly believed in ghosts, spirits, or any of the sort. I refused to watch scary movies or television shows because ghosts and horror scared me. Imagine my surprise when my dead best friend visited me by my bedside in the middle of the night. Yes, there was screaming.

I took one last look in my full-length mirror and decided this was as good as I was going to get. "Take a deep breath, Jessica, and walk out the door." Yep, she was here. I turned slowly to find my mother's spirit standing at the end of my four-poster bed. She was in a white chiffon evening gown, the one that showed off her breasts and clung to her hips. She insisted that she would be buried in it so she wrote it into her will when my father died. Standing here, in the gown, and in death, she was still stunning.

Great, just great, now she shows up. I turned quickly and walked through the door. *I am leaving her in my bedroom. She will have to wait. I have breathing human beings who require my immediate attention. Whose idea was it to give me the ability to see dead people?* I looked up at the ceiling as if my thoughts were floating to God in a serious question and continued to the living room.

My brother, James, sat on my couch with a beer in his hand. I guess he figured it was five o'clock somewhere. He was tall and handsome like my father, and many times I would smile just looking at him. He was very GQ, with his chestnut brown hair and blue eyes. My sister, Jax—short for Jacqueline, was tall and thin. She had long, straight blonde hair, the same color as mother's, with deep green eyes like mine. She stood by what I referred to as the "back wall of windows." I had floor-to-ceiling windows, which went up two stories, all along the back wall of the living room. I was not quite sure what she was looking at, most likely nothing at all.

I had an amazing view of the Patuxent River if you were looking through the windows in the front of my house. However, in the backyard, I had a lawn of mostly grass with a few flower beds, a horse barn, and some trees. Today though the horses were put up in the barn, the grass was turning brown already from the cold, and the trees were practically leafless since it was well past the beginning of fall. Jax looked completely put off and out of her element here. I was glad she had at least put on a dress since she was like I am—a jeans and T-shirt kind of girl. My Uncle Bradley, my father's only sibling, sat on the couch with my brother discussing how peaceful my mother is now that she was in heaven with her husband. *No, she's in my bedroom.* Now I completely understood why my brother was drinking.

"James, you OK, bud?" I asked, sincerely. He raised his eyes to my face and smiled his trademark fake grin.

"Just peachy," he said.

He gets that trademark fake smile from our mother. She was a professional at it. You could put the ugliest baby in front of her, and she would plaster that smile on then tell you the child was the prettiest baby she'd ever seen. My sister and I wore our true thoughts and feelings on our faces. You put an ugly baby in front of us, and we will look like we just saw an ugly baby!

"Uncle Brad, do you need anything?" I said in my finest hostess voice.

"No, sugar, I'm good. We should probably get going. I'm giving her eulogy, and I want to talk to a few people and get their thoughts on Beth as well. I am thinking of just quoting a few wonderful things about her. What do you think?"

I think you are asking to hear stories you do not wish to hear about mother!

"It's a wonderful idea," I replied as sincerely as I could.

"I think you should just stick to the usual BS about going to heaven, how wonderful she was, or just make stuff up." Jax always knew how to cut to the chase.

"Jax, honey, I know you are hurting, but your momma was a good woman." Uncle Brad said, trying to diffuse her before she went any further.

Jax scowled, knowing it was a losing battle. Jax didn't have the easiest childhood, but that's not to say she was not spoiled with material possessions. She just lived in our mother's shadow and

the out-of-wedlock stigma that traditional values tend to label you with. Had she been born twenty years later; she would have been simply fine. Society today tends to accept unwed mothers, no matter their age. Our mother, Elizabeth Leigh Bonner-Hanson, had been a beauty queen and model in her twenties. She met my father and claims it was love at first sight. After a six-month whirlwind romance, they were married. My father, Jonathan Quincey Hanson, a real estate tycoon about twenty years my mother's senior. But he loved her dearly and doted on her. She was his trophy wife. He gave her anything she wanted. He made millions in real estate before he met his precious Beth.

He lavished her with wealth long after his death. He had a heart attack at home and Mother found him in the study with his head on his desk. She was never the same from that point forward. She spiraled into a depression so profound the deepest crevice in the ocean was merely a crack in comparison. She ended up on a plethora of anti-depressants and once tried a holistic approach with natural supplements. Eventually, she turned to painkillers, wine, and margaritas. She filled her bed with whomever she wanted, just so she was never alone. Most were gold diggers after my mother's money, the money she had inherited from my father. Luckily, our attorney, turned family friend, would find a way to get rid of them. He was like a father, or maybe an uncle, more so than my real uncle was to me, and I trusted the man implicitly. Yet, from one of these low-life gold-diggers sprouted my little sister.

I would not say my mother was devastated that she had a baby out of wedlock, but I think she felt some guilt as if she cheated on my father. That led to her not always being the best mom to my little sister. I filled in many times being that I was sixteen when Jax was born but I was not cut out to fill our mother's role. It was only a few years later that I was off to college, followed by law school, and starting my career. When I graduated from law school I went home to live with my mother for a little while to help her with Jax. By then Jax was almost eight years old attending elementary school. She desperately wanted a mom that showed up for VIP Day, the book fair, bake sales, or whatever other "normal" moms would show up for. Unfortunately for Jax our mother turned heads since she was still a notable person in the entertainment world. She once caused an accident in front of the school where two dads were watching our mother, in all her glory, walk into the front doors. Of course, being the "lesser" child in the eyes of our grandmother did not help matters either. Our grandmother adored her daughter, our mother, being that she was the only child. Mother's "indiscretion" was not something my grandmother talked about, but when she did it was full of venom and hurt. Poor Jax had to live with it while mother dulled it with pain pills and alcohol.

"Hey Jax, you want to ride in my limo to the funeral?" I asked sincerely. She shrugged her shoulders. That was the only answer I would get, but I sensed she just did not want to go at all. James stood up, finished his beer, then said he would go with Uncle Bradley. I was glad since I wanted some time alone with Jax in the car, but I would not have denied James riding with us had he wanted to. We all grabbed our coats as we headed out the door. I pulled the door to the house closed, I took one last look in the direction of my bedroom and decided to forget that my mother's spirit was there. I had a funeral to attend.

CHAPTER 2

The funeral was as nice as a funeral could be. There were many people there, some I had never met before. A few business associates of my late father, along with acting and modeling friends of my mother, were in attendance. The actors and models were the biggest grievers of the lot. Most had not had much to do with my mother in the last five years or so, but they sure acted like they lost their best friend. It was stomach turning to be honest. This was a time when one of my mother's fake smiles would have come in handy. Jax and I rolled our eyes at each other repeatedly. My father's longtime friend and the family attorney,

William "Bill" Brothers sat with Jax, James, and me in the front row. It was comforting having him there. He held my hand and let me lean on his shoulders several times when I just did not want to hold my head up anymore. He looked more like a bodyguard than an attorney with his large broad shoulders, cleanly shaven head, and tall muscular body. I used to think he looked like the Mr. Clean man on the cleaning bottle that the maid used in my bathroom when I was a child. He was more handsome than a cartoon drawing and at his age was still a very good-looking man. After my father died, he took care of all of us and there were times I wished he would marry my mother becoming my stepdad.

He would have seen that as a betrayal to my father, but I wished it anyway. Still, he managed to step in at all the right moments when any of us needed him. He was probably the only person, besides James and I, whom Jax listened to or cared about. Mother was good at taking his advice because she knew he was speaking for my father when he advised her on what to do. When I passed the bar exam in Maryland, he allowed me to come work for his firm as an associate. He made sure I worked my way up just like everyone else. Now I was a Junior Partner, but he was still very much my boss. Today, he was filling the role of my father. I missed my daddy now more than ever.

The rest of the funeral was sort of a blur. I shook hands, took hugs, smiled graciously, and dabbed tears when appropriate. I kissed babies and laughed at old stories of my mother. I felt like a politician. I was proud of Jax for plastering the same smile on that I had, although we were not pros like James, we certainly were holding our own. Everyone was going back to my mother's estate for a catered lunch; it was a funeral with style. Jax and I would be riding in the limo back to the estate home near Annapolis, with James and Uncle Brad in Uncle Brad's silver Lexus. This was the extent of our family now - James, Jax, me, and of course Uncle Brad. I considered Bill family since he had been to every family event and holiday for as long as I could remember, but if we are talking blood relations there were four of us left. Of which, only three were the Hanson family since Jax had been given our mother's maiden name of Bonner. I reflected on this as I walked into mother's estate home, our family felt small and pitiful now.

"Don't think so negatively," my mother's voice said near me. Startled, I turned my head to find her spirit form standing in the doorway to the formal living room.

"I thought I left you at home," I responded in a whisper. "Besides how do you know what I was thinking?"

"I can tell by the look on your face that you were thinking negative thoughts. You should really work on hiding your emotions better." She was always so commanding. "Mother, I need you to just be quiet. I'm not sure I'm ready to speak to you right now. I am upset with you for messing up so royally and leaving us already." I picked up my stride toward the main entertaining hall.

"Well for the record I didn't mess up, and you will start to see what is really happening in the coming days," she whispered.

Suddenly my eyes lit up and I turned around to look at her, but where her spirit form had just been now empty, she had vanished. I hate when spirits do that. They drop some piece of information on you and then disappear. I felt like spirits liked to play games for some reason. The ones that have some other purpose, like they were murdered, must help point the living and breathing in the right direction to catch their murderer, so they tend to stay in our world for much longer. There was some cosmic rule that prevents them from just saying, "Hey, Professor Plum did it in the living room with the candle stick." It would make life much easier if they could.

After a nice catered lunch followed by some required host duties, I was ready to leave. With a smile, I walked over to Jax draping my arm over her shoulders to ask, "You ready to blow this taco joint?"

"Yes!" I could feel it was a huge relief for her. I walked to where Bill stood talking to a group of people then smiled broadly. He returned the smile with a look of *what are you up to?* on his face.

"Jax and I are ready to go. Would you be willing to drive us back to my house?" I said as sweetly as a daughter might say to her daddy, with batted eyes and all. He was not exactly my father, but the eyes still worked on him!

"Of course!" He said with a laugh. "I want to discuss a few things with you anyway."

We said our goodbyes then left the house in the capable hands of James and Uncle Brad; they were wrapped up with entertaining the guests with great skill. James was good at charming people like mother was, so this was where he would thrive more than I would. I just wanted to get home take this confining suit off, slip into some comfortable clothes, and have an important chat with Jax. I was hoping my mother's spirit would stay at the estate to watch her funeral reception from afar so I could relax. I often wondered where spirits floated to and from when they were not visible to me. Now, in this moment, I just wanted her spirit to stay here.

I climbed into the passenger seat of Bill's Escalade; it was big, all black, and looked like it belonged in a presidential procession, yet it suited Bill perfectly. Jax got into the back and immediately kicked off her heels to sit in a crossed leg position in the middle. Bill was a gentleman, opening and closing the doors for Jax and I. I smiled as I watched him walk around the front of the vehicle. He shrugged off his suit coat, hung it on a hanger in the back seat, then climbed into the driver's seat loosening his tie as he sat down. There was always such a sense of protection and safety around Bill that I took great comfort in.

We started the drive down the long driveway lined on both sides with apple trees. I peered through the window as we drove by the now hibernating trees reminiscing how mother had always hated them. When I was younger, I would pick the apples from the branches and feed them to my horses. Mother essentially did not like the mess the apples made when they dropped onto the ground. I didn't understand this, since she never had to do yard work, and in her own words once said, "that's what the lawn service is for." My thoughts switched to the memory of taking this same drive with Bill when my father died. I was just a teen at the time. The flashback of watching the trees stream by the window as we drove off caused a tear to slip down my cheek. It was the first real tear I had shed all day.

"Where are you, Jess?" Bill asked.

"I was just remembering this same drive when Daddy died." I looked down at my hands folded in my lap as I said it. Bill reached over taking my hand in a comforting gesture, the tenderness of it made me smile at him.

"We have a few things to discuss," Bill said. "As you know, I am the Executor of your mother's will, you are the primary inheritor, and although there are provisions of trust for both James and Jax, you have primary responsibility for the estate and the possessions. What would you like to do with it all?"

I turned my head to look at Jax who was asleep in the back seat.

"Wait. Isn't it divided evenly amongst us all?" I asked quietly.

"No, it's not. You are listed as the main beneficiary. Although there is a hefty trust for James that was set up before your father died, your mother never truly updated her will in the years since. She added a provision for Jax shortly after her birth, but it was for a smaller trust."

"So basically, whatever my father left, and the way his will was written, that is how my mother left it?"

"Essentially, yes."

"What are the trusts?" I asked.

"Your brother James is still entitled to his half of the trust your father set up for the two of you. This amounts to approximately ten million in cash and assets. You still have your ten million in cash and assets, as well as the real property and material possessions within the physical domain of your mother's Annapolis estate. Jax has a smaller trust for approximately five million that has been invested and is held in trust until she is twenty-five years of age."

"But she's only twenty, what is she to do between now and twenty-five?" I heard the sudden rise in my voice as I spoke.

"Well, that's where you come in. You must decide what to do for her and more than likely will have to support her in the interim."

"Ok, well I don't mind that but what am I supposed to do with the estate? I don't want to live there. I have my own place and my own life. Jax can't live there alone, and James is extremely comfortable living his bachelor life. I expect he will settle down soon being that he's turning thirty this year, but he won't want the responsibility of such a large estate." I carefully laid it all out more so for myself than Bill.

"You may have to live with Jax at the estate for a little while. You won't want to uproot her life just because you are comfortable in your own life." I knew Bill was right.

When I stewed over this revelation, I realized my mother really was selfish at times. *Couldn't she have taken a few moments of her time to plan this out better? Why is this all of a sudden my responsibility and burden? I can't sell the estate and throw Jax out making her fend for herself, she's essentially just a kid. I mean sure she's an adult legally but at twenty you barely know what to do with life much less how to run an estate home. This really is inconvenient. Now I'm being selfish.* Lost in my own thoughts I turned back to glance at Jax again; she was still asleep in the back seat. Our talk was about to be heavier than I had expected. Bill seemed to realize to just let me figure out my thoughts, so we spent the rest of the drive to my house in silence.

I walked through the door of my house, Jax followed in quickly behind me setting off for the guest room to change her clothes. I waved at Bill letting him know we were safely in the home. I knew James would probably stay at the estate tonight and that he'd eventually have to come to my house to get his car. I locked the doors then took a deep breath. I did not feel my mother's presence in the home which was a relief. I needed to figure some things out and process everything. I walked into my room shedding clothes along the way to my bathroom. I just wanted to pull my hair down, wash my face, and put on some pajama bottoms with an oversized t-shirt.

As I entered my bathroom I froze; the air was almost frosty, and I could feel there was a spirit present in my bathroom. This was not a familiar presence. I knew from the aura of the room that I was going to be face to face with a spirit that had been long gone from this earth and possibly not friendly. "Go into the light whoever you are. Just go into the light." I said aloud hoping Jax could not hear me. "Go into the light," I repeated. I had once asked a spiritual woman "hypothetically" if I saw a vision/spirit that was bad or dark what I should do. She told me that a dark spirit was never good, and I needed to just tell that spirit to go into the light. I rarely came across bad spirits, but when I did tell them to go into the light generally did the trick. This spirit was not budging. The hair on the back of my neck stood on end as chills ran down my spine. The room seemed so much colder than my bedroom. I turned on my heel, practically ran over to my bed dropping to the floor to beg the universe, or holy spirit, or whatever was out there for help. *Please, whatever this is make it stop. I don't want to do this not now. Please, I'm begging take this away. I am scared and I just want to rest. Please, please protect me.*

Warmth suddenly swept over the room, and I instantly felt better. I looked all around seeing nothing in my bedroom or my bathroom. Whatever that icy dark spirit is, it was no longer present. I relaxed a little then at once started to cry. A full-on sob washed over me for the first time in many days. I cried for my mother, I cried for my sister, and I cried for my father all over again. I just sat on my floor and cried.

CHAPTER 3

I opened my eyes in my bed around three in the morning as if something had purposefully awakened me. I sat upright looking around my room thinking I would see something or someone. It was dark with only a soft light coming from the moon into my room through the windows on either side of my bed. The air was not frosty so whatever had scared me earlier was not present. I did not see my mother's spirit, nor did I feel her presence, so I was not quite sure what had woken me. I felt a little disoriented, so I padded softly toward my kitchen in search of a bottle of water. My bedroom and bathroom are part of the Master Suite of the house that is found on the main floor with the kitchen and living room.

The guestrooms are all upstairs, as well as my home office, with a large bonus room over the garage that I stored some boxes in. I had expectations of getting married and having children one day when I purchased the home; but so far, I had not found any man worthy of me – ok that reads: I have not found any man willing to put up with lawyer hours and not complain that I did not spend enough time with him. I never told anyone that I went on the occasional date with about my trust fund and inheritance because I deemed it was not a pertinent piece of information. I live very modestly and go to work each day like everyone else. I knew I did not have to work and certainly I could live off the money my father left me, but I wanted to work. I did not want to have gold digging men like my mother had. I know the stigmatism is that women are gold diggers, yet men are just as bad!

I stood in the kitchen which was barely illuminated by the light from the refrigerator when I heard a rustling outside in the backyard. I walked slowly to the wall of windows peering out half expecting to see a wild animal, like a deer. Instead, I saw a man, not a live man of course, a spirit man. He was tall, with chiseled features, and broad shoulders, wearing a uniform of some kind. I could not tell if it was a military or police uniform, but he did not seem threatening toward me as he stood there. I sensed that he was there for protection. I quietly slipped out onto my back deck cautiously approaching the rail. The man did not move, he did not run away, nor did he speak. I stood there in silence for a long moment. It became clear he was not going to approach me or speak to me, so I returned to the warmth of my home. I turned my head once more to see him still standing there when I closed the door. In a strange way, I felt as though he was guarding my home for some reason. I was not sure if I was comforted by his presence or afraid of the reason he needed to be there for protection. I did know one thing for sure he was not there to harm me in anyway.

When I awoke the sun was gleaming throughout my bedroom, the night had ended, and morning was upon me. I felt her presence in the room. Sure enough, when I opened my eyes my mother's spirit was standing near the foot of my bed.

"Wake up sunshine!" she said overly cheerful. "Time to rise and shine and face your day!"

"You are awfully cheerful for a dead woman, mother." I rolled over pulling the covers up to my neck.

About that time, I felt her presence by my side. I looked up to see her watching me carefully. I sat up, although her long blonde hair was perfectly coiffed and she appeared beautiful like always, she now had a worried look on her face. I knew that look.

"What's wrong Mother?" I asked cautiously.

"You have to get out of bed Jess. It's important you get up and check your email this morning sweetie. Oh, and you need to check on Jax." with that she vanished again.

I looked to the door of my room to see if there was movement in the living room. I did not see anything, but I could hear Jax moving about in the house. I slowly got out of bed putting my feet on the floor while I pulled my hair up in a high messy bun. When I got to the living room Jax was on her phone speaking in hushed tones with someone. I waited quietly until she said goodbye, which was followed by "I miss you too." *Interesting.*

"Good morning. Who was that?" I said, with a stronger tone than I intended.

Jax turned around abruptly obviously not expecting me to be standing there. Her mouth dropped open as if she were going to say something, but she shut her mouth just as quickly as it opened.

"Well?" I asked.

"None of your business," she retorted in a grumpy tone. I gave her a disapproving look then changed the subject.

"Jax, we need to have a talk."

"I have things I need to take care of this morning; can we talk this afternoon?" I could sense she was purposefully putting me off.

"No, I think we need to go over some things this morning. It can't wait another minute," I insisted.

"Ok," she said reluctantly, as she fell into the couch now typing a message in her cellphone.

"Did you by any chance hear the conversation with Bill yesterday about Mother's estate?" I asked.

"Some of it. I know you are in charge of it all. What exactly does all that mean?" she stopped texting to look over her phone at me.

"Well, it means you are my responsibility for a bit."

"Why? I'm a grown woman. I don't need you to be responsible for me." She sounded frustrated and angry.

"I understand Jax. I don't want to be your keeper. I am not mother, nor do I want to be. I am your sister. I genuinely want what is best for you. I don't want to make you move out of the home you have known since you were born. Which means there are no plans to sell the estate. but it also means I can't give you your full trust until you are twenty-five. I simply will be guardian of your trust, for now."

"So, what exactly does that mean for me and my life?" She was unhappy, I could feel her emotions coming from her like a tidal wave.

"Well, it means you will still live just as you are. Although I may have to move into the estate with you for a while, but you will basically have the same life. Except I will be running it instead of mother."

"Well, you will certainly do a better job," Jax muttered under her breath.

A few moments passed while Jax seemed to be processing the information I had just given her. "I'm sorry I snapped at you. I'm still trying to figure this out too," she finally said sincerely.

"I know you are. I am here for you," I then paused, "but I still want to know who you were talking to on the phone." I was half joking with an older sister tone.

"Just a guy I've been dating. His name is Brian. He's a professional gamer. He goes to conventions in cities like Las Vegas and plays video games for money. He actually gets paid to play," she perked up as she rambled on.

"That's a real job?" I asked with amazement.

"Yeah. At his last convention he was sponsored by Coke

and played on a competitive team. They took second place which paid $7500 each. Not bad for a gamer," Jax said proudly.

"No, I guess that's not bad for a gamer. I don't understand it but as long as he's cool and treats you right that's all that matters to me," I said with a genuine smile. In the back of my mind, I made a mental note to do internet research on professional gamers.

"Jax, sweetie, we have quite a bit to deal with in the coming days and months. I just need you to be understanding and patient as I sort out things. If you need anything just let me know. I guess we can stay here a few more days. I need some time to figure out what to do with my house and horses, especially if I'm going to be taking up my old room at mother's house." I was now feeling put off a little myself.

"Ok, yeah I just need to go by the house and grab some more clothes if that's cool with you." She was young in so many ways.

"You are a grown woman you may come and go as you please," I stated with a laugh. "No partying though. I must still follow the law you know!" I said with mother-like authority.

"Yeah sure. No partying. I'm out of school for the rest of the year anyway. My college classes won't start until mid-January. So, I'm just going to hang with friends. What about Christmas? Are we still going to go to Saint Croix?" she asked.

"I don't know honestly."

I hadn't been to the island the last two Christmas' due to work. My parents had a vacation home there that I guess I now owned, or the estate owned, that would have to be decided in the coming months. I really was not looking forward to all these issues and major decisions. Add in the frosty spirit, my guardian in the backyard, plus my mother's spirit visiting me. *Yeah, I may need a Christmas vacation this year.*

I ate a croissant for breakfast with a fried egg and sliced cheddar cheese on it. I washed it down with coffee loaded with French vanilla flavored creamer. Bill always made fun of me for drinking "coffee flavored sugar milk" as he put it. I was not a fan of the taste of coffee, but I was certainly a fan of the caffeine that I many times needed in order to go to court for a long morning. I had cleared my calendar for the week postponing two hearings so I could deal with my mother's estate matters. I planned to check in each day with my paralegal and Bill, of course. I was going to need Bill's expertise now more than ever. I mainly dealt with family law and the occasional personal injury case. But matters of estate planning, real estate, and corporate law were Bill's area of expertise. I walked up the stairs of my house to the home office and turned my computer on to check email. *Why would my mother say I needed to check my email? This is a woman who most likely never turned a computer on in her life.* Spirits were different life forms all on their own and most of the time I just did not want to deal with them. "Go into the light" was my favorite go to phrase. I avoided Superior Court if at all possible since that is where the murder cases were held. There were some nasty spirits that hung around that place for sure!

My computer flashed into life as the screen on my laptop lit up with the multi-color windows logo. I logged into my work email remotely and found I had six emails waiting for me. One email was from my paralegal confirming all my appointments had been moved with my hearings rescheduled. Two emails were from clients giving me updates on information, including one with a full pre-deposition questionnaire filled out. An email from Facebook telling me I had notifications pending, straight to the trash that one went. An email from my best friend with an e-card telling me she loved me, and she was praying for me and my family. The last email was from my own email address.

Usually this would be marked as spam and immediately discarded., but my curiosity was piqued by my mother's spirit. When I opened the email, it had a bible verse in it. Luke 11:9-10 (NIV) "And I say unto you, Ask, and it shall be given you; seek, and ye shall find; knock, and it shall be opened unto you. For everyone who asks receives; he who seeks finds; and to him who knocks, the door will be opened." *Ok, cryptic, but ok. Why an email to myself? Who would want me to know this bible verse?* I minimized the inbox screen then opened the internet browser to do a search for professional gamers. They actually have a Major League of Gamers. I put the search in my saved searches figuring I would come back to it. I decided to make my phone calls with my first one going to Bill.

"William Brothers' office, this is Patty how may I help you?" Patty was Bill's secretary and had been by his side for the last twelve years or so. She was a great secretary, a bit gossipy, but a highly organized diligent worker. Patty was an attractive blonde in her mid-forties, with long tanned legs that she liked to show off by wearing short pencil skirts. She also had a way with men that was very handy when you needed to get a case on a judge's full calendar.

"Hey Patty, its Jess, is Bill in?"

"Yes, but he's not taking calls. Of course, as usual, you know that doesn't apply to you. I'll let him know you are on the phone." *Wow she's extra snippy today.*
Some days I felt Patty was resentful of the closeness I had with Bill, but today I was not concerned with her opinion about his open-door policy for me. I had other issues at the forefront of my mind.

"Hey Jess, what do you need?" Bill's voice was warm and soothing as usual.

"Hey Bill, I just wanted to touch base and let you know about a few decisions I have made."

"Ok, tell me."

"Well, Jax and I are going to stay at my house for a few more days before transitioning into mother's estate. I think we need it. Then I will move back into my old room there. I know that mother wasn't really running things as of late, more like just existing there. Would you prefer to still run things as you had been?"

"Jess, it's up to you. I'm here to help however you need it."

"Well maybe you can start handing things over to me a little at a time. I won't sell the estate until Jax is twenty-five, at which point I think the fair thing to do would be to liquidate the estate to split it evenly between James, Jax and I." I was feeling a little proud for making the first real decision in this process.

"That's a good plan," Bill said with a tone of approval.

"I just don't know what to do with my place quite yet. I don't want to sell it; I love it too much. I may end up splitting my time evenly between the estate and my home. That will give me some private time and Jax some alone time when she needs it. Unless she's off at college then I will just stay at my home."

"Sounds good. What about financially supporting her? Have you thought how you want to handle that?" Bill asked.

"Well to be honest, I am no financial guru and you have been running the trusts thus far. I think I will just keep William D. Brothers, PC on retainer through the estate to manage all the finances."

Bill laughed as if I said something funny, "Sweetheart, this firm has not been on retainer in over fifteen years. I stopped billing your mother when she went into her depression. But I will gladly continue managing the accounts for you. It's a gift I don't mind giving!"

That was the most gracious thing I had heard all year. I really did not know what was going on with the estate. I chastised myself internally I should have been more involved but honestly, I was too busy with my career to notice.

"Thanks Bill. Really, I mean it."

"Anything else Jess?"

"No, I am sure I will have more to deal with in the coming months. We can just take things one issue at a time. But I do have a technical question to ask you, how would someone be able to send an email to their self?"

"I'm sorry?" Bill said inquisitively.

"What I am asking, is would it be possible to send an email to myself? I got an email from my own email address this morning that was a bible verse, but I was confused as to how my email sent it to me."

"Sounds like spam Jess. Are you concerned about it? If so, I can have our IT department investigate it."

"No, it's ok. I was simply curious I guess." I didn't want to tell him it was my mother's spirit that alerted me to the email, but really it wasn't that big of a concern. For all I know she just wanted me to see my best friend's e-card. That would be more fitting of my mother anyway.

"Alright Jess, well I need to get back to this case I am working on. Unless you have anything else to discuss?"

"No, thanks for everything Bill. I cleared my calendar for the week, so I won't be in the office until next Monday. I will check in with you each day just in case anything comes up." We both said our cursory goodbyes then we ended the call.

I spent the next few hours on and off the phone with my paralegal Barbara handling a few client issues that could not wait until the following Monday. I pushed the cryptic email out of my mind, along with the professional gamer search, and decided to make some hot tea then take a long bubble bath.

The bubbles tickled my skin as I sunk down into my garden tub. I had always debated whether I should have had a jetted tub installed but I was simply happy that I could sink my entire body into the water. As a teen and young woman, a minor disappointment in my life had been that with my legs being so long it prevented me from fitting into most bathtubs. I was determined to make this bathroom fitting for a tall woman. I did splurge a little and installed a small flat screen television on the wall above my tub. I used the little remote to turn on the TV selecting the music channel. No not the obnoxious channel that shows nothing but reality shows, the music channel that plays music with slideshows of little fun facts about the song playing. I chose a meditation channel so that I could just listen to soothing sounds and relax a bit. After all, I deserved some relaxation.

Just as I settled down into the hot water and finally starting to relax, I felt a familiar eerie iciness come into the room as if someone had just opened a window and let the outside air in. I opened my eyes, scanning the room to see if there was anyone, or anything, in the bathroom with me. I found my mother standing at the doorway of my bathroom white as a ghost, pun intended. I looked toward the mirror seeing no other entity in the room, but I could now see my breath in front of me as I breathed. My heart rate began to rise a little, I felt very vulnerable being that I was naked and alone in the room. I pulled my knees to my chest as the only course of defensive posture I could muster in the moment. With a swift rush of icy air, a figure raced through the room while simultaneously my mother's spirit disappeared.

"Whatever you are, whoever you are, just go into the light already," I yelled. *I don't think this "go into the light" thing is going to work with this particular spirit.*
I waited cautiously for whatever had just shown up in my bathroom to leave, appear, or kill me. I did not know if the spirit could kill me, but it felt evil enough as if it could. This one was definitely not a friendly one. I had not necessarily believed in ghosts or spirits growing up but since a few had shown

themselves to me it was hard not to accept that we lived with spirits among us. I had never discussed it with anyone for fear of ridicule and possible commitment to a loony bin.

"Don't hurt me," I said sheepishly toward whatever was in the room.

"We won't," a deep whisper said into my ear. I nearly jumped out of my own skin and stood so quickly that I splashed water onto the tile floor. I grabbed the towel off the hook on the wall wrapping it around my body as quickly as I could, standing with my back against the wall. The temperature in the room was as cold as if I were standing outside.

"Who are you?" I asked the thing in the room. I couldn't see it. I could only feel and hear it.

"In due time," the voices said louder than a whisper but not much more.

"What do you want?" I tried to ask calmer than I actually felt. I wanted to escape to my bedroom, but my fear rooted me in place.

I waited patiently for an answer when to my relief the icy temperature returned to warmth, the way the room should have felt all along. I knew whomever, whatever it was, had disappeared yet again. My mother's spirit stood once again in the doorway looking more relaxed, almost as if she had something to do with the icy being or beings leaving.

"Mother, they said 'we' who are they?" I asked her spirit.

"I can't tell you," she said sadly, "but you will know soon enough. They will show themselves when the timing is right."

"Are they dangerous, Mother?"

"They can be," she answered.

"Do you know what they want?" I was getting frustrated.

"Yes. But I can't tell you," she said quietly.

I was now completely fed up.

"I WANT YOU ALL TO LEAVE!"

I screamed from the top of my lungs. I felt I was on the verge of crying again when I just wanted to relax. I heard a noise in the living room, I took off running, wrapped in a towel screaming at the top of my lungs, charging toward the spirits in my home. To my surprise, and my poor sister, I ran into her and her new beau looking like a drowned rat in a fluffy white towel.

This was not the best introduction in the world and certainly very embarrassing.

"You expecting a criminal in here sis?" Jax said humorously.

"I'm sorry Jax I didn't know you had come in. I thought there may be an intruder," I stammered.

"And you were going to... What?... maim them in your towel with your bare hands?" she said stifling a laugh.

"I guess I didn't think that one through, did I?" I said looking down at my bare feet.

"Hi, I am Jax's sister Jessica, and you are?" I said extending my hand to the red-faced young man standing in my living room, who was trying desperately not to notice my lack of clothing.

"I'm Brian," he said with a small shake of my hand.

"Oh, you are the professional gamer Jax told me about. Nice to meet you. Please excuse my appearance I wasn't expecting company. "

"No problem," he said shyly. He was a good-looking kid with scraggly auburn hair and blue eyes, wearing an oversized ballcap on sideways. He was a bit on the nerdy side, certainly not what I would have expected to see my sister attracted to, but he was quiet and sweet.

"If you'll both excuse me, I'm going to go get dressed." They both nodded their heads while Jax attempted to hide her smile. I walked as dignified as I could to my bedroom closing the door behind me.

CHAPTER 4

I was determined to figure out this "I see dead people" thing. It was weighing heavily on my mind, and I wanted to stop seeing these spirits. I had a life, a prominent career, a little sister who needed me, and responsibilities that did not include the potential diagnosis of being schizophrenic. I had no idea where to begin. I could go to a psychic, a palm reader, or I could just do some internet research. *You know because everything on the internet is true.* I laughed as that thought crossed my mind. I lived in a very rural area of Southern Maryland, but there was a little beach town named Solomon's Island near my home that held small businesses and restaurants. People liked to travel in the summer to the area for fresh crab, the locally famous Tiki Bar, and festivals that the little town held each year. I liked the intimate atmosphere of the small shops and supported the independently owned businesses whenever I could. There was a small bookstore I had been in several times that had a section dedicated to Spiritualism. 'Little Shop on the Bay,' as it was called, carried other items such as healing crystals, meditation books and CDs, incense, and other forms of enlightening material. I had purchased a book of meditations once before with some incense for my bathroom. I did not necessarily believe all the psychic type of stuff, however if ever there was a place to learn how to not see spirits, I figured this would be a good place to start.

The store was a small tidy place situated on the first floor of an older home turned into a business, which was situated on the main street of the town. The sweet smell of incense filled the air as you passed through the door. A young woman sitting behind the counter had her nose buried in her phone. *Most likely texting* I thought, as she greeted me with a "good afternoon" without taking her eyes off her screen. I smiled as if she could see me through her phone then continued past her to the area where the spiritual books and other enlightenment things were placed. I had no idea where to begin so I grabbed a book on Universalism and quickly glanced over the back cover. It was not exactly what I needed so I returned it to its previous spot. I turned the rack that held the many different titles of books letting out an overwhelmed sigh.

"May I help you?" a sweet voice said from behind me. I turned to find an older woman barely over five feet tall looking up at me with glasses resting on the tip of her nose. I would have described her as Native American or Hawaiian if I had to categorize her looks. I started to open my mouth and describe what I wanted, but second guessed how idiotic I would sound and simply said "No, Thank you," instead.

"You are looking for a way to make the spirits stop visiting you," she stated as if she read the thought right from my brain. I stood there quietly not knowing what to say. "Your mother told me," she said very plainly as if this was a normal conversation to her. I looked around as if I expected to see my mother's spirit, but she was not there.

"I'm sorry. What did you say?" I asked genuinely perplexed.

"I said 'your mother told me' in answer to your unspoken question as to how I know you want to make the spirits stop visiting you."

"Are you a mind reader, or psychic or something?" I asked almost in a whisper so the girl in the front wouldn't hear me.

"No. But I do see and speak to spirits much like you do,"

she said, "I have a letter in the back for you I will go get it. Hold on I'll be right back." And with that she disappeared through the back door of the store. I had no idea what to say or think. I decided it was too weird, I hurried through the front door of the store moving as fast as I could to my car. I was going back to the solace of my home.

Wake up, wake up, wake up. I thought as I pinched my arm in the driver's seat of my little BMW. Ok the pinching was real and hurt so that had to stop. I was so out of my mind that I felt extremely vulnerable and truthfully shaken. Just then a hand knocked on my window unnerving me. This was becoming a reoccurring event in my life, consistently being startled. I looked up to see Bill smiling down at me. *Oh, Thank God!* I rolled the window down and smiled in relief.

"Why are you just sitting here in your car?" he asked.

"You wouldn't believe me if I told you," I said without explaining. "More importantly what are you doing here?"

"I had a client to visit down here, and you know how much I love the restaurant on the pier."

"Yeah, I do," I agreed amused.

"You ok Jess? You look like something is bothering you. I mean I know you just lost your mom, but you look like something is troubling you. Are the affairs of the estate too much right now?" he asked with genuine concern.

"No, it's not that. I just…" I paused trying to figure out how to formulate what I wanted to say without sounding crazy. "I am seeing things that are like bad daydreams, I guess. I don't know how to describe it."

"I see. Well, I am done for the day, want to grab some coffee and talk for a bit? I promise not to make fun of your coffee flavored sugar milk," he said with a wink. I genuinely smiled. "Sounds good to me."

We walked together to the little coffee shop around the corner and sat on the front porch. I grabbed a small piece of coffee cake with a cinnamon swirl to go with my sugar free vanilla latte. I cancelled out the sugar free part with the cake, but I didn't much care at the moment. It was a bit warmer today than it was in the previous days, but it wasn't warm by any means. It felt good to have the warm cup in my hands and the sun shining on my face. I wasn't sure where to begin in my story to Bill but I figured if I could trust anyone with my issue it would be him. We sat in comfortable silence for a few minutes as I got my thoughts together. Bill watched me over the top of his coffee cup. He was good at knowing when to press me for information and when to let me work through my thoughts.

"Bill, without sounding like a movie here, I see dead people. Specifically, I see my mother. I have seen other spirits before including my best friend that died a few years back. I have a military soldier, or police officer, who watches over my house in the middle of the night. And recently a not so nice, possibly very evil, spirit or body of spirits likes to hang out in my bathroom," I rambled in a rushed sentence. *Whew.*

"Ok," he said rather flatly.

"That's it! Just ok," I said exasperated.

"Yep. Just ok." He was very calm.

"You aren't worried about my sanity or thinking I am mental or something?" I asked unbelievably.

"Nope. I'm not." Bill could be a man of very few words at times and this was one of those times I wanted him to be full of words of wisdom, or at the very least something more than just "ok."

"Bill, I feel like I am losing my mind."

"Jessica, there are some things that you probably should have been told a long time ago. Unfortunately, we weren't sure you would understand or accept what needed to be said," he explained with an air of concern for me.

"Some 'things?' And who is the 'we' here?" I said with a noticeable rise in my tone. Bill took my hand closing his eyes for a moment. I could feel a stir in the air around us and before I could blink, we were sitting in the living room of my mother's estate home.

"Holy Crap! How did you do that?" I exclaimed in almost a panic.

"Jess. Please calm down for a moment."

CALM DOWN! CALM DOWN! This is a man who has been a rock for me and now suddenly he's just somehow magically whisked me into my mother's home with a touch and he wants me to calm down! My mind was racing, I felt like my entire world was turning upside down in that very moment. As if seeing spirits wasn't enough for me now Bill was some kind of magical wizard or something. I was surely dreaming.

"Bill! What the hell is going on!" I practically yelled.

"Jess, your mom and I decided a very long time ago to keep some information from you. We wanted to let you have a normal life as much as we could."

"You and my mom decided? What about my father? Was he in on whatever this is?" I said as I twirled my had in the air.

"No Jess. He wasn't," Bill said sadly.

"Why not?" I felt defensive somehow.

"Because he didn't know Jess."

"Didn't know what?" I demanded.

"Jess, your mother and your father had an amazing relationship. They were in love, incredibly happy, and wanted the best that life had to offer them. They had wealth that most people could only fantasize about, and both were healthy.

"Your mother and father had more love than most people experience in a lifetime. They were like a match made in heaven and wanted a family more than anything. But your father was a much older man, he was thought to be 'past his prime' in terms of procreation. Your mother turned to me to help her find a way to have children, by whatever means possible."

"Ok. I'm listening." I had crossed my arms across my chest and began rapidly tapping my foot.

"I on the other hand had no desire to marry, or find love, much less date for that matter, but I knew that I needed to have offspring. It was part of my destiny. So, I offered to give life through your mother."

"Wait. You slept with my mother????" I almost shrieked in response.

"No Jess. I did not. I helped your mother become pregnant, but I did not sleep with her," Bill explained.

"So, what you used a turkey baster or something?" I said almost with disgust.

Bill laughed. "Not exactly. I am not of your realm. No, I am not an alien or some kind of fairy god father. I know what you are thinking!"

No kidding! Wait, how do you know what I'm thinking? Do you know I just thought that?

"Yes. I do know you just thought that," he said amused.

"This is not real. I don't know what to say right now. So does this mean you are my father?" I asked with a sudden realization that I may not be my father's child.

"In creation only. Your 'Daddy' is still the father you have known your entire life. I am just the means through which your mother and father had a family."

Well, that explains the fantasy of my wanting you to marry my mother and be my stepfather. It would only seem natural to my DNA.

"Does that mean you are James' 'creator' as well?" I asked.

"No. Funny enough your father wasn't quite as past his prime as they thought, and James was a pleasant surprise to your parents."

I sat in silence processing what Bill had just said to me. This was about as unreal as "unreal" could get. I had so many questions.

Once again Bill just watched me silently knowing to let me process my thoughts. *WAIT! You always know to let me have my thoughts. You have never interrupted me when I was thinking through an issue! You have known because you know my thoughts!!!!!!!* I screamed this revelation in my head as I watched Bill's face, he smiled broadly at me.

"Not fair," I said petulantly.

"I'm sorry Jess. I wasn't sure you were ready to know the truth. I was afraid the revelation would open resentment toward your mother and I for not saying anything to you sooner. Your mother felt it was in your best interest to allow you to have a perfectly normal existence. I knew you would be able to see other beings and spirits. I kept most of them away from you as a small child and teen. Your best friend's death was the first time I allowed one to approach you. She begged me to let you see her. And I knew how much you were hurting over her sudden departure."

"You 'LET' her!" I felt exasperated.

"Jess, I know this is a shock. I didn't want to tell you in a street side café, or in the office with others watching. We tried to use Leila, but you didn't seem to want to accept her either." He seemed genuinely concerned.

"Leila? Who the hell is Leila?" I asked tartly.

"The spirit medium at Little Shop on the Bay."

"Wait, she knows who you are?"

"She thinks I'm a medium just like she is. She has no idea the extent of it all," he explained.

"Is that the letter she was referring to?"

"The letter was your mother's idea. She felt if she visited Leila and had her write a letter to you that you would be more accepting of the information. I thought it was a bad idea to include a third person in our secret, but you know how demanding your mother can be."

"What? You can't control her in death either?"

Bill laughed knowing I was being a smart ass but telling truth all at the same time. "No, she has a soul all on her own. A very demanding, strong-willed soul at that," he said half amused.

"I don't understand any of this, but I do know somehow you are being honest with me," I said. "What exactly are you? What am I?"

"You are human!" He said with a laugh.

"Seriously Bill!!! What are we?" I wasn't playing now. I wanted answers.

"We are highly evolved beings. The universe doesn't stop just past the edge of the galaxy as most humans believe. There are other worlds out there and other spiritual realms; there are more primitive worlds out there as well. Some of the 'aliens' that humans claim to see that use probing and such are actually more primitive not more intelligent as humans have imagined and created them to be," Bill explained.

When I was in college, I once read a book on the Pleiadean civilization that supposedly was an alien race from the star system called Pleiades. This system was in a small cluster of seven stars located about 500 light years from earth. Supposedly they visited earth and stayed with humans to create civilizations like the Mayans and Incans.
They were here to guide humans toward a more spiritual path.

"No, we are not Pleiadens," Bill said reading my thoughts. "However, we are very much like them and yes, they truly existed. No, they aren't coming in mother ships to save humans." He seemed to be reading my thoughts as fast as I was having them.

"I just don't understand Bill. This is beyond my comprehension," I said almost sadly.

"Jess, you are partly human so you may not understand until your spiritual enlightenment is over. Just know that you are not completely of this earth. Some beings are here to protect humans from the primitive societies in other realms."

"Like gods and goddesses?" I asked.

"That's probably the most accurate of descriptions you could come up with in your human thought process. Yes. We are all of God, made in the likeness of God, all to one day return to God when we have fulfilled our purpose. Some are more evolved than others," Bill explained.

"Are you a God of sorts?" I needed to know.

Bill went on to explain that he was more like a protector than a God, and that he had a higher state of being that included mental abilities others did not possess. He was able to use his mind to create things, just like he was able to move us from one place to another by creating where we were sitting. He explained that in reality we were still physically sitting in the café. He went on to say that we as higher entities were able to be in multiple places as well as multiple realms all at the same time. He tried to explain the space time continuum to me, but I was so lost by the time he got to that I thought my head would literally explode. I listened as carefully as I could to everything he said, like a young Jedi listening to a Jedi Master, but I felt more like JarJar Binks who just would not get it.

When Bill finished speaking, I felt exhausted and like I needed an aspirin for my headache, but I had one particularly important pressing question for him.

"Bill, who, or rather what, is in my bathroom?"
Bill looked like he was taken aback, or at the very least concerned, over my question as if I had just said the world was ending tomorrow.

"Jess, be very careful of the spirits that whisper to you in your bathroom. I cannot protect you fully from them as they are of a different realm than I am. I know they will not hurt you because you are a protected since you are my creation. But don't let that lead you astray and no matter what do **not** trust them," Bill said ominously.

"Should I be scared of them?" As if I did not fear them already.

"No. They will reveal themselves to you when they are ready. You have a higher purpose than I do, and they are an integral part of that but just be cautious. Promise me you will heed my warning on this."

"I promise, I promise." I did not care what Bill said, I **was** scared of them.

"Did you send the soldier in my backyard?"

"Yes. I sent him when Jax came to stay with you," Bill stated.

"Why? Why when Jax came to stay with me?"

"She is like you as well. She sees spirits but she doesn't yet believe they are spirits. She sees them as live people. You have the gift of being able to tell when a spirit is in its human form and when a spirit is in its soul form," he further explained.
I pondered over this revelation for a moment.

"Did you create her with mother as well?" I asked.

"No. She isn't my creation. It wasn't until after your mother was with child that I realized another evolved being created with her. He was in the guise of one of her admirers when he planted a light seed in her. He didn't have honest intentions. This has led to a different path for Jax, much different than your path. It is one of the biggest reasons your mother fell into such a depression. You have a connection with Jax that James will never have but it's not necessarily always going to be a good one."
My jaw dropped open like I just saw the real Santa Claus.

"Is that why I am her guardian for now?" I asked cautiously.

"It's part of the reason. She will fully know her path before she is twenty-five. There is time to ensure she follows a love and light path which is your charge at this time. Others will try to pull her into a path of negativity, like your grandmother did unknowingly," Bill recalled with a frown.

"How do I keep her on a 'love and light' path?" I said using finger quotations.

"You need to love her through anything. Like a mother does her child. Your mother should have done this to keep her off a negative path, but she was merely human, and it was too much for her to manage. Your mother has accepted that she cannot show herself to Jax until she is on the right path. But she now knows she is to help you however she can spiritually." He looked worried as he explained this to me. I contemplated what he had just said then a thought occured me.

"Wait, I have to babysit her for five more years?" I asked with pure exasperation.
Bill laughed out loud.

"No Jess. Her path and destiny will be cemented in the next year. You will need to just watch out for spirits presenting themselves as humans to Jax and help keep them away. I will be here to help you as always. I will protect both of you just as I have your entire lives. It is my ultimate responsibility. I should have protected your mother from Jax's creator, but I missed him somehow."
I could see that this weighed heavily on Bill, and he deemed this as a failure of sorts. I patted his shoulder in a return gesture of comfort as he had done for me many times over my life. I really needed that aspirin now more than ever.

CHAPTER 5

I now had more questions than I had answers and felt more confused than before. I tried to watch the news as I sat in my living room the next evening, but my focus was elsewhere. Jax was on the back deck with Brian, she seemed to be having a good time laughing and smiling with her feet propped up on the railing. I looked past her to the yard, noticing my soldier was standing watch over all of us. I wondered if he would step in and protect us if some bad spirit tried to hurt either Jax or I. I felt better with the knowledge that most other beings could not harm me since I was Bill's "creation." I still worried about the frosty beings in my bathroom and questioned why they only come to me in my bathroom. Strange as that was. My mother died in that bathroom so now I wanted to know if the frosty beings had anything to do with her death. When I was upset with her for dying, she had said she did not mess up and I would know what was really happening in the coming days. I took a deep breath as I continued watching my sister and Brian talking animatedly about whatever young people talk about. I wish I were still that carefree at times.

My cell phone rang, I recognized that it was James calling me.

"Hello," I said stifling a yawn.

"Hey Sis, are you home?" James asked.

"Yeah, I'm home."

"Do you mind if I come by and get my car?"

"No," I laughed, "James you can come by any time you know that."

"I know, but I will have company with me since my car is at your house. I had to ask a buddy for a ride. I just wanted to make sure you didn't mind. That's all." His voice sounded jovial through the phone.

"Yep, that's fine." I really did not want to play host tonight but for James I would. After we exchanged information about Jax and Brian, mainly I was telling James about the guy, we said goodbye. I figured I had about thirty minutes before he would get to my house.

I got up off the couch and set off to my room to put on jeans and a soft baby blue sweater. I brushed my hair and teeth, then applied a small amount of mascara and lip gloss. I was presentable yet comfortable. I had gotten a manicure and pedicure the day before mother's funeral so I could walk around bare foot without worrying if the polish on my toenails would be chipped. I tended to neglect my toes in the colder months since I rarely wore open toed shoes during this time of year. I went to the kitchen then stood staring at an empty refrigerator and freezer. I was going to have to do some shopping or Jax and I were going to starve.

I did the next best thing, ordered a few pizzas from a local pizzeria with garlic knots. I called James back to ask him to pick them up on the way, inviting him and his friend to stay for dinner. I prepaid for the pizza with my credit card, I didn't want James to have to pay for them since I was doing the inviting. I pulled a few glasses out of my cabinet then set out a pitcher of sweet tea from the refrigerator next to them. That was about as far as my host duties were going to go for the night. Everyone could pour their own drinks. I grabbed a bottle of water then sat back down on the couch. I put on some music through my surround sound system looking through the back windows again. My soldier was gone, and Jax had moved closer to Brian on the outdoor chaise lounge. They looked comfortable and admittedly kind of cute together. *Just kind of.* I sat wondering where my soldier had gone when the doorbell rang.

"James, you don't have to ring the doorbell!" I called out toward the door. No one entered the house, so I got up to see who was at my door. A man I did not recognize was standing there holding a package in his hand. I cautiously opened the door.

"May I help you?" I asked.

"Hi, are you Jessica Hanson?" He looked me over with curiosity.

"I am," I said flatly.

"I'm Donovan Wheeler. I just moved in across the street a few months ago, and I apologize for not introducing myself before now, but I have a package that I think was mislabeled and delivered to my house by mistake."

He looked to be in his mid-thirties, obviously well-groomed with dark brown hair that curled around the nape of his neck and behind his ears, with bright ocean blue eyes. He had a short trimmed full beard that was very manly that I found to also be extremely sexy. He was tall, I surmised around six foot two or three since he towered over me. I noticed he stood up straight with broad shoulders, and I imagined that he was also well built under his clothing. He was dressed in a grey polo shirt, with the sleeves rolled to three quarter length, and jeans over what I would describe as "dock" shoes. Around this area it was common to have a boat slip somewhere as marinas were a dime a dozen.

"Would you like me to set it on the porch or..." he said with a grin.

"Oh, I am so sorry! Where are my manners!" I stammered as I realized I had been caught completely checking him out.

41

"Please come in! You can set it right here," I said as I pointed to the little butler desk in the kitchen.

He entered the house, setting the package down as I instructed with a very warm friendly smile. Jax and Brian had come in from the back deck and were standing at the entrance of the kitchen watching me make a fool of myself with my new neighbor.

"Hi, I'm Jax, Jess's sister. And you are?" Jax said abruptly, completely amused.

"I'm Donovan, nice to meet you."

Donovan was very comfortable with himself. He seemed like the kind of guy who could fit into any environment. Jax introduced Brian to Donovan then continued to pour two glasses of sweet tea for herself and Brian. She offered a glass to Donovan who declined graciously saying he had to get back to his house.

"It was nice to meet you, Jessica," Donovan said with a smile and his hand extended toward me.

I put my hand in his warm hand, barely managing more than a smile. It was like my tongue had been cut out and I was suddenly mute. Donovan chuckled, grinning as he walked out through the side door of my home with a wave. I was still standing there like a star struck idiot.

"Earth to Jess!" Jax said giggling, waving her hand in front of my face.

"What?" I said with a shrug of my shoulders. "He was hot. Probably the hottest guy I have met in a very long time." That much was true.

Jax giggled like a little schoolgirl then took Brian by the hand to the living room.

James and his friend, Christian, walked through the door a few minutes later and the package on the butler desk was promptly forgotten. Christian was a little younger than James by approximately two or three years I guessed. He was tall and thin with blonde hair that was styled in a way that would make the boys in the latest K-pop boy band jealous. His deep brown eyes were a little oddly shaped but overall, he was a decent looking guy.

We all agreed to sit on the living room floor with paper plates, napkins, and the pizza boxes on the oversized coffee table to eat because no one wanted to do dishes. Jax was thrilled to be telling the story of her normally talkative sister being mute and "googly eyed" over some guy to James and his friend. She equally enjoyed telling how I ran out of my bedroom scantily clad in a towel and dripping wet to confront a possible intruder. She was amused by the idea that I would maim the would-be intruder with my wet towel and stun them with my nakedness. I just smiled, laughing it off with the rest of them. It was nice to sit around eating pizza and laughing with my siblings, even if it was at my own expense. I noticed that my soldier in my backyard had returned and if I wasn't mistaken, he seemed to be smiling too.

James and Christian were getting ready to leave when I heard a whisper behind me. "Watch him carefully." I did not turn to see who had whispered it as I knew whomever or whatever it was would not be visible right in front of my guests. I was not sure if the voice was referring to Christian or Donovan, but my gut feeling was it was Christian. He seemed like a nice enough guy although I had to admit he was a little off. James was only human, as I had recently learned from Bill the day before, he certainly would not be as in tune with spirits as Jax and I naturally are. I noticed that Jax was cautious around Christian, even though she was smiling and laughing, she seemed slightly uncomfortable. That was not necessarily unusual behavior for Jax, as she could to be stand-offish toward strangers in general, but she was watching him walk toward the bathroom with a scowl on her face.

"Jax!" I whispered with a partial scold veiled in my whisper.

"I don't like him," she whispered back in an unasked explanation.

"Well at least pretend or try to plaster a fake smile on. The scowl is unbecoming," I whispered through my teeth.

"You sound like mother," she whispered.

I laughed out loud, as James eyed us suspiciously from across the room.

He was engaged in conversation with Brian about professional gaming. I knew James was doing the big brother thing at the same time probably warning Brian not to hurt his little sister. I was proud of him. Christian suddenly appeared behind Jax and I and asked what we were laughing about. We both jumped. *Where did he come from?* He was shifty. "Oh, nothing just sister stuff," we said almost simultaneously. Our eyes locked as we sent an unspoken sister message to each other that said *He is creepy!* I noticed my soldier in the back yard had moved closer to the house.

James and Brian joined the three of us to start the goodbye process which usually included several rounds of hugs and handshakes. Christian shook my hand then tried to hug Jax, but Brian practically stood between them. *Good for you Brian!* I wish I could read minds like Bill right then, and I wondered if that was a skill I would eventually learn or if only he had that ability. James thanked me again for the pizza and with that he and Christian were out of the house. I instinctively locked the door, not sure if I was locking them out or us in, but I certainly felt better turning the little lock bolting the door in place.

I noticed the package sitting on the butler area of the kitchen. I smiled as I remembered the hunky man who delivered the package to my door earlier. I pulled out the scissors from the junk drawer, slicing the box open carefully. Inside the box was a small wooden box with a lock on the front. Attached to the little wooden box was an envelope that held a small key on a red ribbon and a letter. The letter was addressed to me in a woman's handwriting. As I began to read the letter, I recognized that it was the letter my mother dictated to Leila. It spelled out the relationship between my mother and my father with a love that only my mother could have conveyed. She discussed how badly she wanted a family with my father and would do just about anything, including make a deal with the devil himself if it meant she could have a child. She described Bill as more of a saint than Satan himself but stopped just short of saying she was ashamed of her dealings with him. I could read between the lines and know ultimately, she was.

She didn't describe how she conceived only emphatically stated she never cheated on my father. She was thankful to God for allowing her to have a beautiful healthy baby girl, then surprised but extremely grateful for her little boy as well. She explained that James was definitely conceived between her and my father, and she felt fulfilled as a woman to give a natural child to him.

She described my father's passing as the worst thing that could have ever happened to her, she felt her life was over and she should have died instead of him. She believed he was taken from her because she had a child with a 'supernatural being' instead of trusting God to give her a child. As I read this part of the letter I wondered if Bill knew that was how she really felt. She explained that she believed that Jax was another beautiful blessing, and it was not until her transition into the spiritual world that she realized Jax was from a non-human father.

She had never known in her human life that Jax was from a highly evolved being as well. *Hmmm. Bill never told her that. Interesting.* She wondered through the rest of the letter if this was some sort of good versus evil type spiritual warfare. She closed the letter with an apology to me for not telling me when she was still in her human life. But she acknowledged her weakness as a human and could not bring herself to admit to her failure as a wife and mother. She closed the letter with a warning to watch over Jax always. Leila wrote her own note with the box as well. She explained that the box was filled with the only thing I would ever need to rid myself of the spirits visiting me. She wished me luck and said her door was always open if I had any questions or needed anything further. She included a twenty percent off coupon for her bookstore. I literally bust out laughing at the coupon.

Jax walked into the kitchen as I was laughing over the coupon in the letter and wanted to know what was so funny. I showed her the coupon to the bookstore and said I found it amusing. Jax looked at me as if I had lost my mind then shook her head like she just did not understand me sometimes. As she walked out of the kitchen, I pulled the letter from behind my back and decided I would need to hide it for now. I folded the paper and neatly placed it back in the envelope. I pulled the key out to open the box but stopped myself and promptly put it back. I decided I would have to open the little wooden box another time, preferably when I was alone in the house. I took it along with the envelop to my bedroom. I placed the wooden box on my night table beside my bed then put the letter in the family bible. I turned the pages to Luke 11:9-10, using the envelop as a bookmark. I figured there was a reason that verse was emailed to me mysteriously, I might as well mark it. *What better way to mark it than with the letter from my mother through Leila the medium.* I laughed at the absurdity of it.

CHAPTER 6

Bill was sitting in his office reading over a case file when I approached his door the next morning. Patty tried her best to stop me or at the very least warn Bill I was coming, basically as another means of stopping me, but it was of no use. I was on a quest of supernatural enlightenment I felt had been forced upon me over the last few days. Bill looked up with amusement at the two women who occupied his time the most and motioned for me to come in the door. I wanted to stick my tongue out at her like a little child who just got her way, but it wasn't appropriate, so I refrained.

"Should I just go ahead and tell her you're my dad? Then we can stop the insanity of her trying to keep me from speaking to you because she feels she should control who you are allowed to see and who you are not?" I said tartly.

Bill laughed at me as he shook his head no, "I don't think that would be wise. I wouldn't want to tarnish your mother's reputation in death. Besides how would you explain that I created you since we never had sex?"

"Yeah Bill, how do you explain that?" I asked with raised eyebrows.

Again, Bill laughed then promptly changed the subject, "What do you need Jess?"

"I was wondering what you know about the little wooden box that was delivered to me yesterday."

Bill was now the one raising his eyebrows as if this was news to him.

"I have no idea what you are talking about," he said. I explained it was delivered with the letter from mother, and about Leila's letter with the coupon. *Which I still find amusing.*

"What kind of thing would work to keep us - highly evolved beings - from seeing spirits?" I asked.

"Well unfortunately for Leila, who obviously doesn't know what she's talking about, there is nothing that will keep you from using your gift," Bill explained.

I had not had time to open the box since Jax was staying at my house, so I had no idea what the contents were, and it was increasingly obvious to me that neither did Bill. I mused that there would be kryptonite type stuff in there and that it would probably be best if I just kept the box locked up for a while. I was still partly human, according to Bill, so truthfully some form of human energy interception could potentially work on me to keep me from seeing spirits. It could not take away all of my abilities just merely dull them Bill guessed. Either way he was not truly sure what the contents were or if they would work on me. I guessed some kind of voodoo type stuff was in there with sprinkles of glitter. My girly imagination was getting the best of me at this point.

"Why didn't you tell mother about Jax while she was alive?" I asked.

"She wasn't in a good place after Jax was born. Half the time she was on whatever latest anti-depressant her whacky doc wanted her to try and she couldn't think straight if I had wanted to explain it to her," he explained. Truthfully as much as I hated to admit it, he was right.

"How did you know Jax was from another higher being?"

"I can tell. Just like with you, I could tell you had more of my qualities in you than human qualities the day I held you in my arms," he answered with a fatherly smile as he remembered holding his creation for the first time. Well, really, he was like my father after all.

"Can you tell other higher beings are around in general? Are there any other beings around us?" Now I really wanted to get to know more about this.

"Yes, I can, and no there aren't. I can tell higher beings at once; they have an aura about them. You probably feel it more than see it. Humans generally call this their intuition. Yours will eventually be attuned to the higher frequencies that evolved beings put out. There are lower frequencies of beings like humans for example. You are currently more attuned to them but won't always recognize them because you haven't expanded your mind to include higher frequencies. All humans are forms of energy. Some are good, some are not. In order for there to be good there must be bad, otherwise we would never know that we are experiencing the good."

This was getting deep philosophically. I had read about this before in a book written by a man who was having conversations with God himself. But it was also seemingly in line with the seven chakras and energy centers that were practiced in the Hindu belief systems.

"Is Jax good or bad?" I asked out of slight concern.

"That is to be decided. Souls have the ability to choose and create whatever they wish. She hasn't quite chosen. She's leaning more toward a negative path because of her past, but this is where you are supposed to influence her with love and light and try to keep her on the path of good instead. Like I explained days ago her path will be fully cemented in the next year."

His reminding me of this part of our conversation sparked something I wanted to tell him about.

I went on to discuss Christian with Bill. I knew he was not all good and I told him about the voice that warned me, as well as Jax's reaction to him. I described my feelings about Christian and how odd I felt. Bill listened very carefully to every detail with interest. He jotted down a few notes as I was speaking then told me he would make some inquires and get back to me. He advised that I should heed to the whisper I heard. I wanted to ask more questions about the whispering voice, but Patty interrupted a little too triumphantly with news that Bill's first client was waiting for him. I stood and went to Bill behind his desk hugging him tightly. I think Bill was just as surprised as I was. My human side was obviously more sentimental and emotional than he was. I felt like I needed a hug from him. He smiled warmly at me as I left his office. I flashed a devilish toothy grin at Patty as I passed her desk and snidely remarked that I was appreciative of her squeezing me into his schedule. She scoffed at my remarks immediately returning to her filing. I felt accomplished at the moment, and I didn't have to stick my tongue out at her.

I rode down the elevator then went ahead through the front doors on the street level of our office building. The building was in the bustling business section of downtown Baltimore. It was a hellish commute from Southern Maryland at times but many days I ended up in court in Annapolis, so it was not too bad. Our office was on the twenty first floor of the Centurion Building on Charles Street. There was a security desk on the main floor of the building although half the time the security personnel were on their personal phone, sleeping, or watching television behind the desk. I mostly felt like they were there for visibility purposes only.

There was a deli across the street I liked to frequent that made the best little Panini sandwiches. As I walked in the deli, I greeted Ralph the owner and his wife Doreen, ordering my usual hot baked ham and cheddar cheese Panini. I selected a bottle of water from the cooler along with a bag of Baked Lays potato chips from the rack. I don't know why I bothered with attempting diet foods, but I did. As I approached the counter to pay for my lunch a familiar voice spoke, "I got it."

I turned my head to see my gorgeous neighbor standing beside me. *How the hell did I miss him walking in here!* Donovan stood next to me in a dark grey three-piece suit, white shirt, and a silver tie with flecks of blue thrown in for a little color. He was just as gorgeous in a suit as he was in a causal polo, ok maybe more so in the suit. Luckily, I had decided to see Bill in nice black pants with a dark maroon blouse and not the yoga pants and t-shirt I was originally considering wearing.

"No, it's ok really. I can pay for my lunch," I said hoping it did not sound feminist or ungrateful.

"I would like to treat you to lunch if you will let me," he said with a dazzling smile as he handed his credit card over to Doreen who was watching the interaction with intrigue. I nodded to Doreen in approval, she smiled at the unfolding situation like a Cheshire cat.

"Thank you very much. Although I feel I owe you an apology for my lusty behavior yesterday," I said slightly embarrassed.

"Oh! **THAT** was lusty behavior for you?" He teased.

"Funny. And not what I meant." I rolled my eyes then continued to change the subject. "What are you doing here? If you don't mind my asking," I asked as I selected a small table by the far wall.

I pulled out the chair facing the window so I could watch the bustling street on the other side. *As if you will see anything past Donovan in front of you!* My mind scolded me.

"I work in the Centurion Building across the street," he said with a grin.

"Really? I work in that building, too." I was surprised by his revelation.

"I know you do."

Donovan was a man of many surprises that began to seem a bit stalkerish. "We just met yesterday, so how do you know I work in that building?" I tried to not imply he was stalking me with my tone.

"I saw you leave it a few minutes ago. I assumed you were leaving to grab lunch as I was," He calmly explained. *Of course, Duh! See not a stalker after all!* I just smiled instead of voicing my thoughts.

I sat quietly as I ate my sandwich while Donovan explained that he worked for an architectural design firm. He mentioned a few prominent buildings in Baltimore and the surrounding areas that his firm had previously designed and built. I politely nodded my head in acknowledgement but honestly, I had no idea which buildings he was referring to. The only buildings of significance that I knew in Baltimore were Camden Yards and the old Power Plant facility that now housed restaurants and clubs, neither of which he mentioned. Outside of those I did not much pay attention to buildings in Baltimore. I was not going to tell him that I was of the philosophy that if you have seen one building, you had seen them all. I did recognize Children's hospital when he mentioned it and that was pretty much the only place I could visually see in my mind. After we finished our lunch together and finished the walk back toward the Centurion building, we paused for a moment not knowing what to say to each other.

"Can I take you out to dinner some time?" Donovan asked sincerely.

"Do you promise not to tell me about buildings again?" I responded just as sincerely.

Donovan threw his head back in laughter and we made a deal. I gave him my cell phone number, told him to call me and let me know when he would like to have dinner. I was not going to bore him with the details of losing my mother, how I was not working, and could go out any night this week. However, come next week he may be out of luck fitting into my schedule. I did not figure a gorgeous man like Donovan would want to stick around me for long anyway, but I was not going to say no if he was asking. He kissed the top of my hand as he parted my company, I blushed and smiled politely then we both said goodbye.

I had parked in the parking garage around the corner. I could park across the street from my building, but they wanted a flat twenty-five dollars a day to park with no hourly rate. Although I could afford it, I found it to be outrageous. Plus, I didn't mind the short block and a half walk to my car, it was sometimes the only exercise I would get during the week. I loved my yoga classes, however if I had to prepare for a case, I would miss it due to late nights in the office. As I stood on the street corner waiting on the crossing signal to go from a red hand to a light person, I felt a presence near me. Of course, there were quite a few people on the street, but this was a spirit presence. The hair on my neck was raised. This was a brand-new presence. The hand changed to a person and the crowd began to cross the street together. I did not see the spirit presence, but I caught a glimpse of Brian, Jax's boyfriend, in the crowd on the other side of the street. When I looked again carefully, I did not see him. *Strange, but I could have sworn that he had just been there.* I walked to the parking garage arriving safely to my car. I normally was not fearful of walking through parking garages or on the streets of Baltimore, but today something had spooked me. I was going to have to ask Bill how to not fear spirits – good or bad.

I noticed I must be more in tune with higher frequencies as Bill had explained since my mother's funeral and the ensuing revelations. I had never felt such presences as I was feeling now. I reflected on all the spirits I had encountered in the last few days on my drive home. When I got into my house, I pulled out my book of meditations to read a calming meditation. I needed to relax a little. I had bought some Herkimer Diamonds to meditate with a while back when I first started seeing the spirits; these are crystals that are known to help you get in touch with your spirit guide(s). They were lying next to my book still in the little pouch they came in. They had never really worked for me, or so I thought, now I realized it was probably Bill who had protected me from some of the spirits. *Maybe he is my spirit guide. Why wasn't he protecting me as much now?* I wondered. He had said I had a higher purpose than he had. But he seemed to be a much higher evolved being than I obviously was. He understood things I did not quite comprehend. I felt I should do some research on human energy.

I headed upstairs to my home office and turned on my computer. I glanced through my email first and noticed another email message to myself. This time the email had a quote from a book in it. "A human soul is not just an individual being but is a part of a soul group together with several other entities that remain in the Spirit World." From the book: The Origin of Love p.70. I wrote down the title of the book noting that I was going to need that twenty percent off coupon after all. *That's funny.* I pondered the "coincidence" of the bookstore coupon followed by the book quote in my email. Who knew spirits used email to communicate I mused. I spent the next hour reading different websites dedicated to energy centers, chakras, and the compilation of the human spirit. Some of it was interesting and some of it was just bizarre.

My cell phone rang, it was Jax calling me. "Hey Jax, what's up?" I answered. Jax was crying and I could barely understand what she was saying through her sobs.

"Slow down sweetie, slow down and breathe."
I tried to soothe her as best I could.

"He's gone!" She cried out into the phone.

"Who's gone Jax?" I wondered if Brian had broken up with her and if this was going to be one of those cookie dough ice cream nights with her.

"Brian's gone," she sobbed. "He's gone Jess. I'll never see him again."

"What do you mean by he's gone? Did you two have a fight?" I couldn't imagine what they would fight about but young people were certain to argue and possibly break up. It was all part of the cycle of life.
Jax continued to sob uncontrollably into the phone, while I tried in vain to calm her.

"Where are you Jax?" I asked. This was going to be a go and get her type of sister moment.

"I'm at home," she said.

"Ok I'm on my way over. Stay there."
I grabbed my keys and purse as I ran out the door.

I drove up the same apple tree lined driveway just as I had a few days before, but I could tell something was not right. The front door to mother's estate was wide open. I parked and ran through the door calling out to Jax. I heard her laughter coming from the kitchen. When I got to the doorway of the kitchen, I saw Jax there and Brian was with her. Only this Brian was not the living and breathing Brian. This was Brian's spirit. I did not move for a long moment as he stared at me from across the Kitchen. Jax saw him looking at me, so she turned to face me. She had dried her tears and smiled at me as if she was relieved to have Brian there.

"I was wrong Jess! He isn't gone!" Jax said very excitedly.

"Where was he?" I asked cautiously. I watched as Brian's expression change to one of grief.

"I thought he was on the plane that crashed with all his gaming teammates. But I was wrong. When I saw him at the front door, I couldn't believe my eyes," Jax explained.

"Jax honey, come over here for a minute." I said to her cautiously while watching Brian's spirit that still stood there by her side.

Jax looked at me and then to Brian. She slowly stood and walked toward me. I could tell she was not happy with my request, and she was not exactly sure what was happening either.

Once she moved closer to me, I reached out and held her hand. "Jax, do you see Brian standing there?" I asked with a nod of my chin in his direction.

"Of course, I see him standing there! Why wouldn't I? Can't you see him standing there?" she asked puzzled.

"Yes, I see him standing there. I'm just surprised that you do," I said cautiously.

"What do you mean you are surprised that I do? Jess he's standing right there. You see him. I see him. What is wrong with you Jess?" she said exasperated as she pulled her hand from mine.

I remembered something that Bill had said to me a few days prior. He said that Jax "sees spirits but she doesn't yet believe they are spirits. She sees them as live beings." *Crap!*

"Brian, do you need to go?" I asked him.

Brian nodded his head yes. I asked him if he was going to be coming back and he nodded his head yes again. *Whew!* That would at least buy me some time to figure out what to do.

"When will you be back?" I asked him. He shrugged his shoulders. I figured his spirit would be tied up with funeral appearances. I knew that spirits like to attend their own funerals as if that provided some comfort to the family and friends who think they "feel their presence there."

Jax was looking back and forth between Brian and me. She was very confused, I could feel her frustration with me, and my interaction with him, as it started to rise out of her. I had to think fast.

"Brian, would you like to come to my house say Saturday night for dinner?" I asked quickly.
He smiled while nodding his head yes.

Good thing Brian was kind of a quiet guy in real life otherwise I'm not sure Jax would buy the "not speaking" to answer my questions conversation we were carrying on at this moment. Jax relaxed her shoulders a bit but began to pout as she realized that Brian had said he needed to leave.

"Where are you going?" she asked Brian. He looked at her very solemnly.

"Honey, I think he has a funeral to attend," I said truthfully.

"Oh," Jax said realizing that Brian had lost all his friends. He was sad, and in her mind that was the reason for his quietness.

"So, dinner Saturday night?" I repeated with a fake cheerful disposition. Brian nodded his head yes once again which made Jax smile. Jax went toward Brian as if to hug him, but he backed away a step or two.

"Jax, why don't you let Brian go take care of what he needs to so he can be at the house Saturday night," I suggested.

Jax looked hurt by Brian backing away but said OK. Brian's spirit turned and exited through the kitchen door. I knew once he was on the other side of the door he would disappear. I was only glad that at that moment Jax was not questioning why he went through the back door or more importantly how he got there without a car. I hugged Jax as she cried on my shoulder. She had just lost her boyfriend, and although she believed for the moment he was still here, she was frightened by the entire ordeal. I was going to need Bill's help for this one.

CHAPTER 7

The news of the plane crash that claimed the lives of the mouse2sports IEM World Championship team was not the top news story on Baltimore news channels, nor did it appear on Good Morning America. It was hardly news on the internet. Truthfully, it was found by obscure searches looking specifically for the names of the team members. Luckily, it was all labeled 'unconfirmed reports at this time' and I was not deeply concerned that Jax would be scouring the internet looking for news about Brian. I had already found an article referencing a press release on the mouse2sports website. One click on the link and a message stating 'Due to technical maintenance, the servers would be down at this time' which appeared in multiple languages. I was relieved.

I had all day today and most of tomorrow to figure out how to handle this with Jax. Brian's spirit would be joining us tomorrow night for "dinner." I was not sure I would be able to do this alone, so my first order of business was to invite Bill over for Saturday night. I was not in the mood to deal with Patty today, so I called Bill's cell phone leaving a short message for him to call me back. I asked him to clear his calendar for Saturday night if he had plans and ended it with an ominous "it's about Jax." I figured he would call me after he checked his messages at lunch.

Bill was a creature of habit. You could count on him to check his messages on his cell phone first thing in the morning, usually around 7:00 a.m., and during whatever lunch break he took some time between 11:00 a.m. and 1:00 p.m. He would start answering calls directly around 6:00 p.m. every day. I did not call his cell phone often since I was able to reach him in the office most of the time. He would know it was serious since I left a message on his cell phone, but he would understand it was not an emergency so to speak.

I was sipping on a homemade caramel macchiato at the desk in my home office when my inbox showed I had a new email message. It was another message to me from my own email address. I stared at the unread email again wondering who was emailing me right now, perceivably from beyond, from my email address. I clicked on the message to open it and found another book quote. "'One of the reasons people are unable to succeed but instead walk a path of failure is spiritual disturbances, the effect of stray spirits.' From the book: The Laws of Happiness | p99." I wrote down this book title on the same notepad I had jotted down the other book title *The Origin of Love*. It was time to go to the bookstore and figure out why someone wanted me to know these quotes.

The Little Shop on the Bay was quiet this morning without any customers in the store. The young woman I had seen the previous visit was not looking at her cell phone this time but was instead playing a game on the computer that sat on the lone desk behind the counter. She looked up momentarily and rotely said "Welcome to Little Shop on the Bay, let me know if there is anything I can do to help you," then she promptly returned to her game.

"Thank you," I replied politely.

I walked directly to the book section of the store and began looking through the titles. Unfortunately for me, they were alphabetized by author's last name and my "email spirit" had not given me that piece of information. Leila came around the corner and saw me standing there. She smiled sweetly but looked as though she was afraid, she would run me off again.

"I'm sorry about the other day," I said to break the ice.

"Not a problem hon."

She was definitely a Baltimorean with her "hon" term of endearment. "Do you need some help today?" she asked.

"I'm looking for two books. I do not have the authors' names just the titles. Do you think you could help me find them?" I asked.

"Let me see what you have."

She pushed her glasses up toward her face and took the piece of paper I had brought with me.

"The Origin of Love is a book written by Ryuho Okawa and The Laws of Happiness is by Dr. Henry Cloud."

She went to the C shelf and pulled the book *The Laws of Happiness*, it had a pretty red cover with a Victorian key on the front. She handed it to me then walked to the O section to pull the next book. I read the first few pages of the book she handed me, I found it to be a book more about finding one's happiness. I flipped to the back cover reading a line that struck me as more pertinent than the email quote. It said "Cloud reveals that true happiness is not about circumstances, physical health, financial success, or even the people in your life. The truth of the matter – confirmed by science and the Bible – is that happiness is not what happens to you; *it is who you are.*" I contemplated this sentence for a moment.

"Here you go!" Leila said to me holding up the second book. It had a basic title in black block lettering and a picture of a diamond on the cover. The back cover blurb described the book as Ryuho Okawa's answer to the origin of love in relation to eternal life.

"It's a used book. I don't have a new one in stock. I can order you one if you would prefer," Leila said almost apologetically.

"It's fine. I will take it as is," I smiled to reassure her that I was ok with a used book.

"Did you get the package I sent you?" Leila asked.

"Yes, thank you very much. I haven't opened the wooden box though," I said as if I needed to explain up front before she asked me questions about the contents.

"That's very wise of you," she stated very quietly.

I smiled not knowing what to say to that, which now piqued my curiosity. If Jax was not home when I got to my house, I was going to open that box and see what kind of contents it held for my "see no more dead people" spell. Ok I was adding a little imaginative witchcraft to it now, I figured a spell was much more appealing than some sort of voodoo glitter or alien kryptonite.

I placed the two books on the front counter to pay for them and realized I had forgotten my twenty percent off coupon. *Figures.* I paid the young lady then walked to my car ready to delve into whatever these books, and the wooden box at home may hold in store for me this afternoon. My cell phone started ringing as I sat in the driver's seat of my car. I did not recognize the number, so I let it go to voicemail. It was then that I noticed my soldier was standing outside The Little Shop on the Bay. I tilted my head to the side and watched him cautiously. *Did he follow me everywhere I went?* This was something else I was going to have to ask Bill about. *I need to start a list. Did he put me on some sort of twenty-four-hour spiritual bodyguard detail?* I hadn't noticed the soldier anywhere but my backyard before today. Maybe I was becoming more in tune to spiritual beings around me as Bill said I would. I started my little car, turned out of the parking lot, and headed directly home.

When I turned into my driveway, I noticed that Donovan was standing on my side porch as if he had just knocked on the door. He turned toward me as I pulled up, he was smiling broadly at me. I couldn't help but smile right back.

"Hi," I said as I opened the door to my car.

"Hello."

He had come to my car door to help me out, always the consummate gentleman.

"To what do I owe the pleasure?" I said with a thick southern accent as I batted my eyes like Scarlet O'Hara would.

"Why, Miss Hanson, you had best be careful or I may just have to carry you over your threshold on my shoulder!"

Donovan was playing a southerner right back. I laughed at the image of him picking me up and carrying me in. It was more likely that he would throw me over his shoulder as I kicked struggling to be put back down. I laughed internally at the mental image.

He held his hand out for my keys to unlock the door for me. I paused for a moment when I realized what he was doing. I decidedly handed them over and waited as he unlocked and opened the door for me. As I walked past him his hand touched very sweetly in the small of my back. It was like a lightning bolt to my heart because it began to pound hard. I was afraid to look up at him for fear he would see right into my eyes and know I was thinking some not so lady like thoughts. Either I had invited him in without asking him, or had he just invited himself in. I was not exactly sure, but I had to admit I enjoyed having him in my kitchen.

I put the books with my purse down on the little butler desk then walked over to the cabinet to pull down two glasses. I offered Donovan a sweet tea, but he requested water. I put fresh ice in the glasses and poured water for each of us. As I handed him his glass, I noticed he was watching me intently.

Not in a scary way but like he was memorizing each movement I made, committing to memory everything. He was wearing jeans paired with a yellow and blue striped button-down shirt. It was not as dressy as the polo he had worn the first time I had met him and this time he had on a pair of work boots.

"Doing some yard work?" I asked as I noticed the boots.

"No, actually I was going to hang some pictures and paint a few rooms. I hadn't made much time lately for domestic things. So, I took the day off and thought I would work on a few projects at home."

"Ah," I responded nonchalantly.

"Actually, that is why I was at your door. I had tried to call your cell phone, but you didn't answer. I don't get the best cell reception around here so I thought I would walk over to see if you were home, in case you didn't receive my call. I was hoping to borrow you," he said with a boyish grin.

"Borrow me?" I questioned with raised eyebrows.

"Yes, borrow you," he laughed.

"For?" I curiously waited for his answer.

"I want a woman's perspective on color for two rooms. I have to pick out paint and I thought maybe you would go with me."

He looked so innocent; it was easy to see it was feigned.

I laughed at his feigned innocence. "What gives? You don't really want me to pick out paint, do you?"

"Actually, yes. I do sincerely need your help, but I may have an ulterior motive."

He was now the wolf in sheep's clothing.

"And that is?" I was thoroughly amused.

"I want to spend the day with you and take you out to dinner tonight."

I looked at the books on the butler desk, my mind instantly went to Jax and Brian. "I... uh... I don't know that I can," I said sadly.

I really would much rather spend the day with this gorgeous man and help him watch paint dry if I had to, but I had to be here for my sister too.

He could see my eyes looking at the books and he followed my gaze to them. "I am so sorry! You were doing something, and I just barged in here and tried to whisk you away. I should have asked if you had plans first." He was a genuine gentleman; I could tell he was sincere in his apology.

"You know what Donovan, I will go with you to pick out paint and I will have dinner with you. Can you give me just a few hours in between? Maybe while you are painting, I can come back home to do a few things I need to do this afternoon. Does that sound like a plan?" I proposed.

"Why yes, Miss Hanson, that is most definitely a plan."

He was satisfied and I was going to spend some time getting to know him, without completely neglecting my tasks for the day.

We walked across the street to his house together. It was a brick colonial home with a circular driveway in the front. He had a detached four car garage, and the back of his home faced the water of the Patuxent River. His property was on the river, whereas my property sat across from it. The entryway to his home boasted a large two-story foyer with a beautiful chandelier. The stairs were to the right of the doorway and curved upward toward a large landing. The wrought iron and wood railing was very manly, he certainly had expensive taste. He took me into the kitchen to grab a tape measure that sat on the top of a large dark granite breakfast bar. He had an incredibly beautiful wall of windows much like mine, only his view of the river was much prettier than my view of brown grass and trees. I had always said I would put a pool in my backyard but just had not made

P. B. Lamb

the time to do it. He of course had a pool with a guest house connected to a full outdoor kitchen.

There was a sunken living room to the right of the kitchen that had exactly what I expected to see - a full sized leather sectional, an oversized ottoman, and a huge flat panel television that looked as though it took up the entire wall. A corner fireplace with floor to ceiling flagstone added just the right finishing touch for the room.

"You want to see the rooms I need to paint?" He asked with a grin as he watched me taking in his home and all the surroundings.

"Of course! How is a girl supposed to know what colors to pick if I don't see the room, feel its aura, and its feng shui!" He rolled his eyes at me as I said it.

He took me by the hand to guide me up the staircase into a guest bedroom that was at the end of the hall. It was completely white walled, with a large sleigh bed, a small night table, and a chest of drawers with a small flat screen television on the top. The furniture was all dark wood with a mahogany finish. There was absolutely no color to the room, including not having sheets or a comforter on the bed, just the mattress and box springs. I started to open my mouth and say something smart but stopped. I saw he was watching my face very carefully. Everything so far in the house was very manly. It was obvious Donovan did not have women in his life, or at least not women who influenced his décor.

"What did you have in mind?" I asked, while looking up into his eyes. He took a step toward me, gently moving a piece of hair away from my face. "I like the color of your eyes. Maybe some green in here." He could have said mustard yellow or glow in the dark pink at that second and I would have thought it was the best idea ever. I had not felt this intensity and attraction toward a man in a long time – if ever. I broke the moment by stepping back away from him, walking to the single window in the room. He had a clear view of my house from this room.

"Greens are good," I said as I cleared my throat. "What other room did you want to paint?" I asked hoping to just get out of this room.

"This way," he said as he again took my hand to lead me to the other end of the hall. He always felt so warm. His hands were so big I wondered if he could palm a basketball. He had a nice body, and his rear was…. *CRAP! Stop looking!* He laughed as if he knew I was checking him out. He led me into the Master Suite. *Of Course, it would be his room! I should have just stayed in the guest room.*

His room was enormous at least double the size of my room. The home had a detached four car garage, but it also had an attached garage, with his room running the entire width of the house directly over the attached one. The room held a large king-sized bed in the center that was covered in plastic, and I was sure the bed was not made underneath. All the walls were soft beige except the wall directly behind the bed which was typical homebuilder white. The furniture had obviously been moved around because there were two night stands off to the right side of the bed, almost in the middle of the room. Behind where the nightstands now sat was a large sitting area with a tan suede couch, two matching armchairs, and a large television. The room also had a huge walk-in closet to the left, and a door that was closed which I assumed went into the master bathroom. There were a few sepia canvas photos of famous buildings leaning against a large dresser. I was not going to ask about them lest I be riddled with boring architectural details again.

"You definitely need some color in your life."
I peered around the room completely in awe of its size.

"That's why you are here," he smiled at me. It was a smile of pride and appreciation all at the same time.

"What were you thinking here?" I asked like an interior decorator would, or the way I thought an interior decorator would. My mother had hired several to redecorate the estate over the time we lived there but I rarely paid attention to them.

"I would like to stay with a warm palate of color in here but mainly I want to paint an accent wall behind the bed."
He had impressively put some thought into this room, so I began to feel that this was not just a ruse to get me into his room.

"What do you think of peaches or an orange sherbet color?" I posed.

"Sherbet?" he asked like I was speaking a foreign language. I laughed out loud. *Such a typical man, primary colors only.* He smiled broadly at me.

"Come on I think I know what to pick out for you," I said walking toward the door of his room. "By the way, you need some throw pillows too." He rolled his eyes.

We drove in his truck to Old Town Alexandria, Virginia which was about an hour drive. He did not want to just buy paint at the large retail hardware store, he had a specific store he wanted to go to. I should have known the 'architect' would use a high-end specialty store rather than just buying paint like normal people. I picked out a color for his accent wall that was called "orange creamsicle" It was a cross between a peach and orange sherbet. He was only concerned with the fact that it was not from the primary color spectrum. "Why are there color names like orange creamsicle?" he pondered aloud. He joked about not wanting to lick his walls.

I selected "silver sage" for the guest room. It was a light green color that had a silver sheen to it. Depending on the lighting and the way you looked at it you would see green or silver. The store we were in was a restoration type store so there were other items like designer throw pillows and comforters. He allowed me to select a few throw pillows for his room that were similar to the orange creamsicle color. I selected a medium sage green duvet and down comforter for the guest bedroom. The duvet was accented with darker sage color embroidered fleur-de-lis patterns around the edges leaving a plain center. There were matching pillows to the duvet that we picked up along with two cream colored faux fur pillows.

After our shopping spree, which I had to admit was very relaxing and entertaining, we stopped at a little café to grab a bite to eat. As soon as I walked through the door, I saw my brother's friend Christian sitting a few feet from the entrance. *Oh please, not him.* I tried to look down in an effort to hide my face, but it was too late, he recognized me and began making his way toward Donovan and me. The air felt cold and creepy, he was definitely trouble.

"Hey Jess! It's me Christian, remember?" He said as he approached me.

"Oh yes, Christian, I remember! How are you?" I sounded so fake.

"I'm good. How is your little sister? I heard about her boyfriend," Christian said.

Donovan gave me a look that I knew meant I would have to explain about Jax and Brian on the drive home.

"She's ok," my answer was short, "by the way, this is my friend Donovan. Donovan this is my brother's friend Christian." I made sure to point out to Donovan that Christian was my brother's friend. I certainly did not want there to be any misconception where Christian and I were concerned. Donovan shook Christian's hand, we exchanged a few more pleasantries before we parted ways. Christian left the café shortly after we ordered our sandwiches, and it felt as if the temperature in the entire place rose ten degrees. I smiled at Donovan who did not look particularly happy at that very moment.

"Sorry, I didn't expect to see him here," I said as if I had something to do with his unhappiness.

"No problem. I am sure if I continue to take you out, there will be other men who will try to take your attention away from me," he said with a wink. I wasn't sure if I was flattered or disgusted by the thought. Not long after that we finished eating so we walked back to where his truck was parked. He helped me into the passenger seat then shut my door. I saw my mother's spirit standing on the street corner about two car lengths ahead of where we were. She stood smiling at me like I had just introduced her to her future son-in-law. *Oh, please mother! It's just a date.* I laughed to myself then shook my head.

On the drive back, I explained about my mother's recent death and my sister's boyfriend dying this week to Donovan. I did not mention I was visited by their spirits nor that I had several others around me - like my soldier guardian. I explained our family history, including Jax being from a different father. It was hard to believe that we were all from different fathers especially since I had spent my entire life thinking otherwise. I did not tell him about the highly evolved beings or about Bill. I just gave him the typical story most people knew of our family. I had not really dated in years, so I did not have to explain seeing spirits to anyone before.

I wondered briefly how I would ever explain something like this to a man. Maybe it was meant to be my secret forever, or worse, I was meant to be like Bill and never date or marry. It made me feel a little sad to think I may have to carry this burden, never telling someone I eventually fall in love with about this part of me.

Donovan dropped me off at my house at a little past two in the afternoon. He was heading back to his house to do some painting, while I was heading into my house to do some reading and attempt to understand the way things truly are.

CHAPTER 8

I had a "missed call" message on the screen of my cell phone.
I must have turned the ringer off because I did not hear my
phone ring at all. It was Bill who had called. He would either
be in court or with clients this time of day, so I decided to wait
until after 6:00 p.m. to call him back. Donovan and I had agreed
to a 7:00 p.m. date, so I had about five hours to delve into the
books and the little wooden box in my room. I fixed a cup of
hot tea then pulled out a blanket from the closet to settle down
on the couch with the books. I wanted to read a little before I
tackled the contents of the wooden box.

I started with *The Origin of Love* book since it was the first
book quote I had received. I felt that was a good place to start.
The book opened with pondering what true love really is and
upon reading such, which was only about three sentences in, I
thought about Donovan. I wondered if what I felt around him
was the beginning of true love. I had never felt as warm nor had
that sense of belonging with any other man. Donovan certainly
produced feelings of security that I had only experienced with
Bill. The difference for me was that with Bill the feelings only
had a fatherly feel, whereas with Donovan they felt more like
a belonging.

I shook these thoughts from my mind returning to the book.
I read on about love and the energy of love. I found much
of the introduction of this book to be things that I already

believed to be true. I became entranced in the theories of love, its beginning, what obstructs love, and then I came to a passage on good and evil. Ryuho theorized that when a person becomes "disconnected from a group this gives rise to evil." He further explained how as humans on earth we are no longer able to read minds, as we are when we are in our soul form. Several pages later there was a discussion on our souls needing light. As I read this first chapter it dawned on me that this book was essentially my instruction manual on how to keep Jax feeling love and light. She had spent her entire life feeling disconnected from our family thus giving rise to the potential for her to not be good, as Bill had warned me. I began internally questioning if Bill's explanation of life was just his summation of the book. I almost felt let down by the possibility that what he was telling me was not necessarily about life beyond earth but simply one man's teaching and theories on love.

I decided to turn to page 70 to find the passage that was in my email. Why I felt the need to skip ahead I did not know but it was what pulled at me in the moment. In red ink I found the following handwritten note in the margin – "He who seeks; Finds. Seeking answers may not always come in a box." My heart started racing. I recognized the first part of the note came directly from the bible verse. I knew somehow, I was receiving a note from someone, or possibly another being, about the wooden box. I stared at the red letters for what seemed like an eternity in disbelief. I closed the book as if to shut out the message, staring blankly at the book cover. I looked through the back windows and noticed my soldier was now watching me very intently. I looked back at the book and heard a whisper from behind me "Open the cover," the voice was cool and quiet, but crystal clear. I slowly opened the front cover of the book and saw the stamp 'This book belongs to:' and handwritten on the little black line was the name Jonathan Quincey Hanson. *CRAP!*

I dropped the book on the couch standing straight up. I turned around to look behind me and sure enough my father's spirit was standing there watching me. My mother's spirit stood behind him, with my soldier now just a few feet on the other side of the window. I had spirits practically surrounding me, I thought I would pass out from the adrenaline that was coursing through my body.

My father's spirit raised his hand to the soldier as if it were an unspoken commandment to stand down. The soldier disappeared altogether. The air in the room was cooler than before and I wondered if my father was the frosty being in my bathroom. *Did he take my mother's life for creating me with another being?* As these thoughts crossed my mind my father's face smiled lovingly, almost reassuringly to me.

"No sweetheart, I did not harm your mother," he said. I started crying, I had not heard my father's voice in over twenty years. I was so overwhelmed with emotion at that moment that I buried my face in my hands uncontrollably sobbing.

"Daddy, why did you leave us?" I asked like a small child.

"Jess, you have so much to learn about the ways of the universe and the return to being One with God. I cannot explain it to you in a way that you would fully understand just yet. Soon you will know the way in which things really are," he explained, "I can tell you that you are much more evolved in your understanding of souls, and how they relate, than most humans are."

I watched my mother move to my father's side; she smiled in a way that told me she was finally at peace being reunited with her one true love. It was true what people believed; that souls were happy to be reunited with their loved ones. I looked down at the book on the couch. "Daddy, did you send me the emails?" I asked.

"No. I did not." He spoke just as composed as I had remembered him.

"Do you know who did?"

"Yes," he offered no further information.

"Does Bill know as well?" I needed to know.

"Bill knows much more than he has let on. He is a more highly evolved being than I am. He is on a level that is closest to God without being God herself."

"God is a woman?" I asked completely surprised.

"She is neither man, nor woman, she is ALL there is. Her qualities of love and understanding are much more linked to that of human women, than of human men," he explained.

I did not know what to say. I was amazed at this revelation of information but miffed at Bill for not telling me everything.

"Do not be angry with Bill," my mother's spirit said, "he is bound by the same universal laws we are."

"Is everyone able to read my thoughts these days?" I asked almost irritably.

"You are able to read thoughts too, you just haven't remembered how yet," my father explained softly.

"Remembered how?" I asked slightly frustrated with this conversation.

My father went on to explain how the book was correct in that we can read thoughts of other souls when we are in our pure soul form. He also explained how transparent everything is in our soul form. This transparency is what keeps things pure with love and light. It's the essential heaven like state of being. When we are in our soul form, we are in the highest state of being, fully evolved, in the likeness of God. It is then, and only then, that we understand every realm of the universe and the relation to all souls. We can read each other's minds, travel through different realms with just a thought, and help more primitive beings, like humans, without necessarily revealing ourselves to them.

"Why are souls, spirits, or whatever they are revealed to me now as a human?" I inquired.

"Because you are already a higher evolution of being. You are higher than a human without being a pure soul," my father answered.

I felt as though I was starting to understand that we were all one spirit, to be reunited with God, and that our relation to each other was not limited by human blood relations. My father was still Jonathan Hanson, and while Bill may have created me, our souls were linked through creation not through love like that of my father. I pondered over all the information I was given and wondered how much more Bill was keeping from me. Suddenly as if I had summoned him with my thoughts Bill was at my door knocking.

I opened the side door and found a very tired looking Bill standing there. "You look like hell," I said to him as a greeting.

"Hello, to you too."

He truly looked older than he usually seemed, but still handsome just the same. Bill walked into the living room greeting my mother and father as if they were standing there in human form. I stood behind Bill watching with interest.

"It's good to see you, old friend," Bill said to my father.

"It's good to see you too," my father smiled broadly just like he would have when he was alive, greeting his longtime friend.

"So, you aren't mad?" I asked my father. Truthfully, I expected my father to be mad at Bill and my mother for having "created" me without his knowledge.

"What is there to be mad about?" my father asked.

"Your father is fully enlightened in his soul form and knows there is a higher purpose here," Bill answered.

They were right. I just did not quite understand everything. I was limited by my human emotions; I felt a little mad on my father's behalf. I knew I had no right to be, nor did I really need to be, but I was. I still loved each entity in the room. My mother and father, albeit in spirit form, were there and it felt peaceful. Bill as my creator, and my confident for so many years, still had my love and respect. I knew I would have to just accept whatever this higher purpose was.

"I already know the answer is you won't tell me, but I have to ask, what is the higher purpose?"

"Jess, all will be revealed soon," Bill said.

I shook my head in frustration as once again some universal law was in play, and I was stuck in my feeble mind. *HA! My feeble mind! These phrases must have derived from souls that return to earth!*

I glanced over at the clock on the wall and noticed it was 5:15 p.m., I had about an hour and forty-five minutes until my "date" with Donovan. I watched the three entities in my living room discuss old times and reminisce like they were truly all standing there. I felt like I should cancel my date with Donovan as I had so much to discover. I had questions to ask about Jax. I wanted to know more about the frosty spirits... *Wait, it was cool when my father's spirit spoke to me.* I froze in place for a moment. Bill, my father's spirit, and my mother's spirit all stopped speaking watching me intently at that very moment.

"Jess, it's not what you are thinking," Bill said very quietly.

"I wasn't thinking much of anything other than questioning why it's warm with my mother, warm with you, but much cooler with my father," I said. Truthfully, I was wondering if my father was evil, or not friendly for some reason.

"Jess, I was your earthly father. And yes, we are bound by love and the energy that a soul possesses with love. But the warmth you feel from other souls is because they are a part of your soul family," my father said solemnly, "I am not part of your soul family."

As he said the last sentence, I felt suddenly incredibly sad then I realized something else important. The frosty beings in my bathroom were not in my soul family, but they also felt unfriendly. I did not feel the same unfriendly feeling from my father's spirit, just coolness.

"You won't feel the unfriendly feeling from me, Jess. I am friendly. I am just not related," my father explained having read my thoughts.

I was starting to understand the difference between feeling coolness and feeling a frosty unfriendliness. I guess I was starting to "remember."

"It's important for you to remember all these things on your own. It's best for you to realize rather than be told. Just like your higher purpose. Once you know your higher purpose, you will have to fulfill it," Bill said.

"I feel overwhelmed," I stated very flatly.

I heard a voice on the other side of the kitchen door. I turned to see who was here and realized Jax had come home. She was talking on her cell phone, standing by her car finishing her conversation before she entered the house. I turned back to my father and mother's spirits only to find they were no longer there. Bill stood beside me quietly, taking my hand for a moment in an effort to pre-emptively comfort me. Something was about to happen I could feel a stir in the air. I wondered if this was what soldiers felt right before they ran into battle. Bill squeezed my hand, then let go as Jax walked through the kitchen door into the living room. She was seething with anger I could feel it.

CHAPTER 9

"Why do I only get five million dollars in trust?" Jax screamed at Bill. My mouth dropped open. *This is what she is mad about? Something that our parents did, that neither Bill nor I had any control of.* I was speechless for a moment.

"Jax, your mother set that up shortly after you were born," Bill said calmly.

"Well once again I am the lesser child!" She spat out.

"Jax, you know that is not true!" I tried to reassure her.

"Really Jess! It's not true? Then why do I get less? Why do you wear a locket from **OUR** grandmother that doesn't have my picture in it? Why am I under a half trust until I am twenty-five while you and James had your trusts released at twenty? Explain all the differences to me Jess, if I am equal to my siblings!" she was worked up and angry.

"Jax, where is all this coming from?" I asked.

"I just got off the phone with Christian. He was telling me how unfair he felt our family was to me. And said I should contest the will, that he would be willing to help me. He's in pre-law at Georgetown, he also has friends and colleagues that could help me. He informed me Bill was working against all of us, taking from our estate for years and not to trust him," she glared at Bill as she spoke.

Christian. I should have known.

"Jax, honey, it's not like that. And you know it. Bill has

worked for this family for free since you were a small child," I defended Bill.

"It's ok I can handle this," Bill stated calm, cool, and collected. He explained the will and trusts to Jax. He explained why my mother had chosen the things she had. He expressed to her how mother was not in her right mind most of the time. He defended me, explained my decision to split all the estate equally when her trust was up, and that he agreed to stay on for free as he had the last fifteen plus years. He went into lawyer mode explaining what would happen if she decided to go to court and contest the will. He further explained with great detail how it could hold up her trust past the age of twenty-five and she would still lose because the wills were completely legal within the scope of law. His voice was very soothing as he was speaking to Jax. I could see her visibly begin to relax; I could tell that she was starting to understand rationally he spoke the truth. When he finished speaking, I had a thought that I hoped would appease Jax.

"Bill, does the will address the vacation home in Saint Croix?" I had to ask because I had not had time to sit down to read the entire will.

"Not specifically, no. It's all considered part of the estate."

"Would it be possible to amend the property division?" I asked sincerely.

"Well, since you are planning to split the main estate and contents equally, you could dissect the vacation property out of the estate. That would be your prerogative." He was smiling, he already knew where I was going with this line of questioning.

"Great. I want to give the vacation property in Saint Croix, with all the material possessions found within and on the property directly to Jax." I felt pleased with myself.
Jax looked shocked when I said it.

"Really?" she practically whispered.

"Really," I said.

"Then it's settled. I can draw up the paperwork, you can put the vacation property and contents in Jax's name," Bill said with a wink. His wink was a reassurance that I had just handled this correctly.

"Wait. Do I have to wait until I'm twenty-five?" she asked.

"I don't see why you should," I said looking to Bill for affirmation.

"I don't see why either," he confirmed.

"Thank you, Jess!"
She threw her arms around my neck; I could feel she was happy again.

I glanced at the clock; it was now 6:20 p.m. I was going to have to either rush to get ready or I was going to need to cancel my date. Bill knew what I was thinking, as he said to me, "You should go get ready."
I smiled at him like I had just gotten permission to go out!

"Get ready?" Jax questioned.

"I have a date…. with Donovan." I turned red then looked down at my bare feet.

"OOOOOOOOO. You have a date with the hottie!" Jax was cooing.

"Yes. I have a date with the hottie." I was trying hard not to look like a little kid in a candy store, but I was beaming, and I knew it.

Jax hugged both Bill and I and started walking in the direction of the guest room she was still staying in. She stopped briefly turning around to face both of us.

"I'm sorry I was angry," she said quietly.
We both nodded, then she set off to her room. I was relieved that her anger was about her inheritance and not her boyfriend. I had not begun to figure out how to manage that yet. I looked up at Bill, he nodded a knowing nod that spoke volumes. He knew about Brian, he knew he had to come to dinner, and he

knew it was going to be tough to deliver the news to Jax. I didn't really read all that from Bill's thoughts, more like felt them. I wondered if that was part of what I had to remember, how to feel other being's thoughts. Bill simply smiled at me. He patted my shoulder, and I pulled him into a hug shocking him yet again with my emotional need of touch. He hugged me back then left quietly. We did not need to say anything else. We were now somehow in sync, although I did not know his thoughts, I could feel his feelings. I understood Bill for the first time, just as Bill had always understood me.

I had less than thirty minutes to get ready which I knew I was going to be rushed. I drew a hot bath so I could at least shave my legs. While the water filled the tub, I began brushing my hair then my teeth. I thought about just putting my hair into a neat little bun for the night since I was not going to have time to wash and dry it. I looked around my bathroom and did not see or feel any frosty presence. I caught a glimpse my mother's spirit in the doorway of the bathroom smiling at me. I smiled back but she was immediately gone. I got in and out of the bath quickly then stood in front of my closet staring at my clothes. I had no idea what Donovan had planned for our date, I was not sure if I should wear pants or a skirt. I thought I might call him to ask about his plans then thought better of it. *That would sound rude.*

I decided on a pair of black dress pants with a soft pink angora sweater. It was classy yet not overly dressy. I slipped on a pair of ankle boots with a small heel. I started to put on the locket that was my grandmothers when I remembered Jax's bitter words about it. I opted for a necklace with a pear-shaped diamond pendant and a diamond tennis bracelet that was hers instead. I had pulled my hair into a neat ponytail instead of working my hair into a bun. I brushed a light dusting of beige and pink eye shadow on my eyes followed by soft brown eyeliner. I put on mascara then my favorite light pink lip gloss. It was more than I wanted to wear, however I felt I should put forth a little effort for a date. One of these days I would learn full glam makeup but today was not the day.

Donovan was promptly knocking on the door at 6:59 p.m. I had to giggle at him being one minute early. I was coming out of my room when I saw Jax had opened the door already to let him in. He was smiling his gorgeous white toothed smile. He combed his hair neatly; it was not long but it was not super short either. The little curls on his neck were just long enough to be cute, but not so long that he needed a haircut. He had trimmed his beard since I had seen him earlier. He wore a pair of black jeans with a button up white dress shirt unbuttoned at the collar. He also wore a black sports coat buttoned by only one button at his waist. He smelled like fresh cologne; I recognized it as my father's cologne which made me smile. Jax stood in the kitchen watching us admire each other with a big smile on her face.

"Hi," I said quietly.

"You look absolutely beautiful," Donovan complimented me. I blushed and couldn't help but instantly look at the floor. I was not accustomed to compliments.

"Thank you. So do you," I said, then rolled my eyes as I realized what I had said.

Jax burst out laughing.

"I mean you look very handsome," I corrected.

"I knew what you meant," Donovan said sweetly.

He approached me and kissed me softly on my forehead. I informed Jax that we would try to be back before midnight and not to wait up for us. She laughed after I said it. I sounded like I was explaining myself to my parents. Donovan and I were both mid-thirties but acting like we were sixteen going on a date for the first time. *It is a first date after all.* Donovan suavely and effortlessly put my coat on me before he walked me to his car. He drove a Mercedes this time instead of his truck. I am not a car person so I could not tell you what model it was, but I knew it was an expensive one. His Mercedes was black and sleek, looked brand new, and when I slid into the leather seat it had that new car smell to it. I smiled in the darkness of the car. I was excited about the date and felt happy for the first time in a quite a while.

As we pulled out of the driveway his car accepted an incoming phone call from his cell phone through the Bluetooth of the car. A male voice said, "Have you secured the package?" Donovan smiled at me apologetically then pushed a button on the touch screen that sent the call back to his cell phone. He held the phone to his ear and spoke about deliveries of some package then gave estimated time in military sounding times. I had watched movies where they said things like "at zero six hundred" and so forth. So, I knew he was using a twenty-four-hour clock, but I could not have deciphered half of what else he was saying. I was not put off by the phone call itself I was more concerned we would get pulled over since he was holding his phone to his ear. Maryland had strict laws that made it so police could pull you over if you were not handsfree while you were driving. He quickly wrapped up his call almost as if he could tell I was concerned about him driving while on the phone.

"I apologize for that," Donovan said.

"It's ok." I smiled sweetly at him to let him know I truly meant it. "Were you in the military?" I asked.

"Yes, a while ago. I served in the Army for twelve years. I received an honorable discharge after I got injured in the line of duty. I took over my father's architectural firm when I returned from my last deployment."

"Oh! What did you do while you were in the army?" I was excited to learn something about him.

"I was a civil engineer. I basically did what I do now, but I designed temporary deployment locations rather than permanent buildings. And I got paid a lot less!" he laughed as he said it.

"I can only imagine." I was in awe of his service to our country.

He reached over to hold my hand as he pulled onto the highway. We were heading toward Washington DC. I was not sure exactly where he was taking me, but I felt relaxed and would have been happy going anywhere honestly. Just being around him was comforting.

"I thought we would go to National Harbor for the evening," he answered my unspoken thoughts.

I raised an eyebrow at him, wondered if he could read my thoughts, then decided I was being silly dismissing the thought almost as soon as I had it. National Harbor is a popular tourist destination in the DC area. It was built on the Potomac River in Maryland but close enough to DC to be associated. It has a waterfront shopping, dining, and casino entertainment complex. There are hotels, high end restaurants - including a few fast-food ones, chocolatiers, fashion retailers, jewelers, a small pier, a marina, and the list goes on. On Friday and Saturday nights after dinner the restaurants became like a club zone with music and dancing. There is a jazz piano place, a country place, and a hip hop dance place. It has a little bit of everything for everyone.

Donovan pulled into the parking garage that was practically in the center of it all. We could walk to wherever we wanted to go. I was grateful I decided to wear my low-heeled ankle boots for the evening instead of high heels. We walked hand in hand to an upscale Mexicana style restaurant. It was brimming with patrons and had a large, muscled security officer outside the door. Donovan nodded politely to the off-duty deputy as he opened the door for me. He gave his name to the hostess then we were immediately taken to our seats. I gave an almost apologetic look to the people who were waiting as we basically walked right in.

"Did you have reservations?" I whispered as Donovan pulled back a chair for me to be seated.

"No," he whispered back with a grin.

He sat across from me as we listened intently to our hostess explain about the current drink and entree specials. This place was apparently known for its specialty drinks. However, since I am not much of a drinker, I opted for a diet coke and Donovan ordered ice water without lemon. The waiter came to our table asked if I had ever been there, which I had not, he proceeded to tell me how they make certain things table side. He handed our menus to us then gave us a few moments to decide. Donovan watched me over the top of his menu more so than he looked at it. I finally laughed at his playfulness. I had decided I was going to get the chicken enchiladas in the Verde sauce. We opted for rice and beans as our sides. The waiter had previously explained that the sides were delivered to the table family style – which meant in large bowls to help ourselves. Donovan ordered Filete con Hongos, which translated to a Filet Mignon with wild mushrooms.

We talked about our childhood, well mostly I spoke of my childhood and growing up as a young woman without my father. Donovan had lived a spoiled life with his father being a prominent architect in Baltimore who procured highly coveted government contracts. Donovan told wild stories of trouble he and his buddies would get into. Including racing their cars down a closed off strip of road that had been abandoned when the new highway overpasses were built just outside of Baltimore. It was nice to learn a little about Donovan and how he joined the military because his father threatened to cut him off if he didn't make something of himself. He told me a scary story of how he had basically died while deployed oversees and he awoke in the hospital. I could not imagine what his parents went through with that ordeal. He started his bachelor's degree while in the Army and obtained an engineering degree when he got out. His father had died several years ago at which time he took over his business. He had no family left really. His mother left his father while he was in the Army, and last he heard she had remarried wanting nothing to do with him or his father. I thought that was the saddest thing I had ever heard. Interestingly enough, we were both without our parents. I felt a pull to him in that moment that made him seem more intrinsically connected to me than before.

Our dinner was absolutely delicious, I ate more than I should have. I was going to need three extra yoga classes to make up for all the food I consumed. Donovan surprised me by ordering guacamole ice cream, which I was thoroughly disgusted by the prospect of guacamole flavored ice cream. He laughed a full hearty belly laugh when he ordered it, and I wrinkled up my nose. It wasn't guacamole flavored after all but a mint ice-cream that they combine ingredients that make it seem like it was guacamole. There were raspberries to represent tomatoes, coconut for onions, and chocolate for something I could not remember, as well as a few other delicious ingredients. It was fun to watch the waiter prepare our guacamole desert at our table just as they would fresh guacamole. It was a fabulous way to end the meal.

"So, what would you like to do now?" Donovan asked as we walked through the front door of the restaurant.
"I have no idea! I have never been down here."
I was just so happy to be around him that I did not mind what we did.
He took me by the hand to lead me down a long set of stairs. I joked at how they were very much like the stairs in the movie Rocky and felt like I should hear the triumphant song associated

with that scene playing overhead. At the bottom of the stairs was a waterfront park that had a man coming up out of the ground. Not a real man, a bronze statue of a man called 'The Awakening.' The piece was a giant man rising from the sand, his head, hands, and legs were all rising from the ground as if reaching for the sky. It was an amazing piece of art. Donovan smiled at my enthusiastic discovery of the giant coming out of the earth.

"It's one of my favorite pieces," Donovan told me.

"Thank you for sharing it with me. It's amazing!" I truly meant it.

Donovan stood remarkably close to me on the platform that overlooked the giant sculpture. I felt a sudden iciness in the air. I could not tell if it was the actual air temperature or something more. Donovan wrapped his arms around me hastily pulling me to him. I was surprised by the sudden movement as it was not a romantic gesture but a protective one. I looked up to see his face, he stared off to the right as if he was watching someone in particular. He shielded me with his body. My heart began to race because I could not see what was happening. Donovan had completely enveloped me with his arms burying me in his chest. I felt a rush of icy air pass by us, I knew then it was a spirit of some kind. I could not see what was happening, I felt very confused. I tried to pull away from Donovan, but he held onto me very tightly. I was debating internally if I should try to explain the icy rush of air to Donovan, but he would not let go to give me the chance to.

A voice whispered in my ear, "it's time to go." I looked up to Donovan who was looking down at my face with concern. Again, a voice whispered, "it's time to go." I felt anxious and apprehensive about if Donovan knew what was happening. The spirit left just as quickly as it approached.

"I think I should go home," I said sullenly. *How am I going to explain all this to Donovan?* I had such an amazing time with him; I did not want to ruin our evening by having to explain that I see dead people, spirits, and I have some higher purpose that even I do not understand.

"Ok," Donovan replied just as sullen as I felt.
We walked in silence to the parking garage; Donovan did not take his arm from around my shoulders. It was nice to feel this protected. I wish I knew how to explain my life to Donovan. I suddenly felt incredibly sad and alone, although being in his presence was comforting.

I knew I would end up not being able to explain fully what my life was like. I did not understand most of it quite yet, mainly because I was partially human, and I had been protected from all this my entire life. How would Donovan attempt to understand it when my own mother certainly could not? I felt like I was going to burst into tears at any moment. Donovan stopped on the street just before the entrance to the parking garage holding me close to him. He was looking into my eyes when he leaned down as if to kiss me. He paused just as his lips were going to touch mine. *Yes, please!* As the thought passed through my mind, he kissed me passionately and purposefully. I melted into his strong arms wanting this moment to last forever.

When we arrived back to my house, I noticed all the lights were out except a small light in the kitchen. I did not want to go into my house. I certainly did not want our date to end. Even with the icy spirit ambushing me at the sculpture I still wanted to be around Donovan. He walked around the front of the car to my side opening the door for me. As I stood, he steadied me by taking my hand. He really was extraordinarily strong and muscular; I felt his entire body as he pressed it against me when he was protecting me. Neither of us spoke of the incident at the sculpture again. He walked me quietly into my kitchen.

He did not have the beaming smile he had when he picked me up earlier in the evening, instead he looked concerned, and I thought I could feel that he was feeling a little sad.

"I had an amazing evening," I said sweetly.

"Jess, it was the best date I have ever had."

He surprised me with that statement. *Wow! Even though it was ruined by a spirit...*

Just then Bill walked into my kitchen from the living room. I yelped a little because he scared me.

"I'm sorry Jess. We have a problem," Bill said.

I turned to Donovan who was looking down at the kitchen floor.

"I am so sorry Donovan," I apologized for our date having to end.

"Nice to see you Donovan," Bill said acknowledging his presence. *Wait!*

"You two know each other?" I asked them both.

"We've had some business dealings," Donovan offered with a look at Bill that I could not decipher.

"Yes, we've had some business dealings. Plus, he owns our office building," Bill further explained.

Oh, yeah. I forgot that part.

"I hate to say goodnight, but I must be going," Donovan said.

"I know me too," I returned the sentiment.

"May I take you out again?" Donovan asked me as he looked at Bill. I was confused as to why he was looking at Bill. I figured he was looking for permission to 'date his daughter' so to speak.

"Yes, I would love that," I answered before Bill could say anything more. Bill excused himself back to the living room. Donovan gave me a kiss on my forehead then bid me goodnight one last time. I watched from the kitchen window as he walked from my house and climbed into his car. I was struck by how empty I felt watching him walk away.

CHAPTER 10

"What is going on?" I felt almost angry with Bill as I walked into my living room.

"Jax is missing," he said without emotion.

"WHAT!?!?!" I had raised my voice to almost a shrill, "When I left, she was smiling and saying she would be here when I got home."
I now felt panicked and anxious.

"I know. She knows about Brian," he again seemed unemotional.

"Oh Shit!" I couldn't help it; the word just flew right out. I never use curse words, but this was one of those times it fit. "What are we going to do?" I asked concerned.

"I don't know yet," he said.

"I can't catch a break, can I?" I asked rhetorically.

"How does she know?"

"Christian," Bill said now with disdain.

"I knew that guy was trouble. First the inheritance and now this!" I was pissed, "how does he know?"
Bill was being awfully quiet and introspective; I could tell he purposefully ignored the question. I wanted answers but he seemed to be working through things in his head. I really wish I was able to read his thoughts. I sat down on the couch closing my eyes in exasperation.

I decided it was best to just try and calm down. Being angry was not going to make things better it would only serve to make things worse. As I sat there, I went into a calming meditative thought process. I was thinking about Jax and Brian. I wondered if I could summon spirits, like Brian. I wanted to be in a peaceful place. I wanted Jax to be home. I wanted to make everything better. Bill reached over and touched my arm as if to wake me. When I opened my eyes, I realized I was in the living room of my mother's estate home.

"I hate when you do that!" I chastised Bill.

"She's here," he said quietly.

I jumped up off the couch almost running to the stairs. I was not sure if I should call to her or if I should just go up to her room. Bill was not coming with me – obviously – and I figured that I had to do this on my own as part of my guardian duties over her. *Remember Love and light, love and light, love and light.* I repeated to myself over and over in my head.

When I got to the closed door of her bedroom, I could hear Jax crying. I felt sad and weak at that very moment. I wanted to rush in wrap my arms around her and tell her everything was going to be ok. I knocked softly. "Jax... it's me," I spoke quietly.

"Go away!" She screamed.

"Jax, I know you are upset. I'm just here to talk."

I tried to sound calm even though I felt anything but calm.

"I don't want to talk!"

She was going to be stubborn this time I could feel it. A vacation home in the Caribbean was not going to solve this problem.

"Jax, I think we need to really talk," I said sweetly.

Her door flew open, she stood there in dark jeans and a black sweater with mascara running down her face. She was red faced and I could feel from her that she was going back and forth between angry and hurt. She could not decide which way to feel now. I was surprised I could feel all this from her. I felt a connection to her I had not felt before and I was grateful I could read her emotions, but I really wanted to know her thoughts.

"Jax, I know you are angry, and I can feel your hurt. I think we should talk." I was still trying to coax her into letting me in.

"I don't trust you," she spewed with venom at me.

That hurt.

"Why Jax? Why don't you trust me? What have I done that has broken your trust with me?" I reasoned.

"You should have told me the truth," she said.

"What truth Jax?" I was not sure which truth she was referring to. I didn't know if she was referring to the spirits, the fact that her creator was a highly evolved being, or that Brian had died, and I led her to believe he was truly standing there in the kitchen.

"STOP IT!" she screamed at me.

I was so caught off guard by her screaming that I did not know what to say.

"STOP IT JESS!" she screamed again.

My jaw dropped and I could feel tears pricking my eyes on the verge of spilling when Bill appeared behind me.

"Get away from us!" Jax yelled at him. She moved around me to get in between Bill and me. She was trying to protect me from Bill.

"Jax, he isn't the enemy here," I said calmly.

Bill looked like he had been stabbed in the heart by her venomous words.

"He's the reason all this is happening!" she yelled.

I looked at Bill for some guidance. Bill just looked at both of us with pain and a look of regret.

"Bill?" I asked cautiously.

"Jax. I'm not the enemy. You are being deceived by the enemy," Bill said authoritatively.

"What is going on?" I asked them both.

"Jax is being influenced by the evil that is welled up inside her. Other negative thoughts are feeding the negative energy she has been exposed to," Bill said calmly, as if that was a perfect explanation for what was happening.

"What negative thoughts?" I asked cautiously.

"Christian is not negative!" Jax stated emphatically, "He's more truthful than either of you have ever been."

"Jax, I don't think Christian has good intentions," I said directly to her, "remember how you didn't like him when you first met him?" again, I tried to reason with her.

"I know my first thoughts of him were that he wasn't good. But I know now that he is at least honest if nothing else," she defended him.

"He's not honest," Bill said.

"Jax what has he told you?" I asked wanting to know exactly what I was dealing with. All while thinking, I wanted to strangle him or find a way to get him out of our lives.

"What do you care?" she spewed, "You are just as guilty as Bill is! You lied to me about Brian! You said he was coming to dinner! How is he coming to dinner when he is DEAD?"
She was sobbing again.

I wrapped my arms around her neck trying to pull her close to me. I figured my own love energy would have to surround her to get through to her. Just like Donovan did to protect me I was going to envelop her in love. I started rocking her back and forth in a soothing calming motion. I thought loving thoughts about her, about our mother, and about James. I thought loving thoughts about Bill and his positive influence in our lives. I figured the more positive thoughts I had the more positive energy I would produce. Bill touched both of us and we were overcome with love and light, so much that the entire world seemed to be a bright white light around us. Both Jax and I had closed our eyes holding onto each other. When we opened our eyes, we were in my living room and Bill was gone. *I really hate when he does that.*

"What the hell?" Jax said shocked, "how did we get here?"

"Oh, we have some things to discuss," I said, slightly upset that it was going to fall on me to explain. I looked through the wall of windows noticing my soldier standing on the back deck. He was there to protect both of us, Bill knew we were safer here than at mother's estate for time being.

I informed Jax about Bill being my creator. I explained that she was also created from a highly evolved being but that her creator wasn't Bill. I told her how James was the only fully human child of the three of us. I added about how she and I would always have a bond that James could never have with us. I also said that according to Bill it may not always be a good one. Jax looked a little sad when I said that.

"I know that part," she said sadly.

"How do you know?" I asked.

"I can hear your thoughts sometimes. I don't always like them," she wasn't kidding.

"How long have you been able to hear my thoughts?" I asked afraid of the answer.

"Since mother died," she said, "At first, I thought I was imagining things. I would only hear snippets of information. Like the night you met Donovan, and when you had that silly coupon. I knew you had a letter too but that you were hiding it from me. I just didn't know where the letter was or what it was about."

I was not sure what to say, instead I asked another question.

"What other thoughts have you heard?"

"I know you really like Donovan. I know you do not like Christian. And I heard you thinking about how to explain to me Brian was dead, but I didn't believe that was one of your thoughts. I felt like I was making it up in my head. After all I saw Brian with my own eyes in the kitchen that night," she sounded very confused.

"Well, you have a gift I don't have yet. I can't hear thoughts. I see people in their truest form. I see them if they are spirits or if they are true humans. I can sense a person or being's aura and whether they are good or bad. Sometimes I can feel their emotions, like with you and Bill at times, but I can't hear any thoughts," I explained.

"I only know your thoughts," she said quietly.

This is our connection.

"What is our connection?" she asked audibly.

"The fact that you can hear my thoughts, it's how I am supposed to fill you with love and light to keep you on the path of good."

I figured something out, or remembered, whichever it was – but I was figuring this out. We had reached a good point in this conversation so far, though we had barely scratched the surface. At least Jax had calmed down and no longer felt as angry.

"What about Brian?" she asked as a tear fell down her cheek.

"What do you mean?" I asked wiping the tear with my thumb.

"Is he really coming tomorrow night?"

"He is. But he isn't human, his spirit is coming."

I was hoping she would not get angry again as I said that.

"I'm not angry," she answered my thought, "Will I be able to say goodbye to him?"

"I guess so. I got the feeling from his spirit that is why he is coming, for closure." I really was not sure about all this myself. "He may appear to you in human form. Bill explained to me that you see spirits too, you just don't have the ability to recognize them as spirits yet. You see them as human."

She nodded her head like she understood.

"I think you need to stay away from Christian though," I said carefully.

"I know. He is truly angry with Bill. I don't know why,

but he wants to hurt Bill." I could feel that she was scared of Christian.

"We can call Bill in the morning and ask him what to do," I suggested.

We were both exhausted emotionally, and physically. I suggested we get some sleep and try to address more of the issues in the morning. I was pretty emotional about all of it myself and did not have nearly all the answers I felt I needed.

"Jax, promise me you won't leave in the middle of the night," I needed the reassurance.

"I promise, besides my car is at mother's - we somehow Star Trek 'beam me up Scottie' got here remember!" she was smiling. My sweet sister Jax was back to joking. *Thank goodness.* I was going to have to ask Bill to stop doing the 'teleportation' thing without warning. It was unnerving.

Once I was in my room, I crawled into my bed pulling my comforter up over me, almost to protect myself like a small child would. I was laying in the darkness with only a hint of moonlight in the room thinking of Donovan. I would have to call him in the morning as well and explain something about the evening to him, I just did not know what to say. As I drifted off to sleep, I thought about our dinner and our kiss. I finally had a smile on my face as I fell into a deep slumber.

CHAPTER 11

I opened my eyes slowly adjusting to the sunlight streaming through my windows. I had dreamt about Donovan; I awoke still feeling the emotions I had in the dream. We were married, incredibly happy, and had children. The strange part was that it did not feel like a dream it felt very real. I stretched and sat up to find my mother's spirit standing at the end of my bed.

"You need to check on Jax," my mother's spirit said sadly. I did not respond to her, I simply got out of bed and rushed to the guest room upstairs. Jax was not in the room, yet her cell phone was on the nightstand. She had to be somewhere. I could hear water running in the bathroom. I knocked lightly on the door but received no answer. I knocked louder, this time calling her name. Still no answer. I opened the door and found her lying on the bathroom floor. She was sobbing. I felt relieved she was ok physically, but I could feel she was hurting emotionally.

I wanted to cry with her as I brushed her wet hair away from her face. I held her and did not speak. I tried not to think any thoughts other than how much I loved her and wanted to take away her pain.

"Thank you," she said after a moment. I smiled as I continued to hold her. We were sitting on the bathroom floor for a few moments when her cell phone began to ring in the next room. She looked frightened. I could feel she was expecting a phone call that she did not want to take.

"What is it?" I asked.

"Christian," she said, "he wants me to meet him this morning."

"Jax…" I started to tell her I did not think it was a good idea.

"I know it's not a good idea," she interrupted me.

"What do you want to do?" I needed to find a way to get rid of him.

"I don't know yet," she said, "I'm concerned about his anti-Bill agenda."

I was honestly concerned by that as well. I was hoping Bill would be able to explain a little of this to both of us. Since Jax was the brunt of Christian's wrath at the moment we needed to know what the real story was. Bill seemed to be hiding something, or at the very least he was not being completely forthcoming.

"Why can't I see mother?" Jax asked sadly.

"I don't know. Bill said something about her not being able to reveal herself to you until you were on the right path."

"I feel like I am the center of some good versus evil war. I feel pulled toward positive things like you and James. Then there are times that the pull toward negative thoughts and feelings are so much stronger."

I could tell she was struggling.

"I want to be good," she said as she started crying again.

"Then be good Jax," I said hoping it was that simple.

We sat in silence for a few moments.

"How was your date with Donovan?" she asked obviously wanting to move on.

I smiled and remembered his kiss again.

"YUCK! Get out of here!" she said as she stood up.

We both laughed out loud.

"Stay out of my thoughts if you don't want to know!" I said as I left the bathroom. I headed downstairs to the kitchen to make some coffee and heat up a couple of cinnamon rolls for us.

After we had our light breakfast, we sat in silence in the living room not really speaking. I could feel she was thinking through everything she had come to realize in the past twenty-four hours. I was just as into my own thoughts as she was in that moment. I saw the books lying on the coffee table which triggered my thoughts about the wooden box in my bedroom. My eyes widened at the same time that I had the thought. Jax stared at me with a question. She knew I had the box.

"I don't know what is in it," I said in answer to her unspoken question.

"Maybe we should look at it together," she suggested.

I thought about it for a second and decided it may be a good idea. I walked toward my bedroom to retrieve the box. The spirits of my mother and father were both standing there when I walked in. The air was frosty, and I could see my breath. I stopped instantly, not wanting to move a muscle, I felt a strong pull but before I knew what was happening, I was knocked to the ground by the frosty being. I closed my eyes tightly trying to muster up enough courage to face whatever this was. I opened my eyes looking for my mother and father, but they had disappeared. *Why do they leave whenever the frosty beings are here?* I pondered.

"Because your parents are different beings from another realm than we are," the frosty beings said in a hushed whisper.

"Why are you here?" I wanted answers, and I would take them from the frosty beings if I had to.

"You keep creating us," they explained.

"I… What?" I was dumbfounded, "what do you mean I keep creating you?"

"For everything good that you experience, we grow in number, as we are the negative which counteracts the good you have."

"How is that possible?" I was more confused than ever.

"We are the beginning and the end of everything in your

realm," the frosty beings moved around me as it spoke, "you are the offspring of the Archangel lineage. Therefore, you are the future creator, and we are aligned with you to create the opposite of what you create."
I sat speechless, not absorbing what I had just been told.

The frosty beings were circling around me in a way that made my pulse race so fast I thought my heart would jump through my chest. The air swirled like it does in a sandstorm. There were flecks of silver and grey swirling around with these beings. I wanted them gone. I figured if what they were saying was true, and I was creating them somehow, then I could un-create them or create that they would vanish.

"You must leave from here NOW!" I commanded, "LEAVE!" The air quickly returned to normal, and they were gone in the blink of an eye. *Wow. That worked.*

I picked up the wooden box, opening my bible to the pages that held the letter from Leila and my mother's spirit. I stared at the page that held the verse which came to my email first. Luke 11:9-10 "And I say unto you, Ask, and it shall be given you; seek, and ye shall find; knock, and it shall be opened unto you. For everyone who asks receives; he who seeks finds; and to him who knocks, the door will be opened." I could tell I was on the verge of figuring something out. It was right there before me; I just could not put my finger on it quite yet. I dropped to the floor as I began to cry in frustration. I felt overwhelmed, emotional, and weak. I wanted a peace that passed all understanding. I felt a warmth fill the room like I had never felt before. "If all I have to do is to seek in order to find the answers then consider this my request. I am knocking on your door. Please let me in," I said aloud.

I heard a whisper in my ear. "Come with me," the soft voice said. It was a warm and soothing feminine voice. "Come with me," the voice repeated. My eyes slowly opened; I realized that I was no longer in my bedroom. I was in a bright white light; I slowly lifted my gaze and I saw the feet of a higher being before me. The light that shone all around this spirit was crisp white. I had never seen such a sight. I fell face first to the ground I knew I was not worthy enough to see such a sight. "Arise my child and know you are worthy," a very soothing voice said to me. I wanted to see the face of this spirit. I found that I could not make myself look up. I was paralyzed in awe of this being. I had no idea exactly who this spirit was, but I could feel it was in my soul family. I felt a touch on my shoulder that filled my entire body with a positive loving energy like I had never experienced in my life. It was like heaven.

"Oh God, am I dying?" I suddenly panicked.

"No, my dear, you are not dead nor dying," a woman's voice said all around me. It was like her voice was in surround sound. I could not see anyone or anything just the bright white light.

"Am I dreaming?"

"You have traveled through the realms," the voice said.
I looked down expecting to see that I was clothed in all white, like you see in movies, except I was still dressed in my pajamas. At least they were my nice ones. *Thank you, Victoria Secret, for pretty pajamas!*

"Which realm am I in?" I asked the voice.

"The second highest realm known as Seraphim," the voice sounded closer to me. A beautiful angelic figure approached me. She was over six feet tall and seemed to float as she moved toward me. She had golden hair, not blonde, golden – like strands of twenty-four carat gold. Her eyes were as blue as the deepest parts of the Caribbean Ocean, she smiled a very warm smile. She wore a beautiful turquoise and gold tunic over a floor length white gown. There appeared a turquoise light that filled the area around her that overtook the white light when she stood in front of me. I was now surrounded by a turquoise light.

"My name is Faelynn. I am one of eight angels of light. We are the messengers of the Archangels and the keepers of this realm."

Her presence felt intoxicating.

"I'm Jessica," I thought I should introduce myself.

"I know who you are Jessica. You are the future creator. I have summoned you here to answer your questions. You called out asking for answers. I have brought you here to answer some of them."

"I have so many questions I do not know where to start."
I sat still, completely in awe of her.

"I can answer your first question. You are of the lineage of the Archangel Gabriel."

"Not Michael?" I had guessed Michael in my mind.

"No. Michael is a protector, and although you have many who protect you, your lineage is of Gabriel."

"Are you speaking of the same Gabriel that visited Mary and informed her of her son Jesus?"

"Yes, the very same Gabriel who also told Mary she would give birth to a son and name him Jesus. The same Gabriel who told Zacharias that his barren wife Elizabeth would have a son named John," Faelynn confirmed.

"Wow." I was trying in vain to think of other questions.

"Is Bill an Archangel?" I asked.

"William is a protector, a messenger, and a descendent himself of Gabriel. He sought out his own barren Elizabeth and created you to continue the lineage." I was once again stunned into silence; this was becoming a regular thing lately.

Faelynn explained more about the Archangels and said they were described in the book of Enoch 40:9. She quoted what Enoch had written "And he said to me 'This first is Michael, the merciful and long-suffering: and the second, who is set over all the diseases and all the wounds of the children of men, is Raphael: and the third, who is set over all the powers, is Gabriel: and the fourth, who is set over the repentance unto hope of those who inherit eternal life, is named Phanuel.' And these are the four angels of the Lord of Spirits and the four voices I heard in those days." Enoch 40:9.

"Gabriel oversees all powers?"

"Yes," she answered.

"Is that why I can see spirits and feel things that other humans cannot?"

"Yes. You will one day have all the same powers of Gabriel being that you are his descendant. You are also the first female descendant of Gabriel, thus making you a creator," she explained. *Double wow.*

"Are you Gabriel's messenger?" I was curious.

"I am the Angel of Faith and Enlightenment," Faelynn said.

"Who are the eight angels you mentioned?"

"We are Majestica, Illuma, Trinaty, Stulliaire, Linnara, Jaselle, myself, and Shastinelle. Each of us has our own purpose. My purpose is Faith, Trust, and Enlightenment."

My heart felt so full of awe, and at such peace, that I was not sure what other questions to ask. I had already had two major questions answered about who, or what Bill is, and which Archangel I was from. I finally thought of the ultimate question.

"What is my higher purpose?"

"Your higher purpose is to create the future," she said.

"That's it?" I felt like that was so simple.

"You will understand the full complexity of your higher purpose when you remember who you really are," she smiled very warmly at me, "I must take my leave of you. You will be visited by others, and all will be complete."

That was a very cryptic way to say goodbye.

CHAPTER 12

"Wake up! Jess! Wake up!" Jax's voice was almost panicked.

I opened my eyes to see Jax standing over me as I lay on the floor of my bedroom holding the wooden box. I was disoriented, somehow, I had blacked out. Donovan rushed through the door of my bedroom instantly lifting me off the floor, placing me gently on my bed.

"What are you doing here?" I asked him.

"I wanted to check on you this morning. I heard Jax yell when she came to get you, so I ran in after her."
He was looking at me with concern.

"I don't know what happened," I tried to explain but I did not have the words. I held the wooden box out to Jax. I was giving it to her to put back on the nightstand. I did not want to have to explain it or its contents to Donovan. Jax took the box setting it down understanding my thoughts. The bible on my nightstand was still turned to the bible verse. Donovan saw the bible and smiled.

"I didn't take you for the religious type," he said with a teasing look.

"I'm not the religious type," I stated truthfully, "I'm more of a spiritual type."

"Well, you are a very beautiful spiritual type," he said flirtatiously.

I smiled broadly up at him from my bed.

"I'm going to the living room!" Jax proclaimed. I could tell she thought we were too icky sweet for her, I also felt she was almost bitter about it. After all she had just lost her boyfriend. She did not want to be around two people in 'love.' *I am not in love....* I crossed my arms defiantly in my thoughts. Donovan simply laughed at the two of us. He was suddenly entertained somehow.

I sat up slowly as Donovan sat down beside me on my bed. I envisioned pulling him on top of me and making out like a hormonal teen. I blushed at my own thoughts. Donovan smiled at me very sweetly then moved several strands of my hair off my shoulder, exposing my neck to him, he leaned in to kiss it softly. I remembered that I did not brush my teeth or hair yet this morning, nor had I washed my face from the night before. *I must look awful.* I pulled away from Donovan quickly standing up. He stood up next to me, he was so much taller and broader than me that I wanted to just melt into him.

"I have to get back home. I have some work to get done that can't wait until Monday," Donovan said quietly, "are you ok?"

"Yeah, I think I am." I was not completely sure if I was truly going to be ok, but I didn't need to worry him.

"I will call you later to check on you, if that is alright." He was so sweet to me.

"Yes, that is fine. I have guests coming for dinner this evening." I felt I needed to explain this in case he called, and I did not answer.

"Ok, let me know if you need anything before then." He kissed my cheek. I wanted to turn my face and make it a real kiss. Instead, I accepted the soft peck on my cheek then walked with him to the kitchen.

I always felt like a part of me walked away each time Donovan left me. It was almost an empty feeling. I returned to the living room to see Jax reading the book I had left on the table.

"What do you think?" I asked.

"It's interesting. Do you buy into all this we are of one God, all to return to God when we die stuff?" she did not seem to agree with the book.

"I think there is merit to it. Yes," I answered plainly.

"I'm not so sure." I could feel she really felt that way.

This was part of her struggle. I had always had faith in God. I had always believed in the universe being much bigger than just the earth and the galaxy we lived in. I believed in spiritual things and angels or guardians, messengers of God. I was just starting to learn the wider scope of God and his, or her, entities, and realms. I believed things were much broader than institutional religions wanted us to believe.

Jax, however, had never really been raised in church or taught to believe in God. She lived in the shadow of our mother and her depression. She was led down this path of negativity that was claiming her soul. I was somehow destined to be the one to pull her into the light, the one who would teach her about love. I was trying to recall anything I could about teachings or readings with regard to Archangels. I knew there were three Archangels Michael, Gabriel, and Raphael that were Catholic Church teachings. I had never heard of Phanuel, the one that Faelynn spoke of. I felt there were others in the universe that I just did not know of. I remembered a passage in the bible from church where Michael argued with Lucifer. Jude 1:9, "But Michael the Archangel, when he disputed with the devil and argued about the body of Moses, did not dare pronounce against him a railing judgment, but said, 'The Lord rebuke you.'" *That is why I was able to get rid of the frosty beings – I rebuked them.* My eyes widened at this revelation.

Jax had watched me carefully work through all my thoughts. I knew she did not understand, nor follow them, especially since they were scattered and jumped from one thought to another.

"I'm sorry. I'm still confused by it all," I offered in explanation to the perplexed look on her face.

"I am too," she said feeling more so than I did. I could feel the anxiety emanating from her.

"What about the wooden box?" she asked returning us to where we were earlier this morning.

"I think I need to do some more research before we open it."

I was frightened of its contents to be honest. Something about that box was ominous and each time I approached it, or thought of the box, I was immediately distracted or kept from it in some way. I had intended to open it the day before when I was distracted by Donovan. Then the red letters in the book saying not all the answers were in a box. Today I was pulled from it quite literally by the frosty beings, as well as my mother and father's spirits were standing in front of it. I started to get the message that I should stay away from it. Leila herself told me I was wise to not have opened it yet. Curiosity killed the cat, or so the saying goes, I resigned myself to not open it for now. *Good thing I am not a cat.*

CHAPTER 13

I wanted to know more about Archangels, the eight angels of light, and the different realms that both Faelynn and the frosty beings spoke of. I called Bill's cell phone, he answered right away.

"How are things this morning?" he asked in greeting.

"Interesting. But ok," I said, "hey, Bill I have some questions that I really need answers to."

"Ok, are these questions that would be better suited to be answered in person?" I could tell he was willing to come over this morning which was probably best since he had disappeared on Jax, and I last night.

"Yes, I believe they are."

"I will be there in less than an hour."

We said our goodbyes. I knew I had enough time to take a shower and get dressed.

Jax sat by the fireplace reading *The Origins of Love* book. She seemed to be, at the very least, taking the book for face value and not discounting everything she had read. I sat down next to her and began playing with her hair, as I had done when she was a small child. She smiled at me; I could feel that she felt at peace right now. I braided her hair then kissed the top of her head.

"I'm going to take a shower and get dressed. Do you need anything before I go?" I asked.

"No, I am good," she was content for the moment.

"Bill will be stopping by in the next hour so that I can ask him a few questions. Would you mind when he is here if I am alone with him for a bit?" I was hoping this would not upset her.

Jax paused thoughtfully, then said she did not mind with a smile. I felt that she meant it as I stood up smiling back at my little sister.

I stood under the hot water letting it pour down my face and body. It was soothing and felt invigorating. I was contemplating everything that Faelynn had said to me. I should have asked her about the frosty beings or the other realms. I should have asked a million other questions. I thought about something both my parents and Bill had said, somehow, I had to "remember" things. Faelynn had said I would better understand my purpose when I remembered who I was. *What is all this remembering about?* I really wanted to remember. It was after all part of my purpose. I let my thoughts wander away from my purpose to my dream this morning it had felt so real. I wondered what it would be like to be married to Donovan. He protected me, perhaps he was my human protector. Faelynn had said there were many who protect me like Donovan, Bill, and my soldier. That is more like a few, but I was sure, just as in other things, that there were more I may not be aware of.

I stepped out of the shower wrapping myself up in my towel. My hair was wet and dripping down onto my shoulders. I ran a comb through my hair staring at my reflection in the mirror. *I want to remember.* I was almost trying to force myself to remember. I moved slowly toward my bedroom to get dressed. I caught a glimpse of movement outside my bedroom window. When I peered outside, I noticed that my soldier was back on duty, so I smiled at him. *I'm going to talk to him today!* I hurried to get dressed, choosing a pair of nice jeans with a Baltimore Ravens pullover sweatshirt. I swept my hair up into a loose bun, slipping my feet into my sheepskin loafers that were knock-off faux fur shoes I bought at a local department store. I thought they were more comfortable than the name brand ones to be honest. I walked with a purpose to where the soldier had been standing just moments before, but he was not there. I looked all around the yard, he had vanished. I put my hands on my hips in displeasure and let out a sigh.

"Were you looking for someone?" I heard a male voice say beside me. I jumped and turned around to find Christian standing there.

"What do you want?" I loathed him.

"I'm here to see Jax. Is she here?" he asked with a slithering snakelike smile.

"Haven't you caused enough damage to this family?" I said through gritted teeth.

"I merely speak the truth," he hissed.

"What is your problem?"

"Privilege is revolting," he spat.

"What does that mean?" I almost laughed at him.

"You and James. You come from privilege. You have always had anything and everything you have ever wanted. Neither of you have worked hard for anything. Yet you let your little sister just falter and fail. She hasn't lived the same life. She's lived a life like mine. I feel for her."

"First of all, she has had a life of privilege as well. She has never wanted for anything. As for your assessment of me, I have worked extremely hard for everything I have in my life. I do not lap at the bowl of luxury like I could. I live a modest life with modest things. I have climbed the ladder just like everyone else to get to where I am in my career. You should know what that is like being a law student yourself." I was angry at his description of our family.

"She has not been loved the same," he spewed practically in my face.

I took a step back acknowledging with my silence that he was probably right on that account. "That was not my fault. I have loved her as my sister and treated her no differently than James our entire life. You cannot blame me for that."

He was seething with hatred. I could feel it. I was not sure where this hatred erupted from. I closed my eyes looking to feel more from him. *"I will win her over. She is destined to be with me."* I heard his voice clearly. My eyes flew open.

"What do you mean she is destined to be with you?" I questioned him.

He looked stunned and I could feel that his hatred grew ten times more. "You are one of them!" he spat out angrily. He started to lunge at me, a large arm grabbed me pulling me backwards. I was suddenly standing behind Bill.

"You need to leave here young man." Bill was authoritative and for the first time in my life he felt very scary. Christian took a step toward Bill, assessed his chances against the large bald man, then decided to back down.

"I will be back to see Jax later," Christian said as if he was demanding to see her. He got in his little Honda Accord then drove off. I hugged Bill tightly, grateful for his impeccable timing. We started to walk arm in arm toward the house when I glanced over my shoulder toward Donovan's house. I thought I saw him in the window of the guest room that I helped to decorate, but when I focused on the window there was noone there.

Jax was standing in the living room with a fireplace poker when Bill and I walked in. He and I both laughed out loud. Here was such a tiny young woman holding a big wrought iron poker in defense of herself, it was amusing at best.

"Well, it was better than a wet towel!" she mused making fun of me, and I rolled my eyes.

"He's gone," I informed her.

"Oh, Thank God! I have been ignoring his phone calls all day. He's practically blown up my phone. I have twenty-two missed calls from him in the last three hours," she said trembling.

I wrapped my arms around her to comfort her. I was her protector now. I noticed my soldier in the back yard as I held her. *Just where were you?* I asked him in my head.

"I was right here in the living room. You didn't expect me to come out there, did you?" she looked at me funny.

"Oh no. Not you." I forgot she could read my thoughts.

"Then who did you think that about?" she asked.

"You can hear thoughts, Jax?" Bill asked.

"I can hear Jess' thoughts."

"Interesting. I knew you would have some of the same powers, I did not expect you to read thoughts. Especially since Jess can't yet," Bill was perplexed by this revelation.

"Actually, I heard my first thought, I heard Christian's voice only I realized when I looked at his face, he hadn't said it out loud," I explained to Bill.

"What was his thought?" Jax asked curiously.

"He thought 'I will win her over. She is destined to be with me,'" I repeated to them.

"That doesn't sound good." Jax now felt anxious and nervous. "I do **NOT** want to be with him. He creeps me out."

"I don't think that is what he meant," Bill said.

"What did he mean?" now, I was curious.

"I don't know, but I will look into it," Bill answered. I could tell he was not saying what he was thinking. I closed my eyes to see if I could do to him what I had just done to Christian.

"That won't work on me," Bill said aloud. I sighed in frustration.

"Can we talk, just the two of us?" I asked, then I looked to Jax to ensure she was still ok with it. Bill nodded in agreement.

Jax picked up the book and walked to the stairs, "I'll be in the guest room if you need me."

Bill and I went to the kitchen. It was the furthest place in my house away from the guest room. I wanted to make sure that Jax could not hear our conversation. I was also concerned she may be able to hear my thoughts so I distanced myself from her as best I could. We both sat down on the high bar stools by the breakfast bar.

"He will be back you know," I said to Bill.

"I know."

"What does he really want?"

"He feeds on negative energy. He is trying to pull Jax away from the love and light path," Bill sounded very sure about what was going on.

"Why? What does he have against us, more specifically you?" I knew I was asking the tough questions, but I needed to know.

Bill sighed deeply.

"I understand you met Faelynn," he changed the subject.

"I did. Don't change the subject."

For the first time in my life, I stood up to Bill. It was the hardest and bravest thing I could do.

"Christian is from a different lineage. He is of the fallen angel lineage," Bill explained resigning himself to answer me.

"What, like, he's from Satan?" I said almost joking.

"Not exactly. Satan does not exist. Neither does the hell that most religions teach of. The fallen angels chose to fall. They are all of the Archangel Lucifer. I have said to you before that in order to know good, you must know evil. Otherwise, how could you ever know you were experiencing good. This is the greatest part of the universe and God's plan. It applies to many things. In order to experience wealth, you must know what it's like to be poor. To experience health, you must know what it's like to be sick. To experience love, you must know what it's like to be unloved," Bill watched my face carefully as he explained this part of the universal plan to me.

"I understand the concept. What does Christian have to do with it?"

"Christian is the negative to your positive. In order for Jax to experience positive and make a choice for love and light, she must know the path of darkness. He is the glimmer of darkness that she must see in order to make a willful choice. God's plan is that all beings – of every realm – must exercise free will."

"She told me she feels a pull toward positive and toward negative, and that sometimes the negative pull is stronger in her."

I now worried that I would fail at my task.

"You cannot think you will fail. What you put into the universe you get back. If you think you will fail, then you will," Bill warned me against my own thoughts.

"Are any of my thoughts private?" I was growing tired of beings reading my mind. Bill laughed.

"I understand your frustration. Once you are used to it, you will be able to clear your mind and free yourself from those who can read your thoughts. The meditation techniques that you started learning about several years ago will help with this process."

"Is that why I can't read your thoughts?" I asked.

"That is part of the reason."

"If Christian is of the Archangel Lucifer line, is he from a non-existent hell?" I could not think of another way to phrase it. My religious upbringing would not allow me to get past hell being non-existent quite yet.

"The Archangel Lucifer chose to go to the lowest realm. He chose to be the negative to everything positive. It was the highest calling for an Archangel at the time. It is the hardest, most challenging purpose to be destined for, for eternity. He took 200 angels with him to descend to the lowest realm and always be the negative to all things good. But that does not make him any less of an Archangel. He just will never reside with the other Archangels."

Bill was very thorough in his explanation. I had to admit it made a bit of sense.

"So, if there is no hell, and there is no burning fiery pit, then why do religions teach of it?"

"Religions teach of such because they do not understand the way that God intended it all to be. God is not a vengeful God, what purpose would be served by that. Why would God want to punish her own creations for choosing to invoke their right to free will? Is that not what all souls were created for? To use free will to love God as God loves each of them? Why then would she punish a soul for making a free choice? God is a merciful and loving God. Period."

Bill was posing some very philosophical questions, and yet they made much more sense to me than any religion could come up with.

"Faelynn said I would be visited by others. Do you know what this is about?"

"Yes, but you will find out soon enough. This is another one of those things you must discover on your own."

Bill was doing his best to be informative without overstepping any boundaries.

"Are the frosty beings from Lucifer?" It was the only explanation I could think of.

"No," Bill said flatly.

"Who are they?"

"They are from another realm. They have a different purpose."

Bill's face told me that I was teetering on the verge of information he was not able to give.

"How many realms are there?" I stepped away from the frosty beings for now.

"There are seven realms. The highest realm is Atzilut. This is where all souls go to be reunited with God. It is essentially the 'heaven' that religions teach of. The second highest is Seraphim which is on the same plane as the realm of Beriya. This is where the Archangels and the Angels of Light reside. They are all the protectors of Atzilut and Beriya. That is as close to heaven as you can get while your soul is in its human form."

"That is where I was," I interrupted.

"Yes, that is where you were. You traveled there with Faelynn." He affirmed and then continued. "The fourth realm is Yetzirah. This is the world of formation. Souls go here when they are descending back to a lower realm to fulfill a purpose, one they may not have fulfilled their first time in the lower realm. The fifth realm is Asiya. This is the realm we reside in. Our realm has living beings as well as angels.

"The human soul is the most complex being because of its ability to be contradictory. It is that which creates a human's ability to distinguish between good and evil, positive and negative. The sixth realm is Ophanin. In this realm the lowest of positive beings exist, they work to connect the lowest beings to the highest beings. The seventh and final realm is the Kelipa. The Kelipa realm has several inner planes, each one holds different types of subversive beings. This is where all negative energy is stored."

"Wow. That's quite a bit of information. It sounds very much like the Jewish teachings I learned about when I studied World Religion in college."

I felt thrilled that I understood most of what Bill had explained.

In one day, I had learned about the Archangels, the existence of the Angels of Light, and the Seven Realms. I was pleased to know that the information I had been taught in World Religion was "almost" correct.

"I'm really pleased to know this information, but I have one looming question. How does all this relate to me and to you, as my creator?" I asked.

"You and I are of the Gabriel lineage. I am a protector of the lineage and have lived on all the realms, from Asiya up to Beriya. I am from the realm of Beriya, I descended to Asiya to create a soul that could transcend to Beriya, as well as have access to Seraphim. I am the last known being from Beriya that may move between all the realms of positive thought. That makes me also a protector of positive energy. It was in my destiny to create a future creator for Gabriel, and a realm traveler like myself," Bill explained.

"Oh." I could not think of anything more intelligent to say.

I sat in silence for a moment contemplating Bill not being human. Although he had explained he was a highly evolved being, actually putting a description to it made it seem much more real.

"Are you called something like a Beriyian?" I sounded foolish as I said it.

"We do not call ourselves by our realm. We are simply highly evolved beings," Bill explained with a soft smile.

"I have been told several times that I am a future creator. How am I supposed to create? I'm not expected to have a lot of babies, am I?"
The thought made my stomach flip.
Bill laughed out loud, almost falling off the stool he was sitting on.

"No Jess. You do not have to have a lot of babies. Although having one or two helps to secure the future of our kind. Your children will possess the same powers you and I have."

"So then how do I become a creator?" I asked again.

"You will figure that part out. It's not something I can explain to you. You have to remember."
I was really tired of hearing how I was supposed to "remember." I found this part of my new instructions to be the most distasteful. I did not know how to "remember."

We sat in silence for a little while, I felt content with the amount of knowledge about the universe I had learned. I was still not completely sure of what my role was supposed to be in it all. Although the knowledge did allow me to become more relaxed about my abilities. I was able to hear Christian's thought, so I hoped that was the start of using that ability more. Of course, I could still see spirits and I hoped I could figure out a way to not see the frosty beings. They still scared me.
I felt a presence in the house as we sat there, so I turned to Bill to see his reaction.

"Brian is here," he said.

We turned around to see Brian's spirit standing at the entrance of the living room. We both stood up moving closer to him, until we were standing a few feet away from his spirit. I could feel he was cool, meaning he was not in my soul family, but he was friendly. I was starting to get the hang of this.

"Hi Brian," I said quietly.
He nodded his head in greeting.

"Why do you not speak?" I asked him.

"He cannot communicate in his spirit form. He must transcend to Yetzirah, the fourth realm, so he can descend back to earth. He did not fulfill his purpose," Bill answered for him. Bill really was a more evolved being than me. I needed to "remember" who I am.

"Should I get Jax?" I asked, feeling like I was not really ready for this.
Both nodding their heads in silence. I had to be honest having Bill there was comforting in the face of what may be coming.

CHAPTER 14

I slowly proceeded up the stairs to the guest bedroom. The door was cracked open slightly with the bedside lamp softly lighting the room. It had started to get dark outside so Jax needed additional lighting to continue reading.

"Jax?" I called her name softly as I knocked on the door. The door opened and I found she was asleep on the bed with the book in her hand. She looked so peaceful.

I quietly walked to her and gently placed my hand on her arm.

"Jax, honey, wake up."

Jax opened her eyes and sitting straight up all at once.

"He's here, isn't he?" she asked in a frightened tone.

"Yes." I replied calmly.

"Tell him to go the hell away! I want nothing to do with him!"

"But I thought you wanted to say goodbye to him," I said confused by her sudden change of heart.

"Why would I want to say goodbye to him? He wants to make me his or take me away or something probably more sinister! I don't want to see him ever again!" she said now visibly upset.

"Ok. Ok. I will tell Brian you have changed your mind."

"No!!!! I thought you meant Christian!" Jax burst into tears burying her face in her hands.

I hugged my sister pulling her close to me, after a few minutes, she pulled away grabbing a tissue to wipe away her tears.

"I'm ready," she said bravely.

We descended together down the stairs, Jax saw Brian's spirit when she was about halfway down. She stopped and stared at him momentarily before she continued. I could feel her love for him, as well as her grief. She did not grieve like this for mother. She reached the bottom of the stairs then went to stand near Brian's spirit.

"He looks human to me," she said barely audible.

"You have not developed the ability to see spirits quite yet Jax," Bill explained to her.

She stepped toward him to touch him, and just like before Brian's spirit stepped back.

"I can't touch you?" she questioned.

He simply shook his head no.

"Is this the last time I will see you?" she was starting to cry.

He nodded his head yes.

I felt the pain and grief surge through her then all around the room as she realized this truly was her final goodbye. Her first love was already gone from this earth and his spirit form was about to be gone forever.

"Where is he going? Is he going to heaven?" Jax asked.

"He is going to a realm of heaven, yes," Bill explained simply.

Jax seemed to accept this answer. She wanted to touch Brian. She wanted to hug him and to kiss him goodbye. She was struggling between grief and anger. I was growing concerned she would give into the anger. I touched her arm to offer a loving touch. She pulled away from me abruptly. She glared at me and then at Bill, "this is the fault of both of you, I blame you both," she stated with venom.

Bill stared at her blankly, I stared wide eyed at her sudden anger and blame toward us.

"How is this our fault?" I said in disbelief.

"She is giving in to the negative energy," Bill said. I noticed my soldier was standing on the back deck. Brian's spirit had moved three steps away from Jax. I could tell he could not be pulled into her negativity.

"Christian did this," Bill declared. I looked at him with disbelief. This was what Bill was keeping from us.

Jax lunged at Bill, he stopped her by grabbing her wrists. I jumped back a few steps, and Brian's spirit suddenly moved to the other side of the windows behind the soldier.

"Jax, stop!" Bill commanded.

"How did Christian do this?" she said through gritted teeth.

"He brought down the plane to get to you," Bill said.

"I don't believe you!" she screamed.

Brian's spirit showed up near her again and he rapidly began nodding his head yes.

Jax saw Brian suddenly nodding his head. She looked at Bill, then back to Brian. I could feel her wrestling internally with this piece of information. I stayed back away from all of them. I did not know what to do.

"How did he bring down the plane?" Jax was trying to understand.

"He used negative forces in the universe," Bill said, and Brian nodded his head yes again. Jax stood still, looking back and forth between Bill and Brian. Bill let go of her arms as she dropped them to her sides. She began to cry again. She dropped to her knees giving in to the heart-wrenching sobs that overtook her. I went to her, enveloped her with my body and all the positive energy I could muster. I could feel her calming down. Jax stopped sobbing for a moment.

"I'm so sorry," she said. "I don't know what came over me." I could tell she really had no idea why she reacted that way. The negative energy in her was much stronger than I realized.

Brian's spirit looked helpless. Bill sat down on the couch sighing heavily. I could tell he was dwelling on something in his mind, but I had no idea what.

Jax stood up slowly to face Brian.

"I love you," she said very quietly. Brian smiled nodding in return. He loved her too. I wanted to cry for her.

"Don't you cry Jess," she said with her finger pointing at me. I smiled a truly fake smile, which made both Jax and Bill laugh.

Brian stayed with us in the living room for about an hour. Jax asked him questions and he nodded 'yes' or shook his head 'no' to answer. Most of the questions were reminiscent of their time together. She wanted to know if he enjoyed things or didn't enjoy other things. She was fairly content when Brian looked to Bill.

"He has to leave Jax," Bill informed her. I decided to go to the kitchen to get a glass of water while they said their goodbyes. I did not really want to watch her struggle emotionally, plus she had Bill there. I picked up my cell phone and noticed I had a text from Donovan.

7:48 p.m. *I just wanted to see if you were ok. D*
8:22 p.m. *I am fine. It's been a rough evening. Jax is grieving her boyfriend. J*
8:23 p.m. *I am here if you need me. D*

I grinned when he answered my text right away. I quickly put my phone down. I did not want Jax to pick up on my joy now. I fixed a glass of water then returned to the living room. Brian was gone and my soldier had disappeared as well. Bill was telling Jax about the different realms, how Brian had to transcend in order to descend. I sat silently listening to them and practiced clearing my mind while they spoke. A little while later Bill touched my shoulder.

"Jess I am going to head home," he said as he pulled me

from my blank mind. I opened my eyes to find Jax was not in the living room.

"Ok. Where's Jax?" I asked.

"She's upstairs."

"Thank you for coming and explaining things… and for helping Jax," I smiled up at him.

"I'll show myself out. Get some rest."

I got up to check on Jax. I paused halfway up the stairs; I could hear she was on the phone. I did not want to interrupt her call, so I quietly backed down the stairs to the kitchen to get my cell phone. I thought I would text Donovan if he was still up.

9:14 p.m. *Hi.*
9:14 p.m. *Hi*
9:15 p.m. *I didn't wake you, did I? J*
9:15 p.m. *Nope. I was working on a CAD design for work. You, ok? D*

I thought about what to say. Part of me wanted to tell him everything that had happened.

9:17 p.m. *Yeah, I am fine. I just thought I would text ya. J*
9:18 p.m. *Would you like to see me instead? (I'm not much of a texter) If that is a word. D*
9:18 p.m. *Actually, yes. I would. J*
9:19 p.m. *Then come over. You can see your colors! D*

I laughed out loud, promptly stopped myself while looking toward the stairs in hope that Jax did not hear me.

9:21 p.m. *See you in 5. J*

I hurried to my room and changed my top from the Ravens sweatshirt to a magenta-colored sweater. I sprayed my favorite body spray on my neck and brushed my teeth. I put on my black shawl, wrapping it around me for warmth. I had taken my shoes off earlier, so I slid the faux fur loafers back on, then picked up my cell phone and keys. It was so dark outside, there wasn't much light from the sliver of moon in the sky. I did not see my soldier anywhere and since I could not see the entire path to Donovan's home, I decided to drive the short distance from my driveway to his. It was not like he was directly across the street. All the properties on our street were each several acres each, so his home sat in more of a diagonal setting to my home. I decided to play it safe.

I pulled into his driveway and parked by the garage door closest to his front walkway. I practically bounded toward his front door, which he opened as I reached the bottom step of his porch. I smiled broadly at him. I felt as though I was a teen who had just snuck out of my parents' house to see him. He greeted me with a bear hug, one of his hands pulled me to him around the middle of my back, while his other hand cradled the back of my head. Both my arms wrapped around his broad chest; I realized I could not touch my fingertips around his back. He felt warm and strong, smelling like men's cologne, it was not the same scent as before, but I liked it just the same. He loosened his arms then pulled back slightly to make eye contact.

"Should we go inside?"

"If you insist," I said playfully.

"I insist!" he said with a laugh.

We stepped down into his living room, where he had a fire going in the fireplace. It was a real wood burning fireplace that had several large logs engulfed in dancing flames. I had a small gas fireplace that I only needed to flip a switch to light the fire. The fireplace tools were merely decor at my house. I had not warmed my hands by a real fire in many years. Mother never lit fires in the estate home. She had most of the fireplaces converted to gas logs after my father died. I watched as Donovan stoked the fire before he came to sit next to me on his couch. The leather was so soft I practically melted into the cushions.

"Are you comfortable?" he asked.

"Yes, very. Thank you."

I just wanted him to sit with me and hold me for a while.

"Can I get you anything?" he was toying with me. *You?* I thought.

"No Thank you," I answered, deciding to use my manners instead.

He smiled broadly at me, then sat beside me pulling me into his arms just like I wanted. I felt a stirring that I would have to ignore because I was not that kind of woman. I had friends that had called me a prude and said I was born in the wrong century. I just had not found anyone I really wanted to share myself with. I was not a virgin, although I wished on many occasions I was. I had toyed with sex with my first boyfriend when I was sixteen years old and naive. He wanted me to have sex with him for his birthday. He had said it was the only birthday present he really wanted from me. I was dumb enough to fall for it, he broke up with me two weeks later. There was a short fling in college that made me feel repulsive since it was based solely on sex and nothing more. I decided to just focus on my career after that.

Now I sat on a couch with one of the most enchanting men I had ever met. I surprised myself with the thought that he was someone that I would share myself with. I convinced myself he would find my inexperience to be a turn off. Someone like Donovan was probably swimming in beautiful women. I laid my head down on his shoulder as he pulled me to him, just watching the flames continue to dance. I was with a man I truly desired to be with. Donovan broke the comfortable silence first.

"May I ask you a question?"

"Of course," I gazed up at his face.
He stroked his hand through my hair pulling my face closer to him.

"Would you think bad of me if I were to say that I have thought of kissing you since I left you this morning?"
He carefully watched my eyes.

"No," I barely whispered.
I could not tell if the crackling in the room was the fire or the chemistry between us.

He leaned closer to me, softly kissing my lips. I could tell he was purposefully being gentle and loving toward me. I opened my eyes to look at him. He stared directly into my eyes, almost peering through my soul.

"I want to be with you." he whispered against my lips.
I want you too.........oh my......... "I want you too, but...." I paused.
He looked at me intensely.

"I am not like that," I said as I turned my eyes down toward his chest.

"I'm not like that either," he reassured me, "I want to be with you in every way." He tilted my chin up forcing my eyes to look at him.

"Really?" I squeaked.

"I've had two lovers in my lifetime. I thought I would be with each of them forever. They both turned out to not be the 'one,'" he confessed very softly.

"Men really look for 'the one?' I always thought most men just wanted sex and that's it," I was being brutally honest.

"I'm not most men," he said just before he kissed me on my lips, this time with more desire. I willingly kissed him back.

He laid me back gently on the couch holding his weight above me with his arms. He was an extremely alluring man. I wanted to strip all my clothes off and be the little slut my friends were in college! He laughed a little.

"What's so funny?"

"I can see your inner thoughts on your face! You look like you are struggling with the angel and the devil on your shoulders," he mused.

"My mother always said I was not good at hiding my thoughts, she said my facial expressions always give them away," I laughed with him.

"I did not ask you here to get you into my bed Jess. I just wanted to see you. Ok, I thought about kissing you, but I would never push for anything we were not ready for."

I **was** struggling with the angel and the devil. Fortunately, the angel was winning. I had pride in the fact that I was 'not that kind of girl.' I wanted it to be special, I wanted it to be with a man I genuinely loved. I felt like I could easily fall for Donovan, but I knew I was not in love yet.

He moved behind me and I rolled on my side with my back to his front. He held me tightly to his body, occasionally kissing my hair and running his hand down the length of my side. It was the most comfortable I had been with a man... ever.

He reached across me for the remote control to turn on his television. I sighed almost in resignation. He had one of those new Roku sticks where you could just pick an application and stream content. He chose the Pandora Music app, then he selected the 'Today's Country Radio' channel. I smiled as the song 'Meant to Be' by the duo Florida Georgia Line filled the speakers all around us.

"I didn't take you for the country type," I said trying to hide my amusement.

"I'm not the country type. I'm the 'all genres' of music type," he laughed as he said it.

I accepted just as the song said, if this was meant to be, it would be.

CHAPTER 15

I replayed Donovan saying he wanted to be with me in "every way" in my mind all morning. I was sitting on the couch in my living room sipping coffee, staring out the wall of windows at the backyard. I had made out like a schoolgirl with Donovan for a few hours before reluctantly coming home. It was well after midnight when I "snuck" back into my own house. I did not want to wake up Jax. I slept soundly, not a trace remembrance of the dreams I had, which was unusual for me. I awoke bright and early, thoroughly enjoying the peace and quiet of the morning. I knew that today I would have to start gathering some things to move to mother's estate. I had to be at work tomorrow morning, and I had two cases that were moved from last week to the end of this week that I needed to be fully prepared for. As much as I tried to think about all the things I had to do today, I kept returning to deviant thoughts of Donovan.

There was a knock on my side door that interrupted my thoughts. I got up to see who was here, it was my brother James. He looked as though he had partied all weekend, and he reeked of alcohol emitting through his pores as he walked past me.

"Good morning, please tell me you have coffee?" he said still wearing his dark sunglasses inside the house.

"I do. Have you slept?" I asked slightly concerned.

"If you call waking up in your car in the middle of Georgetown sleeping, then yes," he said with a sly smile.

I could hear the song "Drunk (And I don't Wanna Go Home)" by Elle King and Miranda Lambart playing in the back of my mind. I shook my head then pointed at the coffee pot. I knew he was here to help pack up things for the move and get Jax and I settled in at mother's estate.

"An all-nighter, huh?" I asked as he joined me in the living room.

"Yeah, Christian came to get me, and we tied on a few."

I practically growled as my face snarled at the mention of Christian.

"Whoa, I'm picking up on some negative vibes sis!" James said with a laugh.

"I don't like him. He may be your friend, but I don't like him."

"He's just a buddy Jess. He's good for going out and drinking. Besides, he's an angry drunk, so we don't go out often. In fact, he expressed his distaste for you last night. So, the love is not lost between you two."

"He's bad news James. I wish you would stay away from him," I cautioned him. I could not explain the intricacies of the situation to James. He was merely human and would not understand.

"So, I'm guessing he won't be invited to the family get togethers and vacays huh?" He joked.

"No, he won't!" I grumbled.

"Who won't?" Jax said from the top of the stairs.

"Christian," James and I said in unison.

"That's too bad. I was hoping we could all be a happy family," Jax said. I was not truthfully sure if she was being sarcastic or serious. She had a way with words that could leave you wondering her intent.

"Anyone up for breakfast?" I asked hoping to change the subject away from Christian.

We opted for pancakes, a quick and easy breakfast that did not require other sides with them. After we cleaned up the breakfast dishes, I checked my cell phone. I did not have any messages or texts. I felt a pang of disappointment. I put the phone down, deciding I needed to clean up and get dressed. I opted for a bath instead of a shower. I wanted to soak and warm up in the hot water. I told both James and Jax I would be out to help after my bath then disappeared behind a locked door. I had not seen any spirits or angels since the morning before, so I was anticipating a visitor. Fortunately for me no visitors decided to interrupt my bath. I needed the break from all the supernatural activities of late. In a matter of days, I had learned of my lineage, Bill's true form, been visited by my mother, my father, Brian, a soldier, and least of all the frosty beings. I had been educated in the ways of the universe from Archangels to the seven realms. I knew a little about the eight Angels of Light and found out that God was potentially a woman. It was quite a bit to process in a week's time. Not having a visitor was refreshing.

I packed up my bathroom necessities after I was dressed in my typical jeans and sweatshirt attire. I was packing and moving after all, so a comfortable outfit was in order. I pulled my luggage set out of my closet, finding that I was staring at my clothes with no idea what I wanted to bring and what I did not. I probably should have just packed all my clothes, but that would have taken days.

Jax knocked on my door. "Jess, I've packed all my things already," she said through the door.

I opened the door to my room and let her in. "I'm going to probably need a few hours to pack everything I need to basically live at mother's estate with you," I said.

"I want to go ahead and go home. Do you mind if James takes me now? He can come back to help you after, it will give you time to pack." I could feel she really wanted to go home. James stepped in my room behind her.

"I don't mind making a few trips," he offered.

"Plus, I need to do some laundry," Jax added.

"Alright, you two can head on. I have some work files and things I should probably pack up in my office as well. That could take a few hours in and of itself."

Her reasoning reminded me that I should probably wash some laundry before I left as well.

Jax and James took what little she had from my house to his car, since her car was still at the estate. They left after a few minutes of goodbyes. I picked up my computer case from the butler area in the kitchen then headed upstairs to my office to pack all the things I may need. I sat at my desk making mental lists of all the things I would need to pack and take with me. I figured I could just use my father's study when I got to the estate, which would eliminate having to pack most things in my home office. I picked up the second book I had purchased from the Little Shop on the Bay placing it in my computer bag. I still needed to finish reading *The Origin of Love*, although I was fairly sure Jax had absconded with it. I made a mental note to double check the guest room before I left. I had a message on the phone in my office. It was from my horse caretaker confirming she would come to the house daily. I sat at my desk looking around the room. *What really is my purpose? What am I supposed to remember? What am I supposed to create?* I had so many unanswered questions still.

I checked my email before I completely packed away my laptop. I had a few client emails that I would deal with in the morning. Some spam that the company spam filter did not catch, and another email from myself. I clicked on the message to open it. Enclosed was a picture attachment to the email. The photo was of Donovan and I at the little café across from our office building. Someone had taken it from the other side of the street through the window. I was smiling and Donovan had his back to the person who took the photo. I clicked on the picture to save it to my hard drive. There were no words with the picture and the subject line was blank as well. *I'm being stalked. I may need Bill to look into the emails now.* I finished what I needed to do in my office. I checked the guest room before I went down the stairs. Jax had pulled the bedding off and left the room very tidy. The book she had been reading was on the nightstand. I picked it up and put it with the other book in my computer case. I took the case to the kitchen propping it near the door.

Donovan was pulling into my driveway as I set it down. I opened the door and stood in the doorway just like he had for me the night before.

"Hi Stranger," I said with a smile.

"Hi beautiful."

He always made me feel that way too. Although, I would probably argue and disagree with him, it was nice that he thought it.

He swept me into his arms kissing me on my lips. I know I must have swooned because he practically pinned me to the door in the kitchen to hold me up. When he pulled away from me, I was practically panting.

"I thought about calling, but I just had to see you again," he said.

I felt thrilled to have him wanting to be around me. I wanted to be near him any chance I could get.

"I am packing to go stay at my mother's estate home with Jax," I informed him sadly.

"Hmmmm, no more late-night rendezvous huh?"

"Nope," I laughed.

"I'll just have to sneak into the estate instead," he winked as he said it.

I pulled him by his hand into the house as I shut the door and led him to my bedroom. I was going to put him to work if he was going to be here. I decided to use my steamer trunk in the closet to fill it with clothes rather than carrying fifteen pieces of luggage. I would save the big piece of luggage for shoes and use the garment bag for my business suits. Donovan carried the steamer trunk to the center of the room for me. I could not help but watch his back flex as he carried it. He was built like a God. I was smiling, and probably drooling, as he set it down.

"Enjoying yourself Miss Hanson?"

"Why yes, Mr. Wheeler!" I grinned.

He picked me up in his arms and laid us down on my bed. I could feel his desire for me, not just in the energy around us, but physically as well. He touched my face with his fingers very softly brushing his thumb across my lips. I looked directly into his eyes, my desire for him had lit my insides on fire. He closed his eyes then placed his forehead on my forehead. Our noses were touching lightly as I also closed my eyes and took a deep breath. With so much desire and intimacy in the air I wanted to just breathe for a moment.

"God she is so beautiful! Thank you for allowing me to find her," Donovan was praying. I read his thoughts! I tried to concentrate to hear more of his thoughts, but the more I concentrated the further his thoughts and feelings seemed from me.

"Relax Jess," he whispered in my ear.

I opened my eyes to find him watching me. He rolled over on my bed pulling me with him so that I was laying on him instead. I propped my hands under my chin and watched him for a moment. This time I was memorizing every beautiful feature of this man.

"I have to keep packing," I did not want to now, "James will be back soon to help me load up these things."

"Why don't you call James, tell him I can bring you and

your things? I have my truck, I think I can handle a steamer trunk and a few pieces of luggage," he smiled as he said it.

"I am sure you can," I giggled.

I got up off the bed to get my cell phone. I had a missed call from James, he was stuck in traffic and had not gotten to mother's estate yet. I called him, told him he could just hang with Jax, and that I had Donovan to help me.

When I walked back into my room Donovan was not on my bed. I looked in the closet and in the bathroom. He was not around. *Strange.* I noticed the French doors to the deck from my room were ajar. My heart started to pound a little. I cautiously opened the doors, but I still did not see Donovan. I called his name, but the only sound I heard was that of my two horses whinnying. I walked slowly toward the barn, my senses hyper aware. I was scanning all around me, trying to find a spirit or another being. I heard movement inside the barn. I could not tell if it was the horses moving or if someone, or something, was in there. I peered through the opening of the two main barn doors. The aisle way of the barn was clear.

"What are you looking at?" Donovan whispered in my ear. I jumped about three feet, screaming like a total girl. He wrapped his arms around me, holding onto me for a moment until I calmed down.

"Hey, hey! I'm so sorry!" he looked upset that he had scared me.

My heart calmed down and I started to laugh hysterically.

"You scared the bejeezus out of me!" I said as I put my head down on his chest. He stroked my hair, and I could sense he was smiling.

"I'm sorry I did not mean to scare you that badly. I saw you creeping toward the barn. I thought you were trying to sneak up on me. So, I went through the back doors of the barn and walked around to where you were."

He was just playing with me! I loved it and hated it all at the same time! "I don't do scared very well!" I said, "I won't watch scary movies because I hate being scared."

He smiled at me, kissed me gently on my forehead, then whispered he was sorry again. We went into the barn, where I introduced Donovan to my horses. I had a cream-colored American Cream Draft horse with beautiful amber eyes named Eros. He was my first horse, he was a bit big for most people, but I loved riding him bareback because I could feel the motion of his shoulders best that way. I also had a Black Percheron named Aphrodite. I wanted a Friesian, but I did not see the point in dropping forty grand on a horse when a Percheron was remarkably similar. She was exceptionally beautiful and such an easy riding horse; anyone could ride her. I let Donovan know my caretaker would be coming by every day. I was a little sad that I would not get to see them every day, but then again, I didn't ride them as often as they needed either.

I fed the horses, then opened their stalls so they could go out into the paddock when they finished eating. Donovan watched with intrigue as I cared for my horses.

"You surprise me all the time," he said honestly.

"Yeah, how so?" I asked as I dropped hay into the feeders.

"You are so beautiful and sophisticated, yet so grounded and a little country," he grinned.

"Yeah, well my heart belongs in the south. I was raised here, but I spent many summers down at my grandmother's home in Georgia. My mother was raised in Georgia. Beneath all her glamour and designer clothes was a southern woman at heart." I loved that aspect of my mother.

Donovan and I walked hand in hand back to the house after I closed up the barn. I was getting a little hungry and offered to fix lunch for us. I made sandwiches served with my favorite veggie chips. Donovan opted for water again to drink while I sipped on my homemade sweet tea. After cleaning up, we finished packing my clothes and shoes in my room. I saw the little wooden box on my nightstand. I was internally debating with myself if I should take it or leave it.

"What is it?" Donovan asked.

"What is what?" I said not understanding his question.

"The box. What is it?" he questioned.

I stood there not knowing how to answer his question, an awkward moment of silence passed between us.

"The other day when you were passed out on the floor you had it in your hand. You handed it off to your sister when I put you on the bed. And now you are staring at it.

"What is it?" he asked again.

"I'm not sure," I said truthfully, "It came in the box you delivered to me the day we met. I have not opened it yet. I am afraid to," I looked up to him literally praying that he would not press the issue.

"Ok," he said as if he knew I did not wish to discuss it.

"Ok." I repeated back.

I left the wooden box on my nightstand. It had been trouble so far. I did not need trouble following me to my mother's estate. *Maybe it will suck up the frosty beings all on its own just by being present in my room.* I was being hopeful yet imaginative in my thinking.

Donovan loaded the trunk and my bags into the back of his truck. He had a pull cover that covered the entire truck bed. I had never seen a truck with such a feature. I put my laptop case into the back seat of the crew cab. Donovan walked with me through the house to make sure everything was turned off, doors were closed and locked, and nothing was left that I may need. I pulled the door to the house closed, suddenly overwhelmed with sadness that I was leaving my own home.

Albeit temporary, I reminded myself I could theoretically come home anytime I wanted, but I was still a little sad. I picked up the hide a key from under a planter that I kept beside the kitchen door. When Donovan climbed into the truck, I held it out to him.

"What's this?" he asked like it was not obvious.

"It's the spare key to my house."

"Do I need to put it under the mat or something?" He did not get it.

"No silly. It's for you to have. Since I won't be here all the time, I figured you could keep an eye on my house. It's just in case," I smiled sheepishly. I had never given my key to any man. This was a big step for me.

"Thanks Jess. I will. And I appreciate that you trust me enough to give me your key." He kissed me sweetly on the lips then put the key on his key ring.

I watched my house disappear from view through the passenger window as we drove away. I was moving back to the house I had grown up in, but on the bright side I was bringing a man that I had just given my house key with me – I would argue I had also given him my heart. I quietly wished my mother and father could meet Donovan. I had not seen my mother or father's spirits, nor the soldier before I left. I wondered if I would see them at the estate. Donovan grabbed my hand then gently kissed it. We were a couple now and it felt perfect. I was so happy and distracted that I had forgotten about the photo I received in my email.

CHAPTER 16

We drove the length of the estate driveway through the apple trees and pulled up in front of the home. This was more of a homecoming, so this time the mood was much lighter. Donovan peered through the front window of his truck in obvious admiration of the house.

"Is this a 1920's home?" he asked.

"Yes, it was built in 1929."

"The classical symmetry, the rhythmic rows of columns and windows, the neoclassical styling and the dentil cornices there are signature 1920s architecture," he said pointing to the roof line of the home.

"I guess," I shrugged.

I had no idea what he had just said. He laughed then tried to explain the different architectural wonders of the 1920s to me and the influence of 18th century French architecture. My eyes glazed over as he spoke.

"I promised to not discuss architecture with you, I know, but this house is amazing."

"I am glad you like it," I laughed.

It was a grand home, not just in the roaring twenties but today as well. It sat on close to eight acres of land with stables, and water access complete with a long pier for boating on the Chesapeake Bay. The stables had been re-built when I was a teen since the original stables were falling apart. They were refurbished to include modern amenities inside but kept the original design of the outside to match the main house on the property. The main house had a circular drive-in front of the two-story columned front portico. The columns of the portico were painted the same shade of white as the face of the portico itself. The home however was deep red brick on all sides. Each of the attached wings were red brick, the additions to the home were attached with glass sunrooms or open brick archways. All the additions to the home had been completed by the 1940s. My father purchased the estate in the late 1960s and made improvements only to the inside of the home over the years while preserving the integrity of the original design of the exterior.

Donovan and I walked through the front door of the home into the grand entrance. The house smelled of home cooking, our cook Ms. Ebby came out of the kitchen and cried when she saw me standing there. Ebby Morgan was our cook, she was an elderly short, stout woman who was born and raised in Georgia. She could cook meals that would rival celebrity chefs. Although we called her Ms. Ebby, her full name was Evelyn Morgan but those close to her called her Ebby, a nickname she was given as a small child. She never married, although she once told me a story about a fiancé she had when she was a young woman, he had cheated on her, and she never dated again. It devastated her. She told me her love for our family was enough for her and she would work for free if it meant she was still a part of us. We had two housekeepers growing up, Ms. Ebby as our cook, a horse caretaker, and a gardener. After my father died my mother hired a lawn service and dismissed the gardener, she felt he could not keep up with demands of the estate. The housekeepers ended up finding other estates to work for, my mother's depression made working for her difficult. Ms. Ebby, stayed on and was still working for the estate to this day. She lived in a little cottage on the back side of the property. She would drive a golf cart over in the mornings to start her day.

My mother bought her a brand-new golf cart every few years. Mother had offered her a car, but Ms. Ebby never learned to drive a car or get a license, and she never wanted to learn.

"Welcome Home Miss Jessica," she said as she threw her arms around my neck. It was a bit of a reach for her because she was much shorter than me. I introduced her to Donovan, then she suddenly announced she had to get back to the kitchen to add a plate for him. She insisted we eat at home, she was preparing a large meal for all five of us.

"Five of us?" I asked with interest.

"Miss Jacquelin has a guest as well. Interesting young man," she said as she looked at me over her wire rimmed glasses. Her tone was that of disapproval, but she certainly knew how to hold her tongue.

I knew in my gut it was Christian. I could feel his presence in the house. I must have looked green because both Donovan and Ms. Ebby offered me some water, forcing me to sit down. I actually felt sick.

"I'm fine," I said unconvincingly.

"Why don't we get you settled into your room?" Donovan offered. I nodded my head in answer and he followed me with the steamer trunk to the east wing. We decided to get the rest of the bags after dinner.

My room was in the east wing of the house on the first floor. I had a large bedroom, my own sitting area, and a full bathroom with large walk-in closets - which all together made a large in-law type suite. It practically took the entire first floor of the east wing. My brother had the second floor above me, and his area mirrored mine except in décor. There were some storage areas on the back side of our wing, as well as an entertainment area with a fully stocked hand carved mahogany bar. My parents chose the east wing for James and me when we became teens because it was connected to the main home with a large enclosed sunroom. My mother did not want us walking through an outdoor breezeway to get to the main home. I liked that it was the closest part of the home to the stables.

I turned the light on in my bedroom and stood in the doorway for a few minutes taking in the room, as memories flooded my thoughts.

"You, ok?" Donovan asked from behind me. He was not struggling to hold the trunk, but I could tell he certainly wanted to put it down.

"I'm sorry Donovan! Here set it there by the bed."
My bed was a regular queen-sized bed with white and pink floral bedding. The walls were a pale pink with white wood trim. I had a small crystal chandelier in the center of the room. The seating area had white plush furniture with pink throw pillows and a TV that had been there since the 1990s. I made a mental note to get a better TV for this room and maybe a Roku like Donovan had. I was not sure if there was cable in the room or if my mother had upgraded to satellite TV as I had recommended years ago. The room was very cold, it felt like the heat had not been turned on in this wing for years. I strode over to the thermostat and turned on the heat setting.

"Want a tour of the rest of the house?" I offered Donovan. He had watched me fully take everything in once inside my room.

"I'm here to help you in whatever way you need it. If you want, we can get you settled in here and you can give me a tour after dinner."
I smiled at how considerate he truly was, always putting me first.

"Thank you, Donovan. For everything. You truly are a Godsend." I walked over to him wrapping my arms around him. He pulled me close to him just holding me. *Anything for you.* I heard his thoughts again. I smiled and relaxed in his arms. This felt like home, being in his arms, it didn't matter what house I was in.

Donovan easily picked me up, sweeping me off my feet then carried me over to the bed. He laid me down gently as he crawled over me. I giggled at his playfulness.

"I figured if you were going to have to move back into the room you lived in as a teen, you should at least experience making out like a teen in here."

His blue eyes were sparkling with devious thoughts.

"Who said I haven't?" I teased.

He narrowed his eyes at me with an inquisitive.

"You told me you only messed around with your boyfriend when you were sixteen for his birthday."

"How do you know it wasn't in this room?" I said deviantly.

He lifted me off the bed to throw me over his knee, like he was going to spank me. I struggled to get off him in vain but couldn't because I was hysterically laughing. He joked about me needing a good spanking while holding me down on his lap. He swatted playfully at my bottom which made me flush with desire and embarrassment all at the same time.

"I'm just kidding! I'm just kidding! I didn't do anything in this room!" I pleaded as I still tried to get off his lap.

He pulled me up to a seated position on his lap with my legs wrapped around him, then softly began kissing my neck. The aura in the room went from a playful feel to a sensual one instantly. I was incredibly hot for him. I felt a desire pulling at me as his lips touched my neck and chin. His breathe was warm and I turned my face down toward his looking directly into his eyes. *I want you in every way too.* I was falling in love with Donovan.

We both took a deep breath sitting back from one another putting just a tiny bit of distance between us. The air around us felt charged and we were both reeling from the intensity of our desires. Donovan stood, picking me up with him then set me gently on my feet. I was enthralled with how easily he maneuvered holding me.

"I want it to be perfect," he said.

I did not have to say anything I fully understood what he was saying. I simply nodded in agreement. He kissed me on my lips, then strode to the bathroom closing the door behind him. I sat down on the edge of the bed. I was going to need to really process my feelings for this man. At some point we would need to talk about more than we had already. I thought back to the other night on our date when he was so protective of me, he probably had no idea what he was protecting me from. I wish I had more trust in him to handle the spirit world side of me so I could share who or 'what' I am with him.

"Why do you look so sad?" Donovan asked me from the doorway of the bathroom as he dried his hands.

"I am pouting," I said with a playful but fake smile.

He did not look like he was buying the fake smile, but he didn't push me to explain. We spent the next little while putting my things in drawers and in the closet, mostly me putting things away and telling him where to put other stuff. He stood in the middle of the oversized mostly empty closet admiring the custom wood organization system.

"I think I should go shopping!" I said to his back.

He laughed a deep laugh, "typical woman."

He turned to face me; his face fell as though he saw a spirit.

"What?" I asked panicked.

I felt a presence behind me. It was cold, unfriendly, and thinking thoughts that I could feel were malicious. I turned on my heel to find Christian standing in the doorway, as a shiver ran through me.

"Ms. Ebby said to tell you dinner was ready," he stared directly at Donovan as he spoke.

"You need to leave," I said while I envisioned strangling him.

"I believe I am a guest of Jax tonight. If she wants me to leave, I will," he spoke arrogantly.

Donovan placed a hand on my shoulder as if to keep me from lunging at him, or it may have been protective, I was not sure which.

"We will be there shortly," Donovan answered for us.

"No time for illicit behavior D," Christian said laughing as he proceeded to leave the room.

"I hate him," I said through gritted teeth.

"Don't say that. Hate is a strong wasted emotion. It fuels him and you don't want to be like him." Donovan sounded incredibly wise.

"I strongly dislike him," I said instead, "he sure can kill a mood, no need for cold showers around him."

Donovan laughed taking my hand to lead me from my room. We were going to have to play nice. For now.

CHAPTER 17

Jax's room was part of the main home, she had been given the nursery when she was born which had a large daytime playroom and a small nanny suite attached to it. The nanny suite had a bedroom, private bathroom, and a kitchenette. Jax moved into the nanny suite as a teen and turned the nursery and playroom into her own apartment like area. We all had to use the main kitchen and dining room for any cooking above using a microwave and our family meals. After my father died the family meals became limited to Thanksgiving and Christmas. Ms. Ebby had cooked for us tonight like it was a holiday, even though Thanksgiving was still a few weeks away. The dining room bustled full of life just like I had remembered it as a child. She had gone all out with a large Turkey and all the sides you would see at a traditional Thanksgiving dinner. She was putting all the final dishes on the table as we walked in.

Donovan and I arrived holding hands through the doors that were just off the main entryway. James came in through the door from the kitchen, he liked to sample food before it made it to the table. I smiled at the memory of Ms. Ebby swatting his hand telling him to wait. Jax, followed by Christian, entered just behind Donovan and me, presumably from the living room. I wrinkled my nose at the thought of the two of them upstairs in her room. Jax looked as if she was nervous or scared, probably both. Christian was smiling a nefarious smile that would have made a fallen angel cringe. Ms. Ebby shook her head in obvious disapproval as she returned to the kitchen.

We all took seats at the table, James the head seat where our father used to sit, Donovan and I to the right of him, Jax and Christian to the left. There was a tension in the air so thick I could feel it and see it stirring around everyone. Donovan placed his hand on my thigh and squeezed. Again, I was not sure if he was holding me down or protecting me. I smiled graciously at him, reminded of his earlier statement that hate was a wasted emotion.

Love and light, love and light, love and light. Jax raised her eyebrows at me in an unspoken question of why I was thinking that phrase over and over. I shot my eyes in the direction of Christian. *Why is he here?* I communicated just for her. She shrugged her shoulders in answer. *Did you invite him?* She discretely shook her head no.

"Is there something I should know about?" James said breaking our internal conversation.

"No, why do you ask?" I asked trying to act like everything was normal.

"Because no one is speaking. And if I didn't know any better, I'd say you and Jax were carrying on a conversation in some kind of sign language or facial language."

Jax and I stared at each other for a moment before we both burst out in laughter. "What's so funny?" Christian asked. I could tell by his countenance he was really uncomfortable. *Good!*

"Nothing. We just know how to speak without speaking. It's a sister thing," Jax giggled.

"Girls!" James said with feigned disgust.

James' comment took a bit of the edge off, so we continued to fill our plates, making small talk with each other. James was interested in grilling Donovan about his job and expressed his personal interest in architecture. James had some knowledge and an appreciation for the same influences on modern buildings. Jax and I sat in silence, both of us pushed more food around on our plate than we ate. It was almost a shame because the food was so tasty. I could see Ms. Ebby looking through the sliver of an opening in the kitchen door every now and then. I would take a bite and curl my lips in an approving closed mouth smile. She was pleased; I could feel her joy to be serving guests again radiating through the room. An idea came to me in that moment. *Come with me to the kitchen.* I watched Jax as she received my thought. She looked up slowly acknowledging me with a very slight nod.

"Hey Jax, will you come to the kitchen with me for a minute?" I spoke out loud.

"Sure," she said nonchalantly.

"Why?" Christian asked.

"Because I have something that I would like for both of us to bring in here to give to the men," I said channeling my mother's fake smile.

Donovan squeezed my thigh in question, so I smiled reassuringly to him.

We both excused ourselves then entered the door to the kitchen. Ms. Ebby met us at the sink wanting to know what was wrong.

"Nothing Ms. Ebby!" I assured her, "I just wanted to let you know that I love being here having a home cooked meal!" Ms. Ebby lit up like I had just told her she won the lottery. The positive energy flowing off her was exactly what I needed for Jax to feel. She wrapped her arms around both Jax and I. The love and light that we all felt in that moment was enough to overcome any negativity that Christian brought with him.

Ms. Ebby told us how amazing it was to have all of us home again. She was sorry for the loss of our mother but reminded us to look at how it brought all of us together. Ms. Ebby was a positive energy center in this house.

"Where is that brandy that Daddy used to keep in the kitchen for special guests?" I asked her.
Her face beamed at the memory, she went to the counter and brought out an old crystal decanter with expensive brandy in it.

"I haven't pulled this out in years," she said as she handed it to me with a huge smile. Jax felt excitement at the thought of being included in a family tradition she had never experienced before.

"Let's go share this with the boys," I said with a grin. Jax was almost skipping back to the dining room she was so happy. I winked at Ms. Ebby who carried the bottle to the table.
James' eyes lit up when he saw the bottle.

"I haven't seen that since I was a child!" he exclaimed.
I smiled a Cheshire cat sized grin at Donovan, he smiled back broadly like he knew what was going on.

"This was my daddy's favorite brandy. He would only bring this out when he had special guests over. I thought we would continue his tradition. Since Jax has never been a part of this tradition, I wanted to include her tonight.

"May the tradition continue through us from hence forth." I was pleased to bind the three of us together with the brandy creating new memories. Ms. Ebby came in with brandy snifters for the men. Jax and I both politely bowed out of drinking. Donovan winked at me thinking *She's going to make it so I have to stay tonight.* I heard his thought, forcing me to stifle an outward giggle, keeping it in my head. I had not considered that he would have to drive home. My devious thoughts of being a bad college girl were rolling through my thoughts when I noticed Jax roll her eyes at me from across the room. I was going to have to work on being able to control my thoughts around her. Christian on the other hand appeared very unhappy with the way the energy in the room changed. He had plastered on a fake smile that rivaled that of my mother. I could feel the resentment coming off him because I had infused positive love into my sister. I was not going to let him win.

Christian only had one drink saying it was because he had to drive. He had law school finals in the coming week that he could not miss. I was still grinning over the small victory at dinner when he left. I had won this round. Jax was smiling and happy when she went to her room for the night. Donovan and I had to practically carry James to his room above mine. He had several drinks and became quite inebriated, but it was worth it. After we plopped him down on his bed Donovan escorted me to my room. It was almost like he was going to kiss me at my door then leave. I carefully mulled through my thoughts deciding what to say.

"I would ask you in for a night cap, but I think I covered that already," I beamed a flirty smile.

Donovan put his hands on both sides of my face, kissing me with such passionate desire I felt overwhelmed by it. My knees nearly buckled under me while he literally held me up. When he finally pulled away from me, I could not speak.

"Goodnight" he whispered as he took a few steps back.

"No please…. please don't go," I pleaded.

I was begging with every fiber of my being.

"Are you sure?" I could feel that he was just as wanting as I was.

I nodded my head 'yes.'

Donovan swept me off my feet, I wrapped my legs around his waist as he carried me to my bed. We gently fell onto the bed together, passionately kissing one another and pulling pieces of our clothes off in the process. I had not undressed in front of a man in so long I suddenly became very conscious of my body. Donovan slowed our frenzied pace down, he carefully moved my hair from my face, exposing my neck and shoulders. He traced his fingers over my collar bones and across the tops of my breasts now barely contained by my bra. My stomach was bare, I used my hands trying to cover it. I did not have the skinny washboard abs that I thought men desired. I was just a normal woman with curves and a soft stomach. Donovan moved my hands to my side continuing to trace his fingers past my belly button. My jeans unbuttoned and partially unzipped but still on. The light pink panties I had on were peeking through the unzipped part of my jeans. I closed my eyes; I did not want to see if Donovan disapproved of what he saw.

"Stop," he said to me in a whisper, "Stop shutting me out. You are beautiful."

I slowly opened my eyes, staring into his gorgeous eyes. He smiled at me as he bent to kiss the soft skin on my ribs and side. His beard tickled me which caused me to let out a soft giggle. I scanned his body up and down memorizing every part of him that was visible to me. He had taken his shirt off, his bare chest covered in just the right amount of soft brown hair. I noticed that he had a few jagged scars by his left pectoral muscle that were near where his heart was. I ran my fingers over each scar. His body was as sculpted as I had envisioned with a broad chest, muscular arms, and well-defined stomach muscles. He was absolutely dreamy, my desire for him was almost exploding deep inside of me. Donovan ran his hand up my left side to my now swollen breast and pushed his way under the bra, gently caressing and lightly squeezing. I took a deep breath letting out a soft moan as I felt the warmth of his hand on my almost fully exposed breast. I wanted him, yet the angel and devil reappeared and were once again at war on my shoulders. He stopped caressing me, pulled the bra back into place, moving his hand down to the curve of my waist.

"I want this to be perfect," he repeated what he said earlier.

"I know."

I wanted it to be perfect too and although I really wanted to feel him deep inside me, it was not the perfect time. I let out a disappointed sound that was very much like an audible pout. Donovan smiled at me and kissed my lips.

"I need to go home," he said after a few minutes.

I literally poked my bottom lip out. I did not want him to leave but I knew he had no change of clothes, and he and I both had work in the morning.

He kissed me on my lips then on my forehead. He was in love with me I could feel it all around him. His aura had a very pretty red hue to it. It was the first time I had ever seen a hue to a person's aura.

"What are you looking at?" he asked looking deeply into my eyes. I would have said he was looking into my soul at that moment.

"You, just you." I whispered.

I could feel his love and desire for me all at once. It was immensely powerful and very fulfilling. I wanted it to last forever.

"I really do need to get home Beautiful. We can have lunch tomorrow if you are free."

He was having just as hard of a time pulling away from me as I was of him.

"I would love that. I will make sure that I do not have any client conflicts first thing in the morning," I paused a moment, "I wish you could just stay."

"I want to stay. I have reasoned in my head a million ways to stay and a million reasons to leave." He was trying so hard to be a gentleman which I loved about him.

"Stay with me. I can ride with you in the morning to your house. I need to pick up my car anyway," I gave him the reason to stay - I still needed his help to get my car.
Clever.

"Twist my arm," he laughed as he said it.

I got up to put on a long silky black gown. I had only worn it once before but never in the presence of a man. I bought it years earlier because it was on sale, and I thought it was pretty. He whistled when I emerged from the bathroom with it on. I blushed. I noticed he was only wearing a pair of boxer briefs. They were black and hugged all the right places. He caught me staring at his 'package' then laughed at me. I crawled into the bed that I had not slept in for many years, next to a man I had never slept with. The sheets smelled clean, so someone obviously prepared for my arrival which I assumed was Ms. Ebby. Donovan wrapped his arms around me from behind as we both comfortably drifted into a deep sleep together.

CHAPTER 18

"Jessica, wake up please," a woman's voice whispered into my ear.

"Jessica," she called again almost cooing.

I slowly opened my eyes; I was surrounded by the bright white light again. I blinked several times to adjust my vision to the brightness. *I must be dreaming.*

"Jessica, you are not dreaming," the woman's voice sounded all around me.

"Faelynn?" I called out to the voice.

A beautiful angelic figure started approaching me. This angel was not Faelynn. She had the same build and height, about six feet tall, but she had long flowing dark red hair. Her eyes were the color of emeralds. She wore the same long flowing white gown Faelynn had worn except this angel's tunic was pale green, similar to prasiolite gemstones, with golden trim. As she approached the white light became the same pastel green color as her tunic.

"My name is Majestica. I am the Angel of Unconditional Love, Healing Love, and Soul Love."

"Hi Majestica. It's nice to meet you," I was just as in awe of her as I had been Faelynn, though I felt a little perplexed as to why I was here with her.

"I have summoned you here to Seraphim to help you," she explained.

"Help me with what?"

"Understanding more about your purpose," she was smiling very sweetly as she spoke.

She had a very calming effect on me.

"What about my purpose?" I was thoroughly intrigued now.

"Love is the beginning and the end. It is that which brings forth healing and peace. You are on your plane to embrace love and light and share the divine energy of the universe with all whom you come into contact with. With each being you encounter you have the choice to give and receive a loving vibration.

"As you release your love and light vibrations you will remember who you truly are, and you will begin to create the future."

"How do I release these vibrations?" I questioned.

"You will know with each encounter. No two encounters are the same," she explained.

"What if I do not know how?"

"You need to listen to your heart. Surround yourself with love, become one with love, live with love. You will always know. But, a word of caution, do not become unequally yoked, to do such would be counterproductive to your purpose."

"What exactly does that mean? I mean… I have heard teachings on being unequally yoked as it is written in the bible. But there are many different thoughts on this," I questioned her caution.

"To be unequally yoked would be like that of a farmer attempting to plow a field with an ox and a donkey yoked together. They would not be of equal strength, proportion, and ability; therefore, the plowing of the field would be far more difficult than necessary," she explained.

"I understand the analogy, but how does that apply to me?" I asked.

"You will understand in time."

She turned to leave, the pale green light began to fade as she moved away from me, returning me to the bright white light again. I had so many other questions that would have to wait it seemed.

I awoke in my childhood bedroom feeling awfully cold. I rolled over to find that Donovan was no longer in the bed with me. I sat up scanning all around, searching for him but he was nowhere to be seen. I stood up and ambled over to the thermostat to see if the setting had been lowered. It was exactly where I had put it the night before. It felt so cold in the room, frosty even. *CRAP! Not again!* I saw the frosty beings in the corner of my room near the sitting area. I do not know why I moved toward the frosty beings instead of running away from them.

"Is today the day for multiple visitors?" I said to the beings.

"We need your help," they whispered in a way that made the hair on the nape of my neck stand on end.

"My help? Why do you need my help?" I asked with tears pricking the corners of my eyes. The frosty beings needing my help sounded scarier to me than anything before.

"You have the key," they said.

"I don't have any key," I felt suddenly very defensive.

"You have the key," they repeated as they began circling around me.

I closed my eyes dropping to the floor as fear overtook me. I sat there rocking back and forth repeating over and over that I did not have the key.

The door to the room opened just at that moment, Donovan started to enter with two cups of coffee. I turned my head suddenly to see that he looked panicked.

"Are you ok?" he said as he rushed toward me.

I started to cry, overcome with emotion and the relief of his presence.

The frosty beings were gone, and the room temperature returned to normal again. Donovan wrapped his arms around my body to comfort me.

"It's ok, it was just a bad dream," he said over and over.
He had no idea that it was more than just a bad dream. How I wished it was just a bad dream. I wiped the tears from my eyes. He smiled lovingly at me as he brushed my disheveled hair from my face.

"I brought you coffee. I was told to make it 'coffee flavored sugar milk,'" he joked.
I laughed out loud, "Bill must be here."

"Yes, he's in the kitchen with Ms. Ebby. Said he needed to see you before you went to work. I guess he's going to drive you in today."

"Oh," I said almost sad that I was not going to get to ride with Donovan. I knew it was because of the visits I had this morning. I really needed to ask Bill a few questions anyway, so it was for the best. I smiled sweetly at Donovan then thanked him for the coffee.

"You are becoming quite the savior lately," I said as I took a sip.

"You don't know the half of it," he mumbled under his breath. I heard him but decided not to question the meaning. I could feel that he was very guarded today. I noted internally to ask him about it later.

Donovan made a few phone calls while I got ready for work. He was explaining to the other person on the phone that he would need to move a few appointments this morning because he would be in late. He seemed agitated by the response he was receiving. I played my favorite playlist on my cell phone, listening to calming music while I put on my make-up, completely tuning out his conversation.

"You don't need all that mess," he said leaning on the doorway of my bathroom.

"HA!" I laughed.

"You do need to brush your teeth though!" he laughed out loud, then I threw a towel at him.

We were joking and laughing with each other as we walked to the kitchen. Bill was sitting at the island in the kitchen with Ms. Ebby having coffee and an English muffin. Ms. Ebby was so happy to have people to cook for and serve. I could feel the joy and happiness in the atmosphere.

"Good morning, Miss Jessica! I have breakfast for you!" she said as she pulled a plate out of the warmer. It had scrambled eggs with bacon, buttered toast, and grits.

"Thank you, Ms. Ebby! It looks wonderful!" I was not very hungry, but I could not disappoint her.

"Good morning, Bill."

"Good morning, Jess. Sleep well?" he questioned with a wink.

He was teasing me about Donovan being there. Donovan chuckled under his breath.

"Funny... Both of you," I said sarcastically, "I slept beautifully thank you!"

I ate my breakfast while Donovan and Bill talked about politics and other boring topics that were not interesting to me. Ms. Ebby scurried around the kitchen busying herself while we sat there. I got up to put the dishes in the sink and Ms. Ebby about had a panic attack.

"No! No! No! Miss Jessica, I can do that for you!" she scolded me.

"It's ok Ms. Ebby, I don't mind."

"Miss Jessica, now you know I have not had anyone to appease in a long time. Don't take this away from me!" she argued.

She was peering up at me over her glasses, I smiled at her as I handed her the plate and mug in resignation.

"Thank you, Ms. Ebby."

I hugged her and she relaxed in my arms. She was like a grandmother to me, and I was glad she was still here.

Donovan, Bill, and I walked out of the house through the front door to the waiting vehicles. I wanted to get in the truck with Donovan, but I knew I had to ride with Bill. Donovan kissed me on my forehead then held me to him for a moment before leaving. I was grinning as I got into the passenger seat of Bill's Escalade.

"He loves you," Bill said plainly.

"I'm sorry?" I was surprised by his statement.

"He loves you. It's written all over his countenance," he said.

"That's nice."

It was all I could think to say. I felt thrilled, a flutter pulsed in my heart having an affirmation from Bill.

"I understand Majestica visited you," he changed the subject.

"Yes. She was a little parabolic in her advice."

"The ox and the donkey?" he asked with a laugh.

"Yep!" I laughed with him.

"That's her favorite."

Bill went on to explain that the unequally yoked was multifaceted and although we could not discount the biblical references to it, many religions interpreted it to be a marital or a sexual reference. It was really meant to be applicable to many situations. He explained that in my case it was a warning not to become involved with beings of a lesser power or realm than myself. I found myself very saddened by this. Did this mean I could not be with Donovan? Would loving him make us unequally yoked because he was human, and I was not? I became so entrenched in my thoughts about how this related to Donovan and me that I did not hear what Bill was saying any more. I found myself being weighed down by the possibility that I may not be able to be with the man I was in love with.

"Jess!" Bill said loudly enough to startle me.

"What? I'm sorry, what were you saying?"

"It has to do with the frosty beings," he repeated.

"Oh? How so?" I questioned.

"They want your help. They know you are a future creator. They will try to influence you to help them."

"They visited me this morning in my room. They kept saying I had the key."

"You do have the key," Bill said matter-of -factly.

"I do?" I was surprised by this revelation.

"The key is your ability to create."

"I don't understand Bill."
I truly did not understand.

"They have to be fed. The only way for you to feed them is to continually create. The more you create the more they are fed," he explained.

"You mean like food?" I was utterly confused.

"No." He was noticeably short with his answers, and I was not understanding what he was saying. "They need you to sacrifice someone to them and in doing so they will be fed. They will have another being in which they can exist through."

"Sacrifice someone!!! Like on an alter with pig blood and stuff???" I was disgusted by the thought.

Bill laughed, "No not with pig blood and stuff, and no alter. No eating bat heads, no evil rituals, nothing like you are thinking."

"Then I don't understand," I said with my arms crossed.

"You will have to sacrifice someone who needs to be loved. One who is desperate for your love. You will have to choose who that person will be, and the lack of your love vibrations will constitute the sacrifice to them," he said sadly.

"Do I have to?" I did not want to do this at all.

"There will come a point where you will have no choice. You will have to choose, and you may not choose wisely. You may very well not be aware you have made the choice until it is too late."

He was watching the road as he was saying this. I could not help but look through the side window saying nothing in response. This was a very heavy burden on me, and one that I may not know how to handle.

"I had to choose," he said quietly, "and I did not realize it when I made the choice. I sacrificed someone who meant quite a bit to me. I knew when it was all said and done, that it was too late. It was part of my path, just as it is part of yours."

"Who did you choose?" I asked just as quietly.

"I chose my business partner Douglas Wyatt."

Bill explained that at the time he was partners with Mr. Wyatt, they were phenomenally successful attorneys. They had represented some high-profile cases and garnered recognition throughout the legal field. They had cases that set the precedence in courts throughout the United States. Their dynamic partnership worked helping them win cases that other law firms refused to touch. It was during this time that he met my father. He represented him in a major land development case that cemented his friendship and respect with my father. My father and Bill became so close that they were perceived by others as a team in not only the legal field but also in the real estate development world. Bill and my father vacationed together, spent holidays together, they became close like brothers.

When my father met, and ultimately married my mother, Bill was the best man in the wedding. Mr. Wyatt became insanely jealous of this budding friendship and business relationship. He demanded Bill remain strictly professional with my father. When Bill refused, Mr. Wyatt threatened to pull his business and separate from Bill closing down their firm. Bill told him to go ahead. Mr. Wyatt left their partnership and opened his own firm, he tried to pull clients, many of whom refused to leave Bill. This infuriated Mr. Wyatt. He changed his practice to a criminal defense practice becoming a terribly angry bitter man. To this day, Mr. Wyatt despises Bill and everything his firm stands for. He has worked on what Bill refers to as "the evil side of the law" as a criminal defense attorney ever since. Although he is an extraordinarily successful lawyer, he is the antithesis to everything Bill is. He is the slime ball lawyer that lawyer jokes are made of. He is the evil to Bill's good.

I sat in silence listening to everything Bill explained.

"Is he human?" I asked, it occurred to me he may not be.

"No. He is not," Bill answered.

"Is he like you?"

"He is a fallen angel. He chose to be a fallen angel when I sacrificed him unknowingly," Bill sounded sad as he spoke, "we grew up together. He was from Beriya just as I was. Although he did not possess the same abilities I did since he was not of the same lineage."

"Bill, what is Christian's last name?" I had a feeling I knew the answer as I asked.

"Wyatt." Bill just then filled in all the blanks for me.

This was the part of the story that was missing. This is why Christian was so angry. He was from the fallen angel lineage as Bill had explained to me several days before. I pieced it all together.

"Is Mr. Wyatt Jax's father?" my heart was pounding in my chest, and I felt like I was going to be sick to my stomach as I asked the question.

"Yes," Bill looked just as ill as I felt.

"He created the same way you did. With my mother," I was not asking, I was stating.

Bill only nodded his head. I was officially stunned once again.

Christian's interest in my sister was as a sibling. *SHIT! He's my sibling too!* I was officially disgusted and sick to my stomach. I was related to him. *I am going to have to learn to accept him, aren't I?*

"Yes. You have to somehow learn to love him," Bill answered my thoughts.

"Is that my purpose?" I asked feeling an empty pit in my stomach.

"It is part of it," he still held something back I could tell, but honestly, I had no desire to know more at this point.

"I guess that explains his disdain and his ramblings about privilege and not being raised in the same way. He is jealous," I surmised.

"His negativity and rage are fueled by his jealousy, just as his father's was over your father," Bill explained.

"So, is this like some Capulet and Montague type feud?"

"More like a Cain and Able type feud," Bill replied.

"Is Mr. Wyatt your brother?"

"Not like humans are brothers related by blood, but in our soul family yes, he is my brother and a very jealous brother at that. We are related much like you and Jax are related. We have the same female creator but are from different lineages. I did not understand that I had to keep him on the love and light path. It is why I am still on this earth to this day. To ensure you do not make the same mistakes that I made."

Bill had just explained so much to me. I understood more of his purpose as well. It was all of our purpose really. We were to remain on the love and light path and keep others on our path as well. It was the beginning and the end. The alpha and the omega – it was love. It all made sense.

"Now you remember," Bill said with a small smile.

I sat back in the seat and sighed. I at least understood my main purpose. I did not quite know how to be a future creator, nor did I understand fully the sacrifice that I may or may not make to the frosty beings, and I still did not know how I would explain any of this to Donovan or if I could. At least I understood the most significant part, to be the love and light to others.

CHAPTER 19

We arrived at our building on Charles Street in downtown Baltimore. Bill was kind enough to drop me off at the main entrance to the building. I waved a small wave to the security guard at the desk, he barely glanced up from whatever it was he was doing. I rode the elevator to the twenty-first floor. I wondered where Donovan's floor was since I had never asked. I knew we were in the same building, but I did not know the name of his firm much less where his office was located. I picked up my messages from the corner of my paralegal's desk. She was not in yet, so I had some time to sit and organize myself before I was bombarded with everything that I was behind on. I put my things down and went ahead to the office kitchen to fix a cup of coffee. There was a tray of cookies on the counter – I really wanted one – but I resisted the urge to eat them. I carried my coffee back to my desk waving at another attorney as he walked by. There were several cards on my desk, most were from co-workers each with a heartfelt sympathy for the loss of my mother. I felt moved by the thoughtfulness.

I put each of them in my computer case to take home. I sifted through my messages then noticed I had a message from Leila at the Little Shop on the Bay. *Interesting.* I would call her later this afternoon. I put my messages in the order in which I would return them (by my own importance of course) and then I turned on my computer.

The phone on my desk rang after a few minutes, and I answered it out of habit.

"Jessica Hanson."

"Good morning, Beautiful! I was just hoping to hear your voice before I am buried in meetings for the day," Donovan said.

I couldn't help but grin knowing he was thinking of me.

"Good morning, are you sure you haven't gotten enough of me yet?" I teased.

"No Ma'am. I was actually hoping to have a little more of you. I believe you were going to check your calendar for a lunch date with me."

I opened the calendar on the computer, I had three appointments all of which were after 1:00 p.m. My paralegal was awesome, she did not overload me on my first day back.

"Well, it seems Mister....., I'm sorry what was your last name again?" I giggled as I said it.

Donovan laughed heartily into the phone.

"Mr. Wheeler," he answered sounding very business-like.

"Oh yes, Mr. Wheeler. Well, it seems that I am available for lunch today. How does 11:00 a.m. sound to you?"

"Perfect! See you at eleven," he said.

"Wait, Mr. Wheeler, where will this lunch take place?" I asked.

"I will come to your office and pick you up!"

"Great, Mr. Wheeler! Have a wonderful day!" I said smiling broadly.

"Goodbye Miss. Hanson."

I hung up the phone feeling pleased. I put a 'personal' time block on my calendar for 11:00 a.m. to 12:30 p.m. just so that my paralegal did not put anything on it at the last minute.

Barbara arrived on time as usual. She had been my paralegal for the last two years. We had acquired her from another firm that had announced it would be closing its doors. The economy had hit some of the smaller firms rather hard but had not affected ours for the most part. Barbara was about ten years older than I was and had been a paralegal since she was nineteen. She was particularly good at her job and very thorough. I knew she could handle anything I asked of her. I trusted her more than most associate attorneys. Every now and then our recruiting team would hire an amazing graduate, but they were so green they were useless. I laughed at them only because I knew that I was once one of those green associates.

I sifted through the pressing issues on my desk, one of my clients had an upcoming Pendante Lite hearing. Pendente lite is a Latin term meaning 'awaiting the litigation' or 'pending the litigation.' It was mainly used in family court cases who were sorting out custody, support, and alimony issues. Many of the women I represented were from abusive relationships, so they needed the PL hearings to survive until a final order was put into place. When I was an intern in my final year of law school, I worked for a domestic violence advocacy group. I knew I would always want to help women in those situations. I took on several 'pro bono,' or free, cases a year for some of the worst cases. I was incredibly careful with who I took on as a client. If I had any inkling that they were gaming the system with protective orders, I would not represent them. I was just beginning to realize that my ability to tell when someone was being truthful, or not, was part of the gifts I had as a higher evolved being. It led to an exceedingly high success rate in the courtroom for me.

No wonder Bill and I made good lawyers.

"You are a good lawyer because you are good at your job," Jax said.

"Hey, what are you doing here?" I asked her as she stood in the doorway to my office.

"I thought I would see if you were free for lunch."

I froze not knowing what to say just yet. I thought about my lunch date with Donovan.

"Oh, I see," Jax said.

"It's ok Jax, I can see him later! You are much more important to me," I said with a genuine smile.

She beamed at me, thrilled that I would cancel my date with Donovan. I picked up my cell phone to send him a text. I knew he was in meetings, so I did not want to interrupt.

10:42 a.m. *Hey, Change in plans. I apologize. Having lunch with Jax. I hope you are not mad! Dinner? J.*

10:43 a.m. *No problem! I do understand and I am not mad! Dinner sounds good. Let me know when you are done with work. D.*

10:43 a.m. *Great! Thank you Love! J.*

10:43 a.m. *Love? D.*

10:44 a.m. *Yep. Term of Endearment. ☺ J.*

10:45 a.m. *Ok Love. ☺ D.*

"You two are disgusting," Jax said in mock disgust. I laughed out loud, literally.

"Have a seat, I have a few things to finish up and then we can go to lunch."

Jax and I walked through the lobby of the building at about five minutes after eleven and headed toward the Harbor. We loved the Cheesecake Factory restaurant located in Harborside; it had been a long time since we had eaten there. It was a few blocks to walk there, we both loved the scenery. Besides getting almost run over by cars trying to run a red light was half the fun of getting there. We were chatty and giggled about girly things that sisters usually talk about. It was a very pleasant lunch. I could tell that Jax was content to have a renewed sisterly bond with me. We were going to split a piece of chocolate cake, no we did not get a piece of cheesecake, and it was actually the waiter who convinced us to splurge and share one. He flirted with Jax the entire time we were there, and I could tell she was genuinely enjoying it. They were talking about college, so I checked my cell phone to see what time it was. I had a text message from Bill.

11:53 a.m. *Issue at office. Hurry back.*
11:57 a.m. *At lunch with Jax. Just waiting on check. Be back shortly. Jess.*

"Jax, we are going to have to get the cake to go sweetie. I have an issue to deal with at the office."

"Everything ok?" she asked concerned.

"I don't know. Bill just said there was an issue, to hurry back."

I was curious but not concerned. He rarely sent a text. I just figured a case had an issue and he needed my help.

Jax and I asked for a 'to go' box with the check. The young waiter gave us two slices in our 'to go' box and his phone number to Jax. We paid, leaving a nice tip for him, then Jax and I discussed if she would call him or not once we left. She said she would think about it, but she was still not sure she wanted to date so soon after Brian's death. I understood where she was coming from. We talked about a pair of shoes we had seen in a display window at the Harbor Place shopping center while we walked back to my office. Jax said goodbye on the street in front of my building and took both pieces of cake with her.

I walked to the bank of elevators and pressed the up button. A hand grabbed my shoulders spinning me around. I was essentially accosted by a handsome man in a gorgeous three-piece suit. He pulled me into a kiss so fast, I had to pull away to breathe.

"Well, hello!" I said with a laugh.

"Hi! How was lunch with Jax?" Donovan asked sincerely.

"Good. It was nice to spend time with her. She showed up unexpectedly. I didn't want to disappoint her," I explained.

"No need to explain. She's your sister," he smiled at me.

"I was more concerned by the term of endearment," he winked at me as he said it. The elevator doors opened then we both got on, he pressed the 21st floor button for me and the 23rd floor button for himself. *Top floor, Impressive.*

"Yes, I own the building," he offered as an explanation for being on the top floor.

"Wow. I learn something new about you every day, Mr. Wheeler," I whistled with an impressive tone.

The elevator stopped on the twenty-first floor, when the doors opened, I started to get off, but Donovan stopped me momentarily then kissed the top of my hand. My heart fluttered as I walked away in the direction of my office completely forgetting about the text from Bill.

"Ms. Hanson, Mr. Brothers said it is urgent that you come to his office," Barbara said to me as I passed her desk.

"Thank you, Barb."

I put my purse and coat down in the chair to my office then pulled my door closed. I hurried down the hall to Bill's office and found that Patty was standing outside Bill's door. It was almost as if she was trying to eavesdrop on what was happening on the other side. I cleared my throat to let my presence be known which startled her in the process.

"Patty, Bill said it was urgent he see me."

"Yes, you may go right in," she said politely for a change.

I walked into Bill's office with a light knock on the door as I opened it. There were two men sitting in the chairs in front of his desk.

"Is this a bad time?" I asked. Both men stood to their feet, as did Bill.

"No Jess. Come in please," Bill said.

I could not tell what exactly was going on, but my pulse began to race, and I realized I was about to be bombarded with something.

"Jessica Hanson, my name is Detective Gregory Talbot. I am a detective with the Washington DC police department. And this is my partner Detective Hank Carlson."

"Gentlemen, nice to meet you," I said with a nod.

"Jess they are investigating an incident in Georgetown over the weekend," Bill said ominously.

"Ok. What incident?" I was completely unaware of what exactly they may be referring to.

"Is James Hanson your brother?" Detective Talbot asked.

"Yes," I replied.

"Were you aware that he was in Georgetown over the past weekend?"

"Yes," I was direct with my answer.

"Were you also aware that he was with another person?" he asked.

"Yes."

I knew he had been there with Christian.

"Do you know who that person was?"

"I know who he **said** he was with. But I do not have direct knowledge of who he was there with," I gave such an attorney answer.

"Miss Hanson, whom did he say he was there with?" he looked directly at me as he asked.

"Before I answer this, what is the incident and why am I being questioned?"

I knew better than to just freely answer any detective. I also knew that if James was in some kind of trouble, I was going to protect him at all costs.

"Miss Hanson, a young woman was raped in Georgetown by two men. She is claiming that the two men were Mr. James Hanson, and a Mr. Christian Wyatt."

"Raped????" I said with a raised voice.

My brother was not the raping type, but I didn't know Christian well enough to know whether or not he was capable.

James may have been a playboy type, but he certainly was no rapist.

"We are not convinced her story is legitimate. She has holes in it that do not make sense. We are just trying to get some basic facts here. No one is being charged with a crime at this time," Det. Talbot explained.

It is common knowledge that cops were good at getting answer when "no one is being charged at this time." I also knew not to answer questions that could incriminate my brother. I was willing to incriminate Christian for all it was worth, but only if he was guilty. I knew he was angry, bitter, and jealous but I did not see him as a rapist.

"Det. Talbot, I know you are just doing your job. But as I said, I only have secondhand information. It is not factual nor is it of any value to your investigation. I can attest to the character of my brother James, but I know very little about Mr. Wyatt. As to their whereabouts, and who or what they were doing, I have no direct knowledge."

"Thank you, Miss Hanson. I appreciate your time this afternoon. If you do think of anything that could help, please do not hesitate to call me." Det. Talbot handed me his business card.

"Bill, I have a client to get to, unless you need something more from me..." I left it open ended in case he wanted me to stay.

"No, we can meet after I finish with the detectives here," Bill said very stone faced. He was giving nothing away, which was one of his signature traits as a lawyer.

I walked back down the hall toward my office. I was caught off guard by the detectives and their investigation. I had a feeling, maybe it was intuition, but I had a feeling that this was about money more than a criminal case. It was something in the way the detective said the woman had holes in her story. I knew that our mother's death had been in the news the prior week and that James, Jax, and I were mentioned in the news as the survivors and heirs to her estate. My client was sitting outside my office when I returned. I had to put whatever this was to the side and focus on my job for the time being.

I had three client meetings that took up the remainder of my afternoon. When I finished with the last client, I returned a few phone calls. It was after 5:00 p.m. when I called The Little Shop on the Bay.

"Little Shop on the Bay, Leila speaking."

"Hi Leila, it's Jess Hanson, I'm returning your call," I said politely.

"Oh Miss Hanson, are you ok?" she asked concerned.

"Yes, I am. Why?"

"I had a visitor about you the other day. He was not very nice. I thought you may be in some trouble."
She seemed genuinely concerned for me.

"I am fine Leila. Who was the visitor?"

"He was an older man. Probably in his sixties. He had a cane, and a terribly angry disposition. He was asking if you had come in for anything recently. I told him you asked about the books. I did not mention the wooden box to him."
Leila was frightened by this man; I could tell by her voice.

"Well, I do not know who it could be, and I am just fine. But I appreciate you checking on me." I thanked her for being so kind then gave her my cell phone number in case the man returns.

I hung up the phone and immediately called Bill's extension.

"Bill speaking," He sounded very curt when he answered.

177

"Bill it's Jess, do you have a minute? I believe we have quite a few things to discuss."

"Yes. Come on to my office."

I hung up, grabbed my coat, purse, and computer case. I did not plan to come back to my office, so I closed up as I headed to talk to Bill.

Patty had turned off the lights outside Bill's office so only a little light was shining under his closed door. I knocked softly on the door waiting to hear him say I could come in. I walked in slowly; he was sitting at his desk with his glasses on reading paperwork very intently.

"Well, that was interesting this afternoon. What do you think that was all about?" I asked.

"Money," he said blankly.

"I got the same vibe," I concurred, "I was thinking as I walked back to my desk that all of us were in the news listed as heirs to mother and father's estate. If some girl saw James out on the town drinking she could very easily make up some story to try and sue him for mother's millions."

"That is exactly what this is," Bill said as he handed me her statement.

"How did you get this?" I asked after I scanned the paper.

"I called a friend higher up in the department and they sent it over," he offered.

"It says here that the two men raped her in the park by the water. Isn't that near Georgetown Park Shopping?" I was such a girl sometimes, knowing all the good shopping areas.

"Yes, with cameras everywhere. I pulled a few strings, had a client pull the tapes from the area. There are no signs of anyone being raped anywhere near there. And her rape kit from the ER is inconclusive. No bodily fluids or signs of trauma," Bill explained.

"James came to the house Sunday morning reeking of alcohol. I know he had been out drinking all night, and he claimed he woke up alone in his car in Georgetown. I didn't ask anything further because he's done that before."

"Well, I do not think this will go anywhere, and I think she will be found to be lying or a fraud somehow." Bill was very frank about the entire thing.

"We have another issue, well two actually," I said timidly.

"What's that?" he said looking over his glasses at me.

"Leila called me and left a message last week. I called her back this afternoon. Seems some older man came to her shop inquiring about me and whether or not I had come to the store for anything recently. She said he was in his sixties, had a cane, and a bad disposition. She thought I may be in some trouble," I carefully explained.

"Hmmm. I'll look into it for you," he offered no further explanation, "what's the second issue?"

"I received another email from myself. This time it had a photo of Donovan and I having lunch together across the street at the little café. It was taken from street level on this side of Charles Street."

"Forward that to me and I will look into that as well," again, he offered no explanation.

"Should I be worried?" I asked frustrated by his lack of response.

"I don't think so. I will investigate each of these for you. The old man sounds familiar, but I don't want to say until I know for sure. As for the photo, I'll have the IT department look into it. Have you told Donovan about the photo?"

"No not yet. I forgot about it until Leila told me about the old man asking about me."

"Ok well, let's keep it between us for now. We can let him know if something comes of it."

Bill was very direct about it all, while not exactly what I was expecting, it was somewhat reassuring.

I left Bill's office shortly after that and headed toward the bank of elevators. I hit the up button instead of the down then rode to the twenty-third floor. When the doors opened, I was standing in front of a wall of frosted glass windows and the clear glass door to Donovan's architectural firm. The door was closed, the lights were off, and no one seemed to be in the office. I stared at the lettering on the door to the architectural firm for a moment. I started to head back to the elevator deciding to ask Bill to give me a ride to my house when Donovan suddenly appeared in the window. I smiled at him, but he didn't smile back.

"We need to talk," he said ominously as he opened the door.

CHAPTER 20

My heart was in my throat, I had no idea what had upset him. "Did I do something to upset you? I'm sorry about lunch," I offered as an apology in case that was it.

"No, it's not you. We may have an issue though," he sounded unhappy about whatever it was.

"What kind of issue?" I was so nervous I started shaking.

"Someone is stalking us," he said grimly.

That's it. Whew. I already knew this.

He looked surprised by my reaction.

"How so?" I asked, much calmer than I had just been.

"I received this in email today."

He handed me a picture of he and I at the café. The same picture I had received in my email. *Ok we were going to have to talk to Bill now.*

"I received the same one in my email last week. Bill is having our IT department investigate it." I explained, feeling much calmer now.

"You didn't tell me you received it."

He sounded a little hurt that I went to Bill and not him. I felt like I read that in his thoughts.

"I didn't want to alarm you," I was truthful, and I had honestly forgotten.

"I think that is something worth alarming me over," he said with an almost commanding tone.

"I'm sorry Donovan. I had forgotten about it until today

when I got back to work. I really did not put much stock into the picture. It's innocent."

"It may be innocent on our part, but it is not innocent on the part of the person who took it and anonymously sent it to us. It comes across as threatening in that someone has access to us, and both our email addresses. I don't know about your firm, but our email addresses are private, only the main email address is advertised."
Donovan sounded overly concerned by this.

I pulled out my cell phone, called Bill in his office, and explained what was going on. Bill got on the phone with Donovan, they had a brief conversation about how to proceed from here. They both were going to have their IT guys investigate the emails and try to trace the origin. I had been getting emails to myself all week so this one did not alarm me. I did not see a sinister message in it, nor did I feel threatened by any of the emails. I felt like someone was communicating with me I just did not know what the message really was yet. Donovan finally hugged me tightly to him after he got off the phone with Bill. He kept kissing my head right on my hair line.

"I'm sorry if I was abrupt with you," he apologized.

"It's ok. I appreciate your concern and protection over me," I smiled at him as I spoke.

"I can't help it. I don't want to lose you and I would cease to exist if something happened to you," his blue eyes were watery as if he was fighting tears. I wrapped my arms tightly around his chest and nuzzled into his neck. I lifted my face and kissed his chin lightly. I was in love with Donovan.

Donovan wrapped his arm around me as he walked me to his car in the parking garage on the bottom floor of the building. There were only ten spaces that were apparently reserved for very few people. I had never realized there was a parking garage under our building. He had driven his Mercedes to work, I instantly looked forward to the seat warmers. The air in the garage was extremely cold, so much so that we could see our breath. Donovan looked as though he was on post in the military, looking out for any combatant that may try to ambush us. I did not feel any presence in the garage human or otherwise.

That was until he opened the door to the passenger side of his car, a sudden burst of icy air rushed by us practically knocking us down. Donovan hovered over me then shoved me into the car as fast as he could. He stood by the door shouting something that was in a language I did not understand. It almost sounded Arabic or Hebrew. I was stunned by the unfriendly spirit that came at us. I had not felt it's presence until it was literally upon us. I had no idea how I was going to explain this to Donovan. I was hoping he would just see this as a ghost or something that most humans would believe existed in this world anyway.

It was only a matter of minutes before Donovan was in the car with me. He looked angry and seemed like he was shaking a bit.

"What was that?" I asked in mock disbelief.

"I... I am not sure exactly," Donovan said as he scrolled through his cell phone. He sent a message to someone then put his phone in his pocket.

"You, ok?" He asked me with true concern.

"Yes, I am fine. I'm a little worried about you though." I observed his reactions very carefully.

"I'm fine Jess. I have seen worse in my lifetime. War is much more intense than some gush of air."

He was minimizing the spirit that practically assaulted us. I was picking up vibrations from Donovan I had not experienced before. It had a mysterious feel to it almost like he was shutting me out. I intuitively had the feeling that Donovan was pulling away from me. He had been upset with me over the photo and now this. He seemed to be slipping away from me, and I needed to either let him go or find a way to explain something to him. I started getting a sinking feeling that even if I explained these spirits, it would most likely push him away from me altogether.

Donovan did not speak for most of the drive. He was very introspective, and I could not read his thoughts, but I could tell he was thinking through something that weighed heavily on him. I sat quietly in the passenger seat enjoying the warmth of the seat warmer. I had never had a vehicle that had such a feature, I decided my next car would have it as it was really a nice feature to have. I was thinking about whether I would get seat warmers in my next car when Donovan's cell phone rang. The car answered the call just as it had on our date. A male voice asked if he was alone, Donovan said it was not a good time and he would call him back later then promptly ended the call.

"Sorry about that," he said quietly.

"It's ok. I don't mind," I tried to place the voice. I had heard it before. I thought it may be the same voice the night of our date that asked him about a package. I was not one hundred percent sure, but I was pretty convinced.

"I'm going to have to take a rain check on dinner tonight," Donovan said interrupting my thoughts. I was surprised but smiled and nodded my head acknowledging what he had said.

Something was up with him, I was sure now, because he was acting strange which made me feel completely out of place. He turned into my driveway across from his home. I needed to get my own car and he knew that. It was sweet that he had remembered, or it was just convenient so that he could just drop me then go home. I preferred to think it was sweet. He was still being a gentleman and opened the door for me to get out of his car.

"You are going straight home, right?" He was almost commanding instead of asking.

"I am home," I said defiantly.

"I mean to your mother's," he said trying to change his tone.

"I may stay here for a bit. I have a few more things I thought of that I want to pack up and bring to the estate." I really did not have anything in particular, but I was not going to just get in my car and drive off just yet.

"Jess, I think you should go to your mother's sooner rather than later."

"What is going on Donovan?" I was not going to just cower to whatever was happening. I had faced frosty beings, spirits, my mother and father, Brian, a soldier, Christian, and two angels in a matter of a week. This seemed miniscule in comparison.

"I wish I knew exactly," he looked down at the ground. He grabbed me suddenly pulling me to his body holding me tightly. So tightly, in fact, I was having a hard time taking a full breath. I could feel fear vibrating through him. He was fighting an internal war that I was just a small part of. *I cannot lose her, not now.* I heard his thought clearly.

"You won't lose me," I said aloud to reassure him.
He held me away from his body looking deeply into my eyes like he was searching for something within me.

"I love you, Donovan," I said hoping it would reassure him that I was not going to leave him.

He kissed me hard and passionately on my lips. I closed my eyes kissing him back. It was so full of love and desire that it almost felt as if we were floating toward the sky. Yet when I opened my eyes, we were firmly planted on the ground in my driveway. It was that good of a kiss that I would have believed we were floating.

"I need you to go to your mother's Jess," he said sounding overprotective.

"Not until you tell me what is happening," I knew I was being petulant.

"You are a stubborn woman," he said with a laugh.

"You have no idea," I winked as I said it.

"Will you please just trust me? I will explain what I can when I can."

"That is not an answer. In fact, I would say that was a lawyer tactic if I have ever seen one. And as a lawyer it doesn't really work on me."

"Jess. Please. Trust me," he pleaded. He put his head on my forehead, his eyes were wide, and I could tell he really did not want to go any further in detail with me. I knew he truly had my best interest at heart.

"Fine. After I get what I need to from my house."

"I will stay here in the driveway until you come back out," he said resolutely.

I walked into the dark house then stood in my kitchen for a moment. I was trying to decide what I was going to take out with me as the "must have" item I needed. I went to my bedroom deciding to get the wooden box. I do not know why it pulled at me just then. As I came around the corner my mother's spirit was standing there, she looked unhappy.

"Mother. What's wrong?" I could feel something was wrong.

"You are in danger here," she warned.

Before I could answer I felt like I had been struck over the head. I fell to my knees grabbing my head as darkness closed in leaving only a pinpoint of light. My head was throbbing, and I could tell I was losing consciousness. I tried to reach out to my mother's spirit, but she had vanished. I felt an evil in the room like none I had ever experienced. *Love and light, Love and light, Love and light.* I was repeating in a rhythmic tone as I closed my eyes.

"Go into the light." I heard an evil hiss whisper in both my ears simultaneously.

My head felt heavy and thick as if I were in a fog. I tried to open my eyes, but I could not. I could hear a soft voice so faint that I had to strain to hear what it was saying.

"You are safe here Jessica," the soft male voice said several times before I comprehended what was being said.

I opened my eyes, finding that I was in the bright white light again, which meant I was in Seraphim again.

"You are not in Seraphim this time," the male voice said. I tried to turn my head finding it was restrictive to do so.

"You are in Beriya," the voice continued.

"How did I get here?" I asked the voice.

"Your guardian brought you here."

I noticed this was not just an empty space like Seraphim was. I was surrounded by what looked like thousands of crystals. Crystals filled the walls, the ceiling, floor, and the tables. All around the room were protruding crystals that were in glass bowls of every color, almost like the crystals were being cultivated in the bowls. I was lying on a bed that was like that of a hospital bed, except smaller and more archaic. I felt warm and safe. I tried to sit up but found I was unable.

"You are in a suspended state that keeps you from further injury," the voice explained.

A very tall male angelic figure appeared before me. He was surrounded in emerald green light. Unlike others I had met, He had angel wings made of emerald rays running the entire length of his body. He carried a large staff, similar to the medical staff symbol on earth. It was golden in color with green wings at the top made entirely of crystals. There were two intertwining blue rays of light that wrapped around the staff like snakes. He was extraordinarily handsome with a chiseled jawline and a muscular herculean body. His hair was deep brown and fell to the middle of his back. He had dark eyes that you could see your own reflection in like black mirrors. He was cloaked in an emerald green gown, the same style of clothing that Jesus is depicted to have worn, except it was a beautiful green. There were gold cords wrapped around his waist like a belt, they looked as though they were literally made of spun gold.

"Who are you?" I asked in awe of this angel before me.

"I am the Archangel Raphael."

"Wow," I had nothing more intelligent to say than wow.

"You were brought to me by your protector and the angel Illuma for healing," he explained.

"Am I dead?" I figured that was the only reason I would be in Beriya with the Archangel Raphael.

"No. You are in a suspended state of existence while you heal," he answered.

"How long will I be here?" I wanted to move but I was completely immobile.

"As long as needed," he said reassuringly.

"I want to go back. I want to see Donovan and Bill. I need to protect Jax." I was explaining all this to the Archangel as if he did not already know this.

"You are almost ready to go back," he stated as he began waving his staff over me.

"Thank you."

I could feel his healing powers begin to flow through my body. The emerald rays infused my body in a way that felt as though I was filled with healing rays of light while simultaneously being lifted off the bed. I began to rise, I was levitating over the archaic bed I had been laying on.

"You are healed," his voice boomed so forcefully that I had to close my eyes.

CHAPTER 21

I could hear Jax and James talking in the room. I could tell I was no longer in Beriya. I tried to move and once again found that I could not. I tried in vain to open my eyes, but I was having an extremely hard time. I attempted to move my arms and hands but could only manage to wiggle my fingers. I hoped someone would notice my movement. I felt that I was not at home, I was unsure of my surroundings, so I tried to use my senses to figure out where I was. It felt very unfamiliar and sterile. *I must be in a hospital.*

"She's waking up," Jax cried out.

"I can hear you thinking," she whispered in my ear.

I can't open my eyes or move.

"You were in a coma," she whispered again.

A Coma!!!! HOW!!!!

"I'll explain later," she whispered so quietly. I figured others were in the room and she was trying to hide that we were communicating.

I want to wake up.

"Can you please get the doctor?" Jax said to someone in the room. There was a flurry of activity then I felt Bill's presence in the room as well as Donovan's.

Oh, please I want to wake up. I want to see Donovan. I should have listened to him and gone home. I need to apologize.

I could feel a tear escape from my eye then run down into my hair.

"It's ok Jess," Bill said to me as he touched the wet streak on my face.

A doctor came in, he was talking to Bill and Jax about decreasing the medication I was on. He spoke to me, but I could not respond except to move my eyes under my eyelids. He opened my eyelid with his finger, shining a light into my eye. It was so bright. He did the same thing with my other eye. He rustled through some papers then told Bill that I had increased brain activity so he did not see any reason they could not bring me out of the coma. He explained to them it may be an hour or more before I was fully awake.

I don't want to wait an hour! I want to wake up.

Jax grabbed my hand and squeezed it tightly. She knew I was upset. I was so glad to have her there to hear my thoughts and know I was trying to communicate.

I love Donovan, Jax. I love him. Please tell him.

She squeezed my hand again then let go. Donovan grabbed my hand and kissed it. I felt complete peace having him touching me. I relaxed and drifted off into sleep holding his hand.

My head was heavy, my neck hurt, and I was trying to move again. I still felt constricted as I tried opening my eyes. It was so bright in the room that I blinked a few times. Donovan was standing at my side speaking softly to me. I could not understand what he was saying. I tried blinking again.

"Jess, the doctor is coming," he said again, this time I understood him.

I nodded my head. I had a tube in my throat, and it felt extremely uncomfortable. I tried to pull at it. Jax and Donovan each grabbed my hands recommending that I stay still, again telling me that the doctor was on his way. The tube was gagging me, and I wanted it out.

Just then a nurse came into the room, she was petite and noticeably young looking. She had deep mocha colored skin with amber eyes and beautiful soft facial features. She was explaining to me that they were going to have to take the tube out of my throat and that I should not try to talk right away. I nodded my head in understanding. The doctor and another older nurse came in, all three starting removing plugs on machines and pulling on cords attached to me. They asked me to take a deep breath through my nose, as I did, they pulled the tube from my throat. It gagged me as it pulled out and I instantly felt nauseous.

"Don't speak," Donovan said when I saw him beside me. I began to cry; the tears fell down the sides of my face into my hair. I could not stop them from falling.

"Shhhhh. It's ok. I'm here," he assured me.

I wanted to sit up; I kept trying but everyone was telling me to just stay where I was. Donovan sat on the side of the bed holding my hand. He was thinking how pitiful I looked and that this was entirely his fault. I shook my head no. He tilted his head to the side watching as I shook my head. I reached my hands up toward him, so he could lift me up. He carefully helped me to a seated position, then I wrapped my arms around him as tightly as I could. I did not ever want to let go of him. He was so tender with me. I could hear in his thoughts that he did not want to hurt me.

You aren't hurting me. I wish you could hear my thoughts so you would know I was ok. He pulled away from me ever so slightly then kissed my forehead like he always did. Jax returned to the room and saw I was sitting up on the bed.

"Jess! I am so glad to see you awake!"

She rushed to the bed throwing her arms around me, much harder than Donovan had, but it was ok I was glad to hug my sister too.

"Are you ok? Do you need anything? Can I get you something? Are you comfortable?" she was rattling off questions non-stop.

I tried to laugh but I couldn't. I pointed to the water pitcher and the cup. She poured me a cup of water and I sipped it very gingerly. I looked around the room at my surroundings. There were several bouquets of flowers, a few balloons, and a teddy bear. I felt warmth and love by the gifts there. Donovan looked like he had not slept in a few days.

How long has he been here? I was thinking for Jax.

She smiled a fake smile then shook her head no. I knew it was her way of saying she could not answer me.

I would like to know what happened to me.

You were attacked. Bill was here now and answered with his thoughts. I looked at the doorway where he stood with flowers and balloons. I was surprised he let me hear his thoughts.

Who attacked me? I asked again with my thoughts.

"We are not sure," this time it was Donovan who answered.

WAIT! Donovan you can read my thoughts?

"Yes, Jessica. I can. I have been able to read your thoughts all along," Donovan answered me.

"You know what I am thinking?" I squeaked out with a scratchy voice.

"Bill and Jax, why don't you let Jess and I have a moment to speak," Donovan suggested as Bill nodded in agreement.

Bill took Jax by the hand recommending that she go with him down the hall for a bit.

"I don't understand," I said hoarsely again.

"Don't speak. You can think and I can answer you. You need to do as the doctors have said," Donovan said very lovingly.

I knew something was going on when you were driving me home. Care to fill me in here?

"Bill and I are both protectors, we are both from Beriya. I was summoned to be your protector," he explained.

I suddenly had a flash of realization. Every time my soldier was around Donovan was not, and whenever Donovan was around my soldier was not. Donovan was always there in the flesh whenever my threat was a human, and my soldier was there whenever my threat was spiritual. Donovan was my soldier.

"Yes. I am your soldier. I am a highly evolved being just like you are. I was brought here to be your protector for several months. I did not count on falling in love with you. I noticed that your aura was red whenever we were together. It was distracting at first. I knew that the red aura was a sign of being destined. Then you noticed it. I read it in your thoughts."

He explained things to me that I may not have figured out on my own. It did explain why he would laugh at thoughts I had then try to cover it up with a side explanation. Like when he said, 'I had my thoughts written on my face.'

"Yes, I knew what you were thinking then, and every time you chastised yourself for checking me out," he laughed.

Not funny. I crossed my arms.

Did you know I was frustrated with not being able to explain things to you?

"Yes. I know you were visited by lesser spirits, and I knew you were dealing with the frosty beings. I could not tell you who I was."

Why can you tell me now?

"Because we are connected by love. I took you to Beriya to see Raphael when I found you. Raphael and Gabriel agreed you should know who I am," he explained. He moved closer to me and placed his hands on my face to look me directly in the eyes. "Jess, I love you. I would give my life for you. I should have protected you and I did not. I am so sorry."

He was genuinely distraught by not protecting me at my house.

Did you know what was happening?
Donovan dropped his hands from my face and held my hands.

"I did not know exactly what was going on. I knew that there was a being that was much more evolved than I am. Like an Archangel or something of similar status. I also knew it was after you. It tried to attack you when we were on our date down by the sculpture and again in the parking garage of my building."

My mother's spirit warned me in my bedroom. It was when I went to get that dang wooden box. Every time I try to go near that box something distracts me, warns me or something else happens.

"Do you know what is in the box?" he asked.

No. I haven't opened it. It was in the package you brought to me from Leila the first night we met. Well, that is the first night we met that I know of.

"It was the first night we met in person, yes. I had been watching you for a few months, but I did not show myself."
Donovan was almost embarrassed by this.

I am glad you are my protector. Will being in love with me change your status as my protector?

"No. It just strengthens our bond to one another."

"I love you, Donovan Wheeler," I said in my scratchy voice. I didn't want to merely think it.

He kissed me lightly on my lips. He was warm and I felt the love radiating through him. This was a love vibration. He was 'the one.'

CHAPTER 22

I still had so many questions, but I was very tired. I did not know what exactly had happened to me in my bedroom. I wanted to know so many more things about Donovan, and now the contents of the wooden box were bugging me. I would have to wait for answers since I needed to close my eyes for a bit. Bill and Jax had come back to the room, Donovan agreed to go home to clean up and get some rest, a hot shower and a change of clothes were in order for him. I closed my eyes as Donovan left the room then drifted off into sleep once again.

The color of Amber filled my mind as I drifted in and out of what I thought was a sleep state. But I knew this time I was traveling between realms. I was heading to another angel I just wasn't sure which one. Everything around me was amber or orange and had a fiery quality. As my vision focused on my surroundings, I was in a warm stone like cave that resembled the inside of a terra cotta pot. It also reminded me of the salt caves people went to for cleansing and healing. The amber light became brighter and brighter until an angel appeared within the light.

"Hello, my child," the man's voice was soothing, warm, and deep.

His hair was long and had a fiery look to it. The air smelled of campfire and wood, but not in the burnt sense, in a way that made you want to roast marshmallows. He laughed a deep bellowing laugh, and I knew he could hear my thoughts about making smores. I had to giggle myself. "Hi, which angel are you?" I asked now knowing all of this was leading me closer to where I needed to be.

"I am Jaselle. I am the Angel of Creation and Vitality."

"Oh! Can you help me create?" I asked with a little too much excitement. I flushed as I realized my words may have been misinterpreted.

"Don't worry, my child, I know your heart and your intent. You do not need to feel any shame in your excitement or asking questions of me. To answer you, I cannot help you create only you can create. I can only show you the path that leads you to creation."

I smiled. I took a deep breath, filling my lungs with the air in the room enjoying in the warmth. I used my senses to take in the environment rather than asking questions. The peace and warmth I felt was inexplicable. I wanted Donovan here; I desired for him to hold me in a place like this. I wished for him to feel as safe as I did here.

"You are always safe in this realm, Jessica," Jaselle said kindly.

"Where exactly am I?"

"You are in Beriya. More specifically you are in the home of Phanuel."

"I don't know much about Phanuel, he wasn't taught in the traditional religious teachings. Sadly, I am uneducated about him," I said.

Jaselle laughed, fire dancing in his deep amber eyes. "Obviously! Phanuel is a woman. She is the Archangel of Hope, Eternal Life, and Relationships. She is essentially all things related to Hope." I was embarrassed by the assumption that all Archangels were male in form. But it made sense that Phanuel would be a divine feminine angel.

"Can **she** help me create?" I asked after a moment of thought.

"Again, She can only show you the path just as I can. You came here on your own. You are beginning to remember. Your powers are brewing and growing infinitely every moment. Time as you know it is just a tool for measurement. It isn't real. You have the ability to create and stop time as you see fit. Just as you have now to be here. You are seeking answers and finding them all on your own now."

I thought for a moment, then felt a stirring within me of excitement and pleasure. Not a sexual pleasure but a loving pleasure, a peace and harmony, like I belonged right where I was. For the first time everything was making complete sense to me. Every step I had taken in my existence had led me to this moment. Everything was working for the greater good. I finally understood that I needed to let go of my own human side and emotional attachments, especially negative ones, to truly thrive and become what I was destined from creation to be. Jaselle laughed out loud again, I looked at his handsome face in complete understanding of why he was laughing. He wasn't laughing at me; he was laughing with me. We understood all in this moment. We laughed at my naivety in human form and my realization I am One with God, and God is One with ME! The moment was electrifying!

"We are all one **with** God," I said aloud.

As I said the words Phanuel appeared in the room. She was stunningly beautiful. My entire life I believed my mother was the most beautiful woman I had ever seen, but Phanuel made my mother look homely. She was electrifying, and her beauty was almost indescribable. Her auburn hair was flowing all around her, her smile radiated warmth, and her golden eyes reflected love directly into your soul. She had beautiful caramel skin, and she wore a long persimmon robe – it was a red-orange color with a golden cord wrapped around her waist that was just like the one that Raphael wore. She exuded love and light. I fell to my knees in complete adoration her.

"Please stand my sweet child. Please, you are not beneath me, nor am I above you."
She held her hand out to me to help me to my feet. I wanted to cry I felt so much love and compassion in her presence. I took her hand, the softness in her touch was beyond anything I had ever felt. She encompassed all things love and motherly that any being could possess.

"I am in absolute awe of you Phanuel," I said without thinking.

"As am I of you. You are the future, my dear. You are the reason we will continue to exist for all beings," her voice was smooth like honey.

"How do I create the future?"

"You fill everything and everyone with love. Good and evil alike." she was saying what I already knew, but I felt like I was understanding it for the first time.
My thoughts again drifted to Donovan. Her golden eyes danced with fire as I looked up to her.

"He is your twin my love. He is your soul. But you already know this," she said.

"But are we unequally yoked?" I asked with trepidation.

"No, my sweet child. He is just as you are. He knows you are his twin. He has known long before you have. He sought you. Long before you began to remember who you are." *Wow.*

"Thank you Phanuel. Thank you." I was teary eyed as she parted from the room, I wanted to just feel her presence there forever. Jaselle laughed his hearty laugh again, and I couldn't help but laugh with him. I closed my eyes and opened them as I woke up in the hospital room. I was remembering all on my own.

CHAPTER 23

A s I awoke, I found myself to be all alone in my hospital room, which was strange as I was sure there was a presence there. I sat up instinctively, scanning the room for whatever it was that was there. Hospitals are always cold and repressive to me, so to feel coolness was not unusual. But I knew in this moment the coolness was another entity. Alive or otherwise.

"I know you are here. Just come out and let me see you," I said into the empty room.

Nothing appeared. No frosty beings. No spirit. Nothing. It was a cold and empty feeling. I closed my eyes and tried to fill the entire room with warmth, my own true love and absolute light. I felt as though I was rising off the bed as I concentrated on the room, still filling it with my love and light.

"What are you doing here?" I heard a voice I recognized. Christian.

When I opened my eyes, I was no longer in my hospital room. I had somehow etheric traveled like Bill could to Christian's college dorm room. I stood in the middle of his shadowy world and couldn't help but laugh. I didn't care what the surroundings were or what they looked like; I didn't even really take notice of it. He snarled at me, "what is so damn funny and how did you get in here?"

"Christian, my brother, I have no idea why I am here, but I

need to just let you know I love you," I said sweetly, trying to channel all the love I could into this moment.

"You are nuts," he spat, "and I am not your brother."
I realized that he was not as evolved yet and that he didn't understand how we were connected or why. He only understood anger and hatred.

"Even if I explained everything to you, you wouldn't understand. I know one day you will know. I also know one day you will find your chosen path."
I didn't know if I could have explained it all to him, even if I had wanted to, I just knew I had to love him.

"For the record, you are my brother. In the spiritual sense of the word," I felt he would at least understand that.

"Look, I know that I am Jax's sibling, but that does **not** make **you** my sister. You are her sister; I refuse to acknowledge or accept that you are related to me. You and your half-retarded brother James, you disgust me. Just because my dad banged your mom doesn't make us brother and sister." He was a truly angry young man. His soul was angry. I knew right then the anger had been learned from his father. And suddenly I realized that at some point I would need to speak to Mr. Wyatt himself.

Days went by as I healed from the head wound that I received in my home. The doctors were amazed at my recovery calling it miraculous. I knew it wasn't miraculous but just was. It was how it was meant to be. Raphael's healing was no miracle, it was just a healing. If only people could understand that healing could be found within themselves. Jesus himself taught "Heal Thyself." It really is that simple. And for those who never healed, it is their souls' purpose to move on in that moment. Our human egos want to believe that the life we know is the end all and be all of existence, and that we are the highest evolved beings out there, but we truly are not. Aliens aren't aliens, they are higher and lower evolved beings. Humans are souls that chose to exist on Asiya for purposes only their souls, or higher selves, understood. But we were all of God, and we were all to return to God, we were all one. While in the hospital I had time to read the books that appeared in my emails. I found the teachings in them to be quite simple. Very biblical, yet not at all. My soul chose this time of healing to grow and evolve more. I was becoming more enlightened as some would say. I practiced my meditation techniques. I also strengthened my ability to close my thoughts off to other beings.

Donovan came and went from my room day in and day out. He stayed some nights and others he went home. At times I felt he was still a soldier on a mission. I never told him I knew we were twin flames, or that I knew he knew, I felt like it was just understood. His presence was a comfort and I craved being near him now more than ever. I felt a love I could only describe as a cross between Eros love and Agape love. Bill visited me every day. He sometimes talked about work since he was handling my cases personally. He filled me in on the progress of the cases I already had, and on some smaller menial tasks he assigned to the newer attorneys. These allowed them the ability to hone their skills as lawyers, like scheduling conferences, depositions, pre-trial meetings. The easy tasks.

Jax was in and out of my room most days several times. She had decided to call the waiter from the restaurant, they had been out on several dates. Turns out he knew Brian and followed Brian's gaming team. It was like Brian himself had arranged their meeting. Jax seemed to be moving toward the love and light path increasingly every day. We had deep meaningful conversations about the books and our own personal journeys. She had managed to forgive momma and grandmother for her treatment in the past. I felt as though I was winning the good vs. evil war. The only thing that puzzled me was James' conspicuous absence. I had seen him once since waking up from the coma. I didn't really pay much attention to it since he was always doing his own thing.

I was finally being released from the hospital, with Donovan, Jax, and Bill all there to help get me home. They fussed over me like I was a delicate butterfly whose wings would crumble if they touched me. I laughed at them. A lot.

"Why are you laughing?" Donovan said with a worried expression on his face as he helped me into his Mercedes.

"Because all of you act like I am going to vanish in thin air if you do the wrong thing."

"We love you and are just trying to make sure you don't hurt yourself," he said with a love so deep in his eyes I couldn't help but smile back at him.

"Baby, I am so appreciative of your protection of me. But I'm not that delicate I assure you," I said reassuring my soldier.

Jax and Bill were going to ride in Bill's escalade to Momma's house. Donovan was supposed to drive me to Momma's as well. Ms. Ebby had been so worried about me, and she was making an enormous meal for my return home. It occurred to me that I was referring to my mother as "Momma" again. The love healed the hurt.

"Donovan?" I said quietly as he drove.

"Yes, love?"

"Drive me to my house please," I stated determined.

"Nope. No way. Hell no. Forgive me for saying that, but No!" he absolutely refused.

"Baby. Look, you can drive me to my house, walk in with me and protect me. Or you can take me to momma's, and I will just travel there by myself. I have learned how to etheric travel myself."

I was being obstinate, and I knew it.

Donovan glared at me with irritation but also with love, ultimately, he knew I was stubborn enough and would do just as I said. He sighed in resignation that he was going to have to protect me. I knew I needed to open the wooden box, and I had best do it with Donovan there.

CHAPTER 24

Donovan had already called Bill, with the hands-free telephone system in the car, and explained to him my "threat." I laughed at his terminology. Bill was very flat in his response, I was not sure if that was out of fear, anger, or resignation that he knew this was part of my path. Bill told Donovan to call him immediately if anything happened at all. I was excited and nervous, yet I had a deep calm and understanding that whatever it was, it was meant to be. Donovan was not thrilled, but he too understood that this was all a part of the path we BOTH had to walk. He knew that as twins we were destined to walk this together.

As we pulled into my driveway, the house looked dark. Eerily dark. It was the last place I had been before I was attacked. I knew now that whoever attacked me was not a spirit, but a human, or at least in human form at the time of attack. I also now knew that as highly evolved beings we could etheric travel, we could travel between realms, and we could be in human or spirit form whenever we chose. I didn't "remember" how to change my form from human to spirit yet. Donovan instructed me he was going to "clear the house" before allowing me to enter it. I smiled then half-giggled at his military instinct and his protectiveness. I simply nodded in acknowledgment then waited for him to give me the "all clear" as he put it.

I turned the radio on as Suite Bergamasque, for piano, L. 75 by Claude Debussy started playing. It was a comforting yet eerie song because it felt like it was played for angels before going into battle. I mused over why angels would need to go into battle, and why did religion teach that it was warlike between good and evil. Why couldn't it just be taught as an existence, not a battle. Not war like at all, merely, walking a path as I have come to know. Or why couldn't it be taught as choosing good or evil. Why must it be war?

Donovan appeared by the car then opened my door. He didn't smile. He wasn't happy, he wasn't angry or sad, he was protective. He seemed to be taller and stronger than ever before. He appeared more like the higher being he truly was in that moment. "Six feet tall and bullet proof" was not an accurate enough description, he seemed more than that in this moment. I felt an extreme attraction to him, so much so I smiled seductively at him. He stared directly into my eyes.

"Not now little girl, not now," he said with slight amusement. He was so damn sexy to me.

"I can't help it, my love. You are a God to me. Zeus has nothing on you right now," I said with a wink.

"Come on," he said with a laugh, as he took my hand and led me toward the house.

My home didn't feel warm or inviting to me, it didn't feel like my home. I felt like the place was crawling with spiders and snakes, of course it wasn't. It felt like a cold empty space, like someone had opened all the windows and allowed the temperature to drop in the home to below freezing. *Shit. The beings were here.* Donovan's grip on my hand was so tight it almost hurt. My mother and father were standing in my living room looking solemn yet supportive. I nodded at them in acknowledgment as I turned into my bedroom. A swirling vortex, like a wormhole, was visible in my room. I walked toward it feeling confident, knowing it could not harm me. Donovan stopped just short of the vortex then looked directly in my eyes.

"I can't go in there," he acknowledged he couldn't protect me.

"I know," I said.

"You can travel right out if you need to. You come right back here to this moment, you got that!" It was more demanding than suggesting.

"Yes, my love. I promise."

Donovan pulled me forcefully to him, his lips mere millimeters from mine, my eyes watching as the blue in his eyes flowed like waves. The ache to feel his kiss took over all my senses. He kissed me deeply. It was the kiss of all kisses. He claimed me, marked me, and made me his all in that moment. I needed to catch my breath after that kiss. I smiled at him then stepped forward into the vortex. Inside the vortex it felt cold and smelled like a mildewy damp basement. I didn't feel love or warmth, instead I felt cold and clammy. I didn't want to walk this part of my path, but I knew it was necessary. As I crossed into the other side of the vortex, I found myself surrounded by dark black cold stones that were shiny like onyx. A dark blue light appeared in the darkness; it resembled the night sky without moonlight. It was surprisingly a beautiful light. Although, it didn't convey beauty or positivity, it was breathtaking on its own.

I waited for what felt like an eternity when a being appeared. It was not a grotesque being like my mind imagined. He was tall like the Archangels with sharp chiseled facial features and small tight lips. His hair was jet black just like the onyx in the space, and his eyes were silver, truly silver. He wore dark clothing tailored perfectly for his body. It was not a tunic, nor did it resemble a tunic, it was more like a suit. But just like Raphael, and Phanuel, he wore a cord around his waist, except his was not gold, it was silver, it resembled spun silver – a cord of silver. I realized in that moment I was standing before Lucifer. The original fallen Angel. I was in Kelipa.

"Very astute observations skills," Lucifer said in a strong baritone voice. His voice was soothing, not evil like I had imagined.

"Why am I here?" I asked him.

"To know the other side. To know why some angels choose to fall, and others choose to stay," he said to the point.

"Why do religions teach that you are so evil and vile?" I asked.

"To maintain control. The ultimate form of evil there is."

"Are you saying religion is evil?" I asked astounded.

"Absolutely not!" he said with a laugh, "I am saying religion is fallible as it is run by humans. Humans follow human instincts. Power and control are a basic human instinct." *Interesting.*

"What is so interesting about that?" he asked, almost as inquisitive about me as I was about him.

"It just is. I have often said similar things before I 'remembered' the things I now know."

I made the quotation marks with my fingers as I spoke.

"Well, have you 'remembered' how to create yet?" he retorted with the same finger quotation gesture.

"No," I said flatly, "truthfully, I am starting to think I am just not ready to."

"You will. Sooner rather than later."

"What are the frosty beings? Did you send them?" I asked.

"Yes and no. I didn't send them per say, as they are their own entity. They can come and go, move at will. They are just that. That which is."

"That which is?" I was really confused now.

"They aren't really anything. You have personified them as if they are some sort of being or human. Truthfully, it is more of an It, than a They," he explained, "you refer to it as 'frosty beings,' with that personification of being soul like, but it is actually soul less."

"So, IT is nothing?" I asked.

"Exactly. Nothing. And Everything," he enunciated as he twirled a coin in his fingers.

I was momentarily mesmerized by the coin he twirled through his long fingers. It rolled through his fingers with a smooth grace like motion. Like he had done this for eternity. I continued to watch the coin almost in a trance. My mind and vision so focused on the coin that I forgot about the topic of conversation. The coin caught a flash of light blinding me for a second. Instantaneously I was back in my bathroom with the frosty "it" now. Lucifer was nowhere to be found; I became fully aware that he purposefully ended our time together.

The absolute frostiness of the air was bone chilling. It felt the same as every encounter before and I could see my breath as I spoke. It still unnerved me, as fear welled within my chest that I had a hard time tamping down. The familiar hiss of the frosty voices spoke.

"Welcome back," It said.

"I am not sure it truly is welcome," I said shakily.

"You have the key," It repeated as if our conversation from my bedroom at my momma's estate had merely paused.

"I know, or rather, so I have been told."

"Who have you chosen?" It said.

"I haven't chosen anyone," I said firmly, "I am not going to choose. If I am the future creator, and I have such powers to create, then I don't have to. I can choose not to choose!"

A rush of icy frigid air forced me across the room pinning me to the wall. The feeling of pin pricks all over my body was painful. I felt helpless in that moment. I was shivering, like I was out in the ice tundra naked and freezing to death. Death.

It felt like death. That was it. Death. My eyes opened wide in comprehension. It is nothing and everything. It is Death. My momma's death replayed before my eyes. She encountered the frosty beings here in this very spot.

I could see she was taking a bath, just as I had been the first time the frosty "it" showed itself to me. She did not want death; she wanted her pain to end. She wanted my father. She wanted a normal life for her children. The only way was to succumb to death. Hence why she said she didn't mess up and I would see what was coming. She could never come around when it was there because it was death. It had already taken her. I was life. It was death. The antithesis to my existence. I created; it took away. The Alpha and Omega. The Beginning and the End. It could not hurt me or end me, it had no power over me, it just was.

The frosty it instantly released me from its grip, and warmth surrounded me like I was glowing in light. I **was** glowing in light. I felt god like. A thought occurred to me, death needed to take in order for me to give life. I instantly felt saddened by this realization. I didn't want to create life and death all at the same time. I didn't want to be like God herself. I didn't want that type of burden on my consciousness. I just didn't. I just wanted love and light.

"Death is not negative," It whispered ominously, "it just is. Let go of your human ego and understand it just is. We just are."

I took a deep steadying breath, thinking of all I had been through in the last few weeks since my momma's death. I recounted all the entities, all the spirits, the people who entered my life, those who had left. With each new person who entered my life, one also left it seemed. All the things I was "remembering" and all I didn't know but I wanted to remember. I thought of Jax and her struggle to stay on a love and light path. I thought of her creator/father. Her need to come into her own powers, but I knew she had to do it on her own. The only influence I had was to love her and infuse her with such love. I thought of Christian and his disdain for all of us – except Jax – because he saw her as an equal. I thought of Bill and all the knowledge he had with his ability to control the outcome of human relations, especially in court, because he knew truth from lies immediately.

I thought of Donovan and our destiny. I was filled with light and complete love as thoughts of a future with him flooded my mind. I knew he was my one. He was my love. My agape. My eros. He was truly a co-creator. He would help me create life. In every way. Then I thought of my earthly parents. My mother and my father, they were part of my Asiyan existence and the support system all beings need on this plane. My thoughts drifted to James. My Asiyan brother, brother only by birth on earth, not soul related nor having any powers. A simple being whose life and death would be just that - simple. In that very millisecond the frosty beings burst into laughter and disappeared.

"JAMES!" I screamed out.

CHAPTER 25

Donovan came running into the bathroom after I screamed. I kept screaming in shocked horror. I had in that moment chosen James and I didn't even realize it. In my mind I was simply going through all my emotions toward each being in my life. Each entity. I chose James as expendable based on his inabilities to be a higher being. That isn't what I wanted. That wasn't my intent. I crumpled to the floor in pure grief. My human ego still fully operational, as Donovan scooped me up off the floor and carried me to the living room. My parents, Bill, Donovan, Jax all present. I sobbed with a grief so deep I was inconsolable, and they all knew it. I sobbed in Donovan's arms anguished over what I had done. I didn't mean to. I wasn't trying to. I had been forced into it. I was cornered quite literally and coerced into it. I felt devastated.

As tears spilled down my cheeks, I remembered the box. I was now angrier than ever. I felt pure anger mixed with grief. I pushed away from Donovan running into my room. Donovan chased me knowing what I was after. It wasn't there. The box wasn't there. I tore the room apart looking for the box. It was missing. I looked at Donovan standing before me with a look of defeat on his face. I felt defeated too. I was defeated. I would never know what was in that box. It was gone.

Bill appeared in the doorway of my bedroom clearing his throat to get my attention. "What!" I practically yelled at him.

"James called. He needs a lawyer, he's been arrested," he said with concern.

"SHIT!" I had to save him. I just didn't know how.

Donovan drove us in total silence to the police station, while Bill worked to bail James out. As we walked toward the police station Christian strode out. He smirked at us with such evil intent that I knew he was the reason James had been arrested. *I hate him.*

"You can't think that Jess," Donovan said lovingly.

"I'm not fully evolved YET! I can think what I want."
I was angry and rebelling more now than ever. The desire to rebel was rising within me like my own good vs evil war waging internally.

I walked into the police station, the negative energy that filled the place was staggering. It had a stench like no other. A mixture of vomit, pee, and body odor so overwhelming that I wanted to run in the opposite direction. I told the desk sergeant who I was there for. Detective Talbot came out from the locked double doors to the waiting area then walked directly to me. He held his hand out to shake Donovan's hand and introduce himself to him first. Donovan politely shook his hand then steered Det. Talbot toward me. I was angry, I knew this was all wrong. I knew this was not a truth finding mission. This was about money, I read it from Det. Talbot's mind. He knew it too, but his hands were tied. He had to follow the leads and the leads were that James had raped this young woman.

"Detective," I said coolly as I shook his hand.

"Miss Hansen," he returned the greeting.

"Why did you arrest my brother?" I was seething with anger.

"Miss Hansen, you know I cannot divulge anything to you."

He thought about the taped interview with Christian and I knew Bill would need to get a hold of it.

"I understand. What are the charges?" I decided to cool the anger and be a lawyer in this moment. If I was going to save my brother, it was going to be by representing him the best way I knew how. As a lawyer.

"He's charged with felony rape and drug charges," he said matter-of-factly.

"Drug charges! What drug charges!" I exclaimed, feeling a rise of anger again. Donovan squeezed my hand that I hadn't realized he was still holding.

"The victim was drugged with Rohypnol. And we have evidence that states your brother drugged the victim, then raped her."

"What evidence?"

"You know I can't share that with you."
He thought about how weak the case was with physical evidence but that he had eyewitness testimony – Christian.

"Thank you, Detective," I said as I turned on my heels to leave.

CHAPTER 26

Donovan didn't speak in the car as we drove to Momma's estate. I was lost in my thoughts about James and how to save him. I worked through every legal angle I could think of. This was a disaster. We all knew this girl wanted money, even the detective believed so, but he was bound by his rules and regulations. Cops all knew their job was just to investigate and charge, the courts would weed the truth out. They truly didn't care one way or another what the outcome was. To them everyone was guilty.

As we pulled into the driveway Bill, Jax, and James were stepping out of Bill's Escalade. I ran to James to hug him. He looked at me with such contempt, holding an arm out to me as if to push me away, and keep me from hugging him. "Not now," he spat as he turned walking away from me. Jax hurried over to me and wrapped her arms around me. She knew. *I'm sorry Jess.* I could hear her thoughts now. I stared at the open front door of the estate in disbelief. *That quickly. That quickly he could turn on me.* Merely an hour earlier I was with the frosty "It" and didn't mean to choose him. *How did that happen so quickly.* A tear fell down my cheek.

Donovan used his thumb to wipe the tear and kissed my forehead.

"It will all work out," he whispered against my head, trying to reassure me.

"No, it won't. And this is way out of my league of understanding," I was sullen in my response.

"Baby, look at me," he said as he pulled my chin to look up into his eyes.

The blue in his eyes were always fluid like water. I always felt calm and reassured when I looked into his eyes.

"It will all work out. And you know it will. Maybe not the way you believe or want, but it will all work out for our higher good."

He kissed my forehead again, holding me close to him before taking my hand. We walked holding hands into the house.

Ms. Ebby had prepared a feast of Roast Pork and Beef, mashed potatoes, green beans, and honey glazed carrots. It smelled so delicious, although I didn't want to eat at all, my stomach betrayed me and gurgled at the scents filling the room. She smiled and said, "good you are hungry!" Then she darted into the kitchen to get the fresh bread in the oven. All of us sat at the table, except James, he went directly to his room and stayed there. He didn't come out at all the rest of the evening.

After dinner Donovan and I went to my room. I could feel the negative energy from James's room radiating through the floor. It amazed me how energy was so transparent to me now. I lay in Donovan's arms with my head on his bare chest. I loved his bare chest. I loved his scent. I loved his warmth. I loved him period. Yet, I worried about James. My concern for Jax had waned as she was happy and flitting through the house like a typical college girl. She had her new crush to concentrate on. Brian visited her a few times, and although he still appeared human to her, she knew he was a spirit. She had been researching spiritualism in the past few weeks and had starting to come into her own path. She was happy. She was filled with love and light. And for the time being it seemed Christian was leaving her alone.

I pondered why Christian would attack James. Why him? He was so adamant that Jax would be "his," why would he shift his focus to James. What piece of this was I missing? And what was in that wooden box? Why was it missing? Was Christian the one who attacked me? I knew deep within me it was not Christian that hurt me. He couldn't have, not with Donovan in the driveway. It would have had to be someone stronger, more evolved than Donovan. I drifted off into a comfortable sleep laying with Donovan, my mind so full of questions that I did not have any answers for.

I felt a hand touching my shoulder, then another hand touching my heart, and a third hand touching my forehead. "Wake up Jessica," three voices said in unison. When I opened my eyes I was in the light space again. Whether Beriya or Seraphim I wasn't sure, but it was a different space than I had been in before. I saw three angels standing over me. I blinked my eyes a few times to adjust to the white light. I sat up with a heavy heart as I took in my surroundings. My previous visits with angels all felt loving and filled with light. This visit felt heavier.

"Hello Jessica. I am Stullaire," a male angel with big beautiful light blue wings said. None of the other light angels that I previously encountered had wings like he had. "This is Linnara," he said pointing at a female angel with big light-yellow wings. Linnara had pale yellow hair and held a yellow book in her hands. "And this is Shastinelle," he said pointing to another female angel with big light pink wings. Shastinelle had wavy light brown hair that had a pink hue to it, and she held a red scepter. Stullaire had silver gray hair and he held a blue scale – like the ones depicted in courtroom seals. They each wore tunics with the respective colors to the objects they were holding.

"Hello. Why do you all have wings?"

It was the most pressing question on my mind in that moment. They each grinned, then half giggled. Instantly they hid their wings behind their bodies, the wings disappeared like they somehow tucked within themselves.

Whoa! How did they do that!

"Sorry, we sometimes forget to put them away when we go to someone," Linnara said.

"We all have wings, even the angels you have already met, we just usually tuck them away," Shastinelle said.

Stullaire laughed, "because we are a little more impish than the others!" They all laughed.

"Why did you come to me?" I asked.

"You seem lost in all this. You see, I am the Angel of Patience, Obedience, and Perseverance," Linnara said.

"And I am the Angel of Meekness and Humility," Shastinelle said.

"I am the Angel of Truth and Counselling," Stullaire said.

"I carry the Book of Prophecy," Linnara explained showing me her yellow book.

"I carry the Scepter of Humility," Shastinelle proudly waved her scepter as she spoke.

"And you carry the Scale of Justice?" I asked pointing at Stullaire's scales.

"Close," he said, "I carry the Scale of Truth."

"I see," I stated.

I didn't quite see, but I could see how each item they carried related to their angelic gifts.

Shastinelle began explaining how meekness and humility would help me to overcome my frustration with not knowing all the answers. If I humbled myself, letting go of my Asiyan ego, I would have more answers than ever before. But I needed to find true humility and meekness. She further explained,

I was not above nor below anyone, and my thoughts truly do create all reality. I thought of being in the bathroom with the frosty things and how I instinctively thought of James as below me, then unknowingly and unwillingly chose him to be "sacrificed" to the frosty things. I didn't quite understand how it would play out, but I knew it was the "necessary evil," so to speak.

Linnara explained how patience, obedience, and perseverance were all fruits of the spirit. That I would need to truly embrace each of them in order to fulfill my path and learn to create with meekness and humility. Without obedience, patience, and perseverance I would never create a meek and humble life. I thought about my impatience with the speed in which things were being revealed to me. I thought about my frustration and anger, neither emotion meek, humble, obedient, or patient. I was starting to understand how each part that these three angels represented were all connected.

Stullaire then showed me his scales without speaking a single word. Engraved on each scale were the words "Wise" and "Unwise," and on the front was the phrase "Be very careful how you live, not as unwise but as wise, making the most of every opportunity." He never spoke a word after that, he didn't need to. Each of them worked conjunctively together to fulfill the fruits of the spirit.

CHAPTER 27

I opened my eyes and found myself alone in bed, Donovan had awakened before me again. *How does he silently get out of bed without me knowing?* I sat up slowly and thought of my dream travel. I knew it was astral travel, plane travel, whatever you want to call it. I was apparently really good at it when I was sleeping. I wondered if recurrent dreams I had when I was a child and young teen meant I was traveling to other planes and fulfilling some played out destiny. I walked to my bathroom to brush my teeth and hair, then wash my face with cool water. I felt flushed and hot, at least there were no frosty things in my bathroom today.

As I bent over to spit out my toothpaste, Donovan appeared in the doorway. "I could totally get used to this view every day," he said with a smile and a wink.

"Perv!" I laughed, as I finished brushing my teeth and rinsed. He held me from behind in the bathroom, inhaled deeply taking in the scent of my hair. "I love you," he said.

"I love you most," and I did. At least I felt like I did.

"No way," he said as he swatted my butt then walked into the bedroom.

It was my first full day back at the office in close to a month, I would need to catch up on a lot. Donovan drove me to work, we rode in the elevator together with me stopping at the usual twenty-first floor and the top floor for him again. I kissed him on the cheek as I went to exit. He grabbed me by my elbow, pulling me back to him like he did the first time, but this time he kissed me passionately. When he was done, he pushed me into the lobby of my office and closed the elevator doors behind me. I was still gushing from the kiss when the second set of elevator doors opened, and James stepped out. He again glared at me but didn't say a word. I called out is name, "James!" but he just kept walking straight to Bill's office. He was teeming with anger toward me, which I surmised was because of the choice I made, but I didn't know how he knew. There seemed to be something else I was missing.

I spent time catching up with Barbara over what I still had pending in my cases. A young, fresh out of law school, attorney named Chad was working on my cases. He was so green he stammered when talking to me.

"Chad. I'm going to stop you right there," I said as patiently as I could. "Take a deep breath. You don't need to be so nervous. Own what you are saying and doing. Even if what you are arguing isn't going to win, you argue it like it is the end all and be all of existence. Have some confidence. This is your case. Own it," I tried to be direct in my advice. I wasn't criticizing and I hoped he wouldn't see it that way. He instantly relaxed his shoulders.

"I just don't want to disappoint you," he was so young and fresh in his approach to law.

Chad was twenty-eight years old, had graduated from Georgetown Law, then worked for a Judge in Baltimore County courts a few years. He had seen a lot of criminal law cases, so he knew how the judges generally were. He knew which judges would be lenient, which weren't, which ones liked our law firm, and which judges did not. He also knew which judges had a good guy reputation, and which ones did not. Essentially, he knew the ins and outs of the Baltimore County judicial system. I instantly thought about my brother James and his situation.

"Hey Chad. Do you have any friends you went to school with that ended up working in the DC court system? One that might know which judges to have, and which one you wouldn't want presiding in a rape case?"

"Yeah, my friend Christian Wyatt. He knows all the judges there," I winced when he spoke. *Great!!!* I felt officially exasperated.

"What?" Chad said at my obvious reaction.

"Nothing Chad. Nothing. Tell me about Ms. Grainger's case."

I moved on past my brother's case and delved into my own assigned cases. Chad rattled off different filings that had been done for Ms. Grainger and informed me of the upcoming calendar dates for her. As he spoke, I saw James walk past my office toward the elevators. He didn't even look my direction. Didn't stop. Didn't say hi or bye. Nothing. It was as if I didn't exist. Barbara poked her head in my office at that moment and said Bill needed me, right now! I grabbed my notepad, heading straight to Bill's office. I knew a brain storming session was about to begin with regard to my brother's case.

Patty was not at her desk when I approached. That was odd. She never missed a day of work. I lightly knocked on Bill's door. "Come in."

I walked to the conference table in his office where he was sitting with files and papers laid out in order and what appeared to be a small thumb drive by his computer.

"Hey, you wanted to see me," I said as I greeted him.

"Yeah, take a seat," he said motioning toward a chair in front of him.

I sat quietly, watching him type away on his laptop.

Dammit. Why can't I find this file!

"Excuse me?" I said to Bill. I had never heard Bill curse a day in his life. He looked up at me surprised, almost shocked.

"Did you just hear my thoughts?" he asked me.

"Did you not say that out loud?" I didn't realize he hadn't spoken.

"No, I didn't," he closed his mouth.

"Then I guess I did. Unless you have someone else around here upset that they can't find a file," I smirked at him.

"Well, look who is truly mastering her skills," he said as he sat back in his chair, pulling his glasses off his face to look at me.

I shrugged my shoulders.

We have a problem. Bill thought.

What's the problem? I thought back.

"James thinks you are the one who turned him in. He said Christian showed him an email from you to Detective Talbot, in which you explained that you knew James was guilty and while you didn't have all the evidence, you knew Christian was with him. He said you provided a written statement, saying Christian had told you they had raped this girl after drugging her with a date rape drug." I sat with my mouth hanging open, stunned. Absolutely stunned.

Christian! I hate him!

"Don't Jess. You can't hate him. That feeds him and you know it," Bill warned.

"I did no such thing Bill."

"I know you didn't," he said, "the problem is the email came from here. From your work account. And it is on our servers here, I had our IT guys look into it." I sat in stunned silence for a moment.

"And worse, they traced the origin to your laptop, at your desk. Here. In this office," he continued, "the emails to yourself, same thing. All traced to your laptop here. In this office. They swear upside down and backwards there is no possible way these emails came from a remote location."

"Bill, I swear I didn't do this," I said defensively.

"I know you didn't Jess," he tried to reassure me, "but James doesn't know this. And he feels betrayed. He is truly angry," Bill dropped his head and then said the one thing I was expecting to hear, "He's gone into the dark Jess. You cannot bring him back."

I sat there and cried. I just simply cried.

I left Bills office feeling defeated. I was not going to be allowed on the case at all. I couldn't help him since I worked for the law firm, and with the emails coming from my laptop we may be facing a conflict of interest if we represented James in the case. It was an absolute worst-case scenario playing out before our eyes.

CHAPTER 28

Sitting at momma's estate I twirled pasta around on my plate, not eating, not really hungry either. I couldn't help but think about the turn of events. I knew somehow Christian was involved in all this. I knew he orchestrated this entire thing; I just didn't know how. Probably paid this girl to say they raped her, and conveniently she has no memory of all the events because she was drugged. I was trying to piece all the information together in my mind when Jax walked into the kitchen. She was quiet and didn't seem as bubbly as she had been lately. I watched her walk across the kitchen to get a glass.

"Hey," I said quietly.

"Oh crap!" she cried out, "you scared me! I didn't see you sitting there."

"Sorry! I didn't mean to scare you," I said sullenly.

"Hey, what's wrong Jess?" she was concerned for me for a change.

"It's James. And all this mess. He thinks I did this to him," I explained as a tear slipped down my cheek.

"I know Jess. I know. I spoke to him," she said.

She knew I didn't do this, and she knew it was Christian. She knew this was part of a bigger plan that neither of us could fathom. She knew. James didn't. She sat next to me and fixed a plate of noodles for herself. We both ate in silence, until her cell phone rang. It was Christian.

Her face fell when she saw the name on the screen. She had gone as far as to label his contact information as 'Evil Christian. Do Not Answer' with a devil emoji under it. I couldn't help but laugh when I saw it.

"What does he want I wonder?" I asked.

"I don't know, and I don't want to find out," she dismissed the call, sending him to voicemail. We both returned to eating when her phone pinged with a text.

6:28 p.m. *You shouldn't ignore me if you want to see James again.*

She turned the phone toward me to read it, another text came through at that moment.

6:29 p.m. *I can make all this go away and it will only cost you and your sister $10mil.*

We both looked at one another in disbelief.

"BILL!" we said simultaneously. This was a Bill issue now.

Bill and Donovan both showed up to the estate. Jax called Bill, I called Donovan, and they both arrived about the same time. No other texts had come in while we waited on them to arrive, and we didn't answer the ones already sent. James hadn't answered his phone when each of us called him. We didn't text or leave a message. We instinctively knew he wouldn't answer. Bill called Detective Talbot who agreed to come to the estate right away. Donovan was on the phone with someone, I recognized the voice as the one I heard in the car, he was discussing running a background check on Christian Wyatt and Chad Obleski. *Chad? My new green attorney Chad?*
Donovan looked at me and held his finger to his lips to shush me. I grinned. I was distracting him with my thoughts. He was still on the phone, but we were that connected that my thoughts interrupted everything else to him.

Bill and Donovan began talking strategic ways to handle this. Jax and I were watching the two of them like military generals preparing for war. They were strategizing while Jax and I were sipping on milkshakes Ms. Ebby had made for us. Ms. Ebby happily moved about the kitchen, putting away the dishes when I caught a flash of her thoughts. *I wonder if my teddy bear will come see me tonight.* She continued to work through the kitchen when the next thought stopped all of us dead in our tracks. *I should invite Douglas to meet these kids.*

"Ms. Ebby! Who is Douglas?" I blurted without thinking how she would react. She turned on her heel, her face bright red with embarrassment. She cleared her throat.

"How... How did you find out about Douglas?" she stammered.

"Ms. Ebby, I will explain another time but please tell us who Douglas is." my heart was pounding, and I felt sick to my stomach.

Bill stood to his feet. We all felt the tension in the room. We all knew. "Douglas" was Douglas Wyatt, THE Douglas Wyatt. Jax's creator, Bill's ex-partner, Christian's father, and now James's attorney. James had hired Mr. Wyatt when he learned there may be a conflict of interest with our firm.

Again, Ms. Ebby, who was now teeming with embarrassment, cleared her throat. "He is a man that has been courting me for the last month or so. He happened upon the estate by accident one afternoon when I was out pulling some vegetables from the garden. He's very charming, we have been having lunch a few times a week, and one dinner."

She looked down at the ground like she had done something wrong.

"Ms. Ebby, you have done nothing wrong," Bill was trying to reassure her as he spoke, "but I need to know. Is his last name Wyatt by any chance?"

He was trying to calm himself, but I could see the anger rising within him as well. She simply nodded her head before she burst into tears. Jax and I both jumped up to wrap our arms around Ms. Ebby. We both knew we needed to be the love and light for her right now. We held onto her infusing so much love and light into her that she instantly calmed down then smiled at us.

Douglas Wyatt had infiltrated our family in a way that Christian had failed to do. And we didn't see it happening.

CHAPTER 29

All the pieces of the puzzle were coming together. We were up against all forces of good and evil. My abilities were still being honed which meant I was nowhere near prepared in my mind. I was truly frightened of Mr. Wyatt. I felt his evil presence even if I couldn't see him. Things were starting to make sense. If I were out of commission, meaning not at work, my laptop would be open. My office would not be watched, or rather, no concern would be raised if some young attorney handling my cases and files was seen sitting at my desk. My momma dies so I am out of the office, mysterious emails start appearing. Christian conveniently showed up in my brother's life to get to Jax, but that didn't pan out like Douglas and Christian thought, because they didn't count on my abilities coming into focus. They also tried to play on Jax's insecurities over her place in the family in the wake of my mother's death, feeding into her anger. They didn't count on my generosity, giving her anything she wanted or needed. They expected human greed on my part. The plan for my brother to go out drinking on an all-night bender with Christian gave way to get money, and to get James charged with a crime, again causing strife.

What we had come to believe is that the goal was to further push Jax into anger if they painted me as the bad guy. They didn't count on her having the ability to read thoughts and know my heart. There were parts that were still a mystery, like were who bashed me in the head and why, and where was the wooden box. We knew Mr. Wyatt had visited Layla at the Little Shop on the Bay and inquired if I had gotten anything. Bill confirmed that was who he had suspected when I told him about Layla calling me because the "bad man" asked questions about me. We also figured that it must have been Chad who would have taken photos of Donovan and me. He would have known my schedule, when I left the building, and he would have been inconspicuous being on the street since he worked in the building.

He's Fired! We all thought it at the same time – except Jax who loudly said, "Who's fired?" Ms. Ebby looked at all of us with her eyebrows raised.

"Chad," I said aloud, hoping Ms. Ebby didn't get any more freaked out than she was.

"Who's Chad?" Jax asked.

"A spy!" I said, feeling betrayed.

Bill immediately called someone in the IT department and told them to shut off Chad's access to everything. That, of course, would tip off Mr. Wyatt we were figuring it all out, but it was a necessary step. At that precise moment, a bright white light appeared in the kitchen. It was so bright we all had to cover our eyes. Out of the light stepped an Angel that easily was eight feet tall and had the build of a god-like warrior. He had long flowing light-colored hair, a strong jaw, with an extremely muscular body, and wore a cobalt blue tunic with the same spun gold tasseled rope around his waist. He was an Archangel. He carried a large sword with a shield strapped to his back. The Archangel Michael had appeared before us, Ms. Ebby instantly passed out.

CHAPTER 30

I was dumbstruck. THE Archangel Michael stood in my momma's kitchen. THE ARCHANGEL MICHAEL. If there was ever a moment that a girl would act girly and fangirl over an angel, this was it. Jax and I both were staring at this large powerful angel in complete awe. The highest of all Archangels was standing before us. He strode over to Bill and Donovan then shook their hands like they were long lost pals, his voice boomed so deeply it shook the walls. He was enthralling.

"Ummmm… excuse me?" I stuttered as I tried to get their attention with my very small weak voice. Jax was tending to Ms. Ebby by escorting her to her cabin.

Archangel Michael turned to face me, his face smiling like he was seeing a beautiful angel himself.

"Hello Jessica. It is an absolute honor to meet you."
He took my hand in his and slightly bowed his head toward me. My hand looked so tiny in his large hand. He appeared larger than life. Literally. I curtsied like a fool because I didn't know what else to do. I stood in front of him peering up at him like he was royalty. In my mind he was like royalty, albeit spiritual royalty. Bill and Donovan stifled their laughs.

When he spoke, there was a familiarity to his voice. I tilted my head and pondered on it for a moment. Then it occurred to me where I had heard him speak. It was his voice in Donovan's car on the speaker phone. That is who Donovan was speaking to when he said he had the package. It was who he spoke to about a background check. *Wait why would he need to do a background check?*

Both Donovan and Michael laughed out loud.

"It wasn't truly a background check like you are thinking here on this plane. I was asking Michael to look in the Book. To tell us what we were dealing with here. Was this a human issue or was this a spiritual war issue? The fact that Michael is here in front of us, tells me this is a war issue," Donovan looked to Michael for affirmation.

"This is indeed a spiritual war issue. The time is here," Michael said as he turned to face me, "we all have known for an exceptionally long time that your presence, the future creator, would bring about this war.

"We were not sure when exactly the war would occur, but we knew that your spiritual awakening would start the events that begin the next war. We have been preparing for a long time for this," Michael explained.

Wow. Wow. Wow.

I sat down in complete and utter disbelief. I listened as Michael, Bill, and Donovan all explained the events that would cause the next war. Starting with the birth of the future creator from the Gabriel lineage. That the first female born within that lineage would be the creator, and that female was... me. As I remembered who I was, it would trigger my counterpart to become who they are as well. I knew this, but I didn't know the gravity of this. Donovan explained that he and Michael had fought in the previous war.

My thoughts turned to Donovan's scars on his chest. He touched them and knew I was thinking of them. "Yes, my love, they are from war. Here on Asiya, not spiritual war," he touched my cheek to reassure me that he was right here and would not get hurt. I looked to Michael and Bill as they explained that Bill was one of the oldest remaining souls from Beriya in Gabriel's lineage and considered one of the most heralded angels beneath Gabriel. I was like royalty so to speak myself, they explained. *Like a princess.*

"No, not like a princess, more like a goddess," Michael interrupted my thoughts.

I sighed as I took all this information in.

War was coming, I was the reason, my brother James was the sacrificial tool, Mr. Wyatt and his son orchestrated these events to kick off the Great Spiritual War, and I could do nothing to stop it all. What I didn't quite get or fit into the puzzle was where Mr. Wyatt fit into all this.

"That's easy," Bill said, "Douglas is my brother, remember when I explained this to you? We grew up together in Beriya. We had the same mother, but not the same creator. I am of the Gabriel lineage; he is of the Lucifer lineage."

Bill stopped speaking and let the words sink in. *Cain and Abel.*

"Exactly Jess," Bill confirmed, "the biblical teachings leave out the part that Cain was Adam's son – the first Godlike being – and Abel was Lucifer's son. Remember Adam was created in the likeness of God. She created the masculine form of the divine feminine. Eve was made from Adam to be the first creator."

"Wait. So, I am like Eve?" I widened my eyes as I asked.

"Not exactly, you are a creator of an angelic lineage, Eve was a creator of God's personal lineage," Michael explained.

"But what about the apple and the snake, and all that?" my head was spinning.

"The story of Adam and Eve and falling from the Garden of Eden, is not retold as it truly occurred. Lucifer and Eve had to create. It was part of the plan all along. She didn't commit some sin behind Adam's back. This was all part of it. She bore a son

Cain of Godlike status, and she bore a son Able from Lucifer. Lucifer chose to fall.

"He chose to take up the most noble of all quests. To be the opposite of all things positive, it was the closest an angel could be to being Godlike, and Lucifer humbly accepted the task. He wasn't a jealous angel. It isn't really good vs. evil. This isn't a war like Vikings or Trojans. This is the next step in the creation of the next realm. You are creating the next realm, my dear," Michael said, "you are creating the next positive position of creation, and your antithesis will create the next negative position. It is all as it should be."

CHAPTER 31

I watched as the three men, or angels, whatever they were, discuss how to manage this situation here in Asiya. They spoke of other angels from other realms I had never heard of, nor could I even begin to try to understand. The "armies" were coming in a matter of... Minutes, hours, days, weeks... Who knew as time was not real anyway. Time was not real.

Time is not real.
I can stop time.
Why don't I just stop time.

I closed my eyes as I began a deep meditation. I pulled from deep within me to stop all time. I wanted to find a way to create without a war. I wanted to pull from the entire existence a love so deep all things fell into place, without anger, hurt, or frustration. I wanted to pull from my soul. I opened my eyes when the room was silent and found myself sitting across from James in a dark room, a dark void.

"James?" I was sincerely surprised to see him across from me.

"Hello Jess," he was not angry with me. He was not anything toward me. He just was. He sat across from me looking directly at me.

"What are you doing here? How are you here?" *Wherever*

here is. I was careful in my questions. I felt confused at the moment.

"Jess, I am your opposite. Your antithesis," he was very plain in how he spoke to me.

"I don't understand James. I thought Christian was my antithesis."

"Nope. You gave me up. You showed Death I was sacrificial," he did not sound hurt by this statement.

"James, I didn't want to. I didn't mean to. I wasn't even trying to," I was defensive as I spoke.

"I know," James said, "I know you were not sacrificing me intentionally. But it was meant to be this way. Don't you know: The way. The truth. And The light," he was quoting the bible.

"Yes, but how does that pertain to us?" I was not following.

"Jess you are the Light. You are the creator. You are love and light. Jax is the Truth. She sees through everyone and everything. She knows the truth. She speaks truth. And I am the Way. By allowing me to fall, I paved the way for the light. The light exists where darkness does not," he was more knowledgeable than I had ever given him credit for.

"What? But how?" I was so confused.

"Jess, we are all creators. All of us. We are all one, all created in the likeness of God, all created to love and be love. But to know love, one must know what love is not. It's so basic. You have been told this before. You know this," he said.

"But you are human."

"Jess, each of us are human, we all have souls that ascend and descend. You just moved my descension from proverbial to reality. My body is human, my soul is eternal."

"James, I am sorry," I truly felt sorrowful.

"Why? You should rejoice. A new realm is born. A new light is starting. A new lineage has begun. Just look!" He pointed to my stomach.

I was pregnant. Hugely pregnant.

Wait! WHAT!?!?!?
This cannot be happening. I am not pregnant. I didn't have sex. Donovan and I haven't had sex. I felt so confused, tears spilled from my eyes, I felt like I was going to burst into a million pieces. I felt overwhelmed.

I instantly found myself to be back in the kitchen. I thought I was going to pass out from the extreme amount of energy flowing through me in that moment. I could feel the molecules of my body charged with so much positive energy that I felt as though I would explode light from every pore. The stirring within me was ramping up to escape, like an internal combustion. I could envision a star being born in the universe, a star - created from the energy of the realms, a star about to burst light throughout all existence. I mumbled about James. Michael scooped me up, telling Bill and Donovan I needed to be in Beriya. Before I could say anything more, I blacked out. I awoke lying in a beautiful crystal room with fractured rainbow light all around me. I felt comfort and peace, I felt safe again.

There was no more sorrow, anger, or pain. I didn't feel anything negative. I only felt love and light. Donovan appeared beside me. He stood there wearing a long white tunic with metallic threading around the edges. The metallic threading had almost a rainbow hue to it like the crystals in the walls. I felt so relieved and happy that he was with me. This was the first time I had seen him in another realm. I instinctively knew this time I was in Beriya. I remembered there was one last light angel that I had not met. Trinaty. As quickly as I had the thought, she appeared as if my thought called to the one angel I had left to meet.

"Hello Trinaty," I greeted her.
She appeared in an indigo light. There was a purplish-blue hue to her tunic, and she had long flowing raven like black hair. Her

olive skin was perfection, she was incredibly beautiful just as all the angels had been.

"Hello Jessica, or may I call you by your angel name, Yiskah?" she spoke in reverence.

"Wow, Yiskah is my angel name?"
I had no idea I even had an angel name.

"Yes, Yiskah means the gift, and Jessica means 'God beholds'," she said.

"Trinaty, you may call me whatever you wish," I said in returned reverence.

"Yiskah it is then. You have summoned me what may I do for you?" she asked.

"I just wanted to meet you. What are you the Angel of?"

"I am the Angel of Spiritual Awakening. You are meeting me now because you are now fully enlightened my dear. You have awoken your true gifts and are one with your higher self," she smiled then bowed her head toward me.

"Does this mean I can transcend through all the realms?" I recalled something Bill had told me weeks earlier.

"Of course, my dear. You have all your gifts from Gabriel now!" she proudly exclaimed. I looked up to Donovan, he was beaming with pride. He looked like a proud man who was with his twin flame, his soul mate, his true love, his forever.

"What about the Great War?" I inquired softly.

"It rages on as we speak," Donovan said, "it's not a war in the sense you are thinking my love, it is more like a dance between positive and negative. It is a repelling of forces in opposition.

"It is a fragmentation of light and dark against one another. As the sun sets the moon lights, as the moon descends the sun arises. It's the new life in a new realm, and a new beginning being sorted, with sides being chosen. You gave birth to new life. New Hope."

"I did?"

I realized I was feeling similar to how I felt when I awoke from my coma. Life was moving on around me while I stood still in time.

I remembered the feeling of combusting and light coursing all around me. I looked down at my stomach to find it was just as flat as it had been before. I didn't feel pregnant, nor did I look pregnant. I wasn't blasted into a million pieces like I felt I was going to be. I felt calm and well rested. I felt love and peace. I remembered the birth of a star like it was movie playing before me. I created a new realm, a new galaxy, a new bright star for new planets to revolve around. I created life. *I created!* And the new life was being filled with positive and negative energy just as Asiya has been. It was a new beginning.

Donovan held my hand then kissed each of my fingers, "are you ready to return to Asiya my love?"

I was.

I nodded my head and together we returned.

WE returned. As one.

EPILOGUE

Donovan held me closely against his chest as he carried me over the threshold of OUR home. Okay really it was his home, but now we were married, and I loved his view so much more than mine! We kept my home and offered it to Ms. Ebby. She was going to come over, cook for us and be our caretaker here in our home. She was so happy we decided to support her, plus, she got a much bigger house. She still didn't want to drive a car so her brand new golf cart would be her transportation to get to our home.

Jax was happily gallivanting all over Europe with her love Randy – the young waiter from the Cheesecake Factory – turns out he was a gamer too. He just wasn't sponsored like Brian was, he in a way idolized Brian though. He was a rich kid too, Randall Louis Jennings III to be exact, and he was on break from college. He had been attending the University of Maryland on a math scholarship. Randy and Jax fell in love, and Jax felt Brian had blessed their relationship. They used their personal trusts to travel around spreading love and light. Jax started a foundation for orphans and traveled the world ensuring orphanages were well supplied with books and toys, and anything the children could want or need. She knew some of the children would grow to be positive and some would be negative, but she wanted to ensure she spread as much love and light as she possibly could. She felt sad she missed my wedding to Donovan, but he and I wanted to keep it extremely small anyway, as in just us, and Bill of course.

Bill 'gave me away' to Donovan, my creator giving my hand in union to my twin flame. Archangel Gabriel presided over the ceremony. I finally got to meet the Archangel Gabriel of whom our lineage was from. Gabriel's hair was pure silver, it almost reflected the light it was so shiny, and he wore a pure white tunic. He had very fatherly features, handsome but older gentleman father features, with laugh lines around his eyes. I felt as if he was my father truly. I should mention we were married in Beriya, our marriage bond is beyond any legal paper in Asiya, although we do plan to have a wedding on Asiya one day too.

I felt like a princess getting married that day. All the angels in Beriya were there. Faelynn, Majestica, Illuma, Jaselle, Stullaire-Linnara-Shastinelle, and Trinaty of course were all there. Jaselle laughed his amazing deep laugh. The Archangels were all there too - Raphael, Michael, and Phanuel. All of Seraphim rejoiced with trumpets blaring when we sealed our union with a kiss. It was so beautiful. Surreal.

James. Oh James. He rose to be the next in line to Douglas Wyatt, Lucifer's right-hand man, and where I created - James too created. When I created the star, he created a black hole to pull darkness into. It was the negative to the new realm that kept the balance in place. He felt neither anger nor sadness, he just existed. I never saw him again, but I knew he existed. Speaking of Mr. Wyatt, as a fully enlightened being nothing was secret from me, I was able to see all things. It was Mr. Wyatt who struck me in the head. He took matters into his own hands since he felt like his creation Christian had failed. Christian is a criminal lawyer on Asiya at Mr. Wyatt's law firm. Still negative, angry, and now truly despises James above all. James ascended, or rather descended, to where Christian should have been, which made the anger fester more within Christian. He's actually a really good criminal lawyer though. Oh, I almost forgot, James and the rape charges – turns out the girl who was lying – she finally admitted to it when Det. Talbot pressured her. She caved, and all the charges were dropped. James didn't care one way or another, he had bigger universal issues to attend to. The frosty death, it appears from time to time on Asiya to continue the cycle of life and death. I no longer fear it. It cannot touch me or harm me in any way. Besides Gabriel would descend and destroy all of Asiya if it did! My Asiyan mother and father, Mr., and Mrs. Jonathan Quincey Hanson, they had fulfilled their purpose on Asiya. It turns out they were twin flames too. They ascended together to Atzilut. Trinaty gives me messages from them every now and then. I still carry so much love for them in my soul.

"Hey, Mrs. Wheeler, earth to Yiskah," Donovan said waving his hand in my face as he set me down in the foyer of our home. Donovan now referred to me by my angel name, Yiskah. He loved that he was the only one on Asiya that called me by my angel name.

"Yes, Mr. Wheeler?" I said as I stuck my tongue out at him.

"You were lost in thought there thinking of all our loved ones," he said.

"Yeah, just counting all my blessings."

He then scooped me up and threw me over his shoulder as he practically ran up the stairs to our bedroom. I was laughing and telling him to put me down, kicking in protest, although it was mostly feigned.

He gently set me down on the bed, kneeling before me. He pulled the high heels off each foot gingerly, caressing my legs.

"I have something for you," he said with a sheepish grin.

"A present for me?" I grinned like a schoolgirl.

"Ok, close your eyes and hold out your hands." I laughed as he instructed me, as if I wouldn't be able to read his thoughts and know exactly what the present was. *I'm only thinking of getting you naked and making love to you, so no you won't know the gift, because I'm thinking of your perky......*
LA – stop it, Donovan Wheeler!
He placed a box on my hands, and I carefully opened my eyes. It was wrapped in white satin paper, with a white satin ribbon tied carefully around it in a bow. It wasn't a small box, more like medium in size. I looked at Donovan through my lashes and blinked seductively at him.

"What is it?" I asked.

"Open it and find out," he smirked.
I gently pulled the satin ribbon then carefully opened the paper. It was the wooden box from months and months ago. The same wooden box Donovan originally delivered to my door. My breath caught as I stared at the box in my lap. I looked at him searching for answers.

"I am the one who took it from your house months ago," he explained.

"Why?" I was getting the feeling this was extremely important.

"You weren't ready to open it yet. Every being in the universe knew you weren't ready. You had to evolve first."

"Is that why so many 'beings' kept me from opening it?" Now I truly needed to know what was in this box once and for all.

"In a way, yes and no," he said, "go ahead and open it."
On the front of the box was a keyhole. I looked under the box to see if there was a key.

"I can't. I don't have the key."
Donovan then handed me the small dainty key with a deep red ribbon on it. I took the key, put it in the keyhole and turned slowly until it clicked.

The lid slightly cracked and what appeared to be light glimmered from the cracked lid. My heart started racing as excitement welled up inside me. I wasn't scared at all, nor was I nervous, I felt calm yet curious. I was ready to see the light. I slowly opened the lid peering at Donovan's face as I opened it. When I looked down there appeared a light, a tiny light the size of a mustard seed. It was tiny but so incredibly bright.

"What is this?" I asked as I stared at the beautiful little, tiny light in my hands.

"It's our child," he said proudly.

"What?" I looked at him in amazement, "what did you just say?"

"That small light, that tiny little seed, that my love is our baby Archangel. Our creation. The spark that begins a whole new lineage of angels."

I was completely awestruck. This tiny little mustard seed of light, this, was our new life and creation.

Donovan made love to me that evening in our beautiful light filled room. We exuded the connection that all love is created from. Our love is a love that transcended all realms and connects two souls for eternity. Our little seed of light was conceived that night, and nine months later a beautiful little baby girl was born. The second female born in Gabriel's lineage. Thus began the story of the Archangel Sarathiel. Our little Sara.

CPSIA information can be obtained
at www.ICGtesting.com
Printed in the USA
JSHW020410180123
36277JS00001B/46